BEYOND

MW01489803

To Genean Granger

Thanks for the support.
How's Claire?

Ev Barnes

Celebrate the Journey

ISBN 978-1-61434-483-4

Published in the United States by Booklocker.com, Inc., Bangor, Maine.

Printed in the United States of America on acid-free paper.

ErvBarnes.com
2011

First Edition

BEYOND THE BLOOD CHIT

Erv Barnes

COVER PHOTO printed with gracious permission from **theBattleZone.com**. It is a leather Vietnam era **Blood Chit**, a promissory note of reward issued by our government and carried by uniformed service members at risk of finding themselves in enemy territory, e.g. flyers. It offers a reward to anyone helping such service members return to safety.

AUTHOR PHOTO by **Beanie Leffler**

MOON PHASE NOTES

Phase	Rise	High	Set
New Moon	Sunrise	Noon	Sunset
Waxing Crescent	Morning	Afternoon	Evening
First Quarter	Noon	Sunset	Midnight
Waxing Gibbous	Afternoon	Evening	Wee hrs
Full Moon	Sunset	Midnight	Sunrise
Waning Gibbous	Evening	Wee hrs	Morning
Last Quarter	Midnight	Sunrise	Noon
Waning Crescent	Wee hrs	Morning	Afternoon

Salute

This work is dedicated to the faces in The Wall of The Vietnam Veterans Memorial—the faces behind the names engraved in black granite and the reflections of those who come to pay respects.

I am grateful beyond words to family, friends, teachers, and students for walking some of this journey with me. My wife, Nancy, is my biggest fan and most helpful critic, reading more drafts than seem possible. My daughters, Bethany and Hannah Lei, encourage me entirely. Friends like Tom Wacker and former students continue to ask about progress. Then there is Write on the Edge, my local writing group, reading and critiquing my work while offering technical and moral support. I may write a first draft alone, but without encouragement, I remain adrift and unpublished. Thank you, all.

Special appreciation goes to Tom Brown, Jr. and the "Tracker School", Tom Brown's Tracking, Nature, and Wilderness Survival School. I read his books and attended several classes. For any mistakes or misrepresentations of his teachings about Grandfather Stalking Wolf's philosophy and red sky prophecy, I accept responsibility.

My deep gratitude is for the Veterans Administration that continues to provide care, for my PTSD recovery group led by Ashley B. Hart II, Ph.D., and for Navy Don, who asked me to seek help.

Chapter One

Dawn, 17 May

Sunlight filtered through the jungle canopy as silence lay upon the land. A low, morning mist haunted dank earth, light and shadow dancing to the rhythm of treetop breezes. Through the shadows of his mind, Kenny Brewster ran alone and unarmed, pursued by angry Vietnamese faces, hearing only his own desperate breaths and uneven footfalls until the distant whop-whop-whop of a helicopter invaded his dream.

He ran through the shadows and the vegetation, feeling both brush against his face and arms. He ran from the pursuing shadows, the small ones with faces and the big one he could only feel. He ran for the helicopter much too far away.

Kenny snatched a look behind him at the faces that were no longer Vietnamese but American-looking kids, young men and women wearing expressions of surprised death. He felt his left foot snag on something hard and he fell, tumbling onto his back. All went silent. His eyes opened in search of reality.

Kenny's heart pounded in his chest, gulping blood from his veins, forcing it through his arteries, and throbbing in his ears. He felt the stillness of his abdomen and his tongue pressing hard against the roof of his mouth, and he commanded himself to breathe.

Twenty minutes. That's how much time he had to prevent the release of fight or flight hormones that would thrust the amygdala of his primitive brain into a wild ride of hyper vigilance, anxiety, and irrational judgment lasting three or four days. It was already too late to prevent a Post Traumatic Stress

Disorder reaction, but he might stop escalation into the wild ride his recovery group called the dinosaur dump. 'Breathe deep. Again.'

Soft light invaded the tiny window above the gray door of his little plastic shed at the edge of the hospital grounds. 'VA,' he reminded himself. 'Okay, it was just The Dream.' Kenny stretched his tired, old body and sat up. He heard the helicopter, closer now, and realized it was for him. Cold water on his face, a few toiletries, and he would be ready to report for duty.

Kenny Brewster was at war again—or yet—and a new mission called him. Any war is testament to the proposition that human life is expendable. This war was even more confusing than Vietnam, awarding relevance to the service of warriors too old to die young.

The Dream was back, only different now with the young American faces. His tired mind swam with memories and with blank spaces where memories should have been. He willed his conscious thoughts back to the present.

0737 Hours, 17 May

Kenny buckled himself into the old Huey, like himself, called out of retirement for desperate duty. He settled into his seat, aware of familiar smells of hydraulic fluid and gun oil, riding the pitch and yaw of the climb away from the VA Hospital. Seeing the amoeba shape of the Northern Wisconsin lake beyond the open right door, he longed to be back there. Kenny heard the ringing in both ears and felt the aches and pains in his legs and back as he stretched uneasily in his lap belt.

He rubbed his scruffy beard and thinning hair, adjusted his glasses, and gazed upon the wrinkles and brown age spots on his hands as he watched the helicopter's shadow swim along the green landscape below. 'When did I get so old?' He was used to asking himself questions almost audibly in his mind—and answering them. 'Yesterday,' he replied, thinking back to that conversation with Rick. Yesterday, everything changed. Today, yesterday still existed in his mind, and he held onto that like breath itself.

Yesterday, his friend and tactical partner, Rick Kowalski, told him about their last two-man mission together for the Wisconsin Army National Guard as LGs, or Last Generation Soldiers. Rick gave back what the prescribed anti-PTSD blackout drugs had stolen—his memories. The American faces in recent episodes of The Dream now made sense. Kenny sat sick in thoughts of what they had done in the name of duty, sick with apprehension for the next mission, sick and tired of fighting.

He looked back toward the lake, now just a dark smudge in the woods. 'Next time,' he promised himself. Next time he would stay home, stalk a few bass on the deep gravel bars, and maybe land an elusive walleye. He liked catching bass, but he loved eating walleye. Mostly, though, he missed the spirit of the few acres that had adopted him, the land he called Lonesome Pines. And, he longed for freedom from the shackles of duty and guilt that compelled him to serve and kill again.

He would see Rick today, the only best friend he ever had. They met at the Vietnam Memorial as both realized they had been in country in 1970 and had been at almost the same place in different units. Rick helped him through those dark times in 1984 after Bonnie kicked him out and his son, Kenny Junior, stopped talking to him. Rick later became a business partner with Vicky while she picked up the pieces and built a marriage with Kenny. He walked through grief with them when Amy, Kenny's sweet daughter with Bonnie, died in the sands of Desert Storm. He was there through Vicky's battle with, and surrender, to cancer. Rick was there through all their murky missions as LG volunteers for General Williams.

Kenny was on his way to report to the general today, his old friend and honorary nephew whom he had watched grow from a young boy, had taught history and psychology, and had coached in wrestling. Dick Williams was one bright spot of success in Kenny's life. He now commanded the Wisconsin National Guard and had created the LG paramilitary program that gave these tired old soldiers a way to help, a way of hoping to keep a few kids from dying young (or worse), and a way to repay the debt he and Rick and others like them felt for surviving Vietnam.

Kenny did not fully understand the economic and ethnic clashes spreading across America. He tried to avoid talk about ideological and political conflicts because it enraged him so, triggering PTSD flare-ups. He tried to avoid thoughts of conspiracy and treachery in the intelligence that drove their missions. He tried, but he failed.

Rick had chosen to work their last mission without the drugs, so he served as Kenny's memory. Like an old wound in his soul, Kenny's heart ached over what they had done, and he couldn't remember it at all. But, Rick could, and Kenny trusted that.

Memories are like dreams, but some dreams are nightmares. Kenny had asked himself yesterday, 'Should all nightmares be forgotten?' and had deliberately decided, 'no.'

For the first time, he was working this mission without the safety net of the drug patch, and he was worried about what else he did not remember.

He became aware, then concerned, that they were heading south along US 141 rather than making a beeline toward headquarters. He studied the body language of the crew intent on the horizon ahead. Looking through the windscreen, he observed several smoke spires rising in the distance. Only then did he notice the large volume of traffic heading north. With a glance back at the smoke, he realized, 'Green Bay is burning.'

They proceeded just far enough to see that Lambeau Field was still there, and he felt relief settle upon the souls on board the helicopter. As they turned to the west, Kenny saw the military convoy heading up WI 29 away from Green Bay. He was acutely aware of the incongruity of the scene, yet his mind refused to consciously process the information. He had heard about troubles in Green Bay and other places around America since the previous election, but he was surprised it had become this bad.

'Why are they going away from Green Bay?' he wondered. They were pulling out. The Wisconsin Army National Guard was retreating. Immediately, he suspected their next mission would somehow be related.

Awareness had become his most important survival skill. Now he sat in a form of trance, perceiving everything around him as though he were watching himself in a movie. Rick's words about their last mission reverberated in his head while his recoil at hearing them churned in his belly. Even without memory, he knew—he felt—that what Rick said was true. Kenny understood that his little life approached a critical moment, and he visualized himself alone in a canoe hurtling downstream toward Niagara Falls.

0843 Hours, 17 May

They landed. Time had become strange to Kenny. That ride seemed so brief, yet almost an eternity, as dream and reality merged. He stepped gingerly from the chopper and signaled a wave of thanks to the crew. The chief gave him a thumbs-up, but the others just watched him go. He walked off the pad to a waiting utility vehicle.

The young driver greeted him, "Hey, LG, the general is waiting for you." Kenny smiled, almost, and sat down without response. Robins sang of spring, but the air whispered summer as they drove up the trail on the ski hill called Rib Mountain. Kenny became mindful of his breathing again, taking in the life and freedom of forest and meadow and exhaling dread. He hated that feeling, but he was in this thing now, he had made a commitment, and he was going over the falls.

Nestled in the beautiful woods on the highest point in Wisconsin was a plastic monster, a prefab structure serving as field headquarters for the Guard. It was out of place here, but Kenny knew the general preferred this setting to Madison or Fort McCoy. Kenny placed each foot on the gravel driveway with the deliberate movement of a fox or feral cat. Although he had ceased fussing over his appearance the day he buried Vicky, he straightened his camouflage hunting shirt and pants out of habit and tucked his boonie hat into a side leg pocket. He opened the door into a small lobby where a young lady sat in battle dress uniform. Well, she was young to Kenny.

She looked up at him and smiled, "Good morning, Kenny." Her big brown eyes flashed a sincerity that shortened his breath. He thought she was pretty with shiny brown hair tied back, a round and slightly freckled face, well-defined and naturally pink lips, and a simple, healthy figure. He guessed thirty something and nearly as tall as he was, perhaps five seven.

'She knows me?' He looked at her nameplate: CWO 3 Lois J. Anderson.

"Good morning, Ms. Anderson."

She stood up and leaned over the desk, looking directly into his eyes, first one and then the other. Then she stared ever so briefly but intently at him. He thought he could feel her looking into his soul, and he almost liked it.

"I sent for you, LG. The general will see you in a few minutes."

Kenny backed away and sat down in a chair against a wall.

"So, how about brunch, Kenny?"

"Brunch?" He struggled to process her offer.

"Yeah, you know, substitutes for breakfast and lunch."

"Why would you want to have brunch with a scruffy old fogey like me?"

She looked down at some papers on her desk as though they had suddenly become important. "Brunch," she confirmed. "You're my favorite LG. Besides, it's my way of repaying you for saving my life."

'Saving her life?' Now, that was a memory Kenny dearly wished had not been stolen from him.

"Okay, brunch," he said, "after the meeting?"

"Immediately after," she nodded, turned her head, and pushed a button on the desk. "The general will see you now."

Kenny stood as tall as he could, squared his shoulders, stepped to the door and snapped it open. General Williams was an imposing figure, six three and two forty, solid as the linebacker and All American wrestler he had been at West Point with a voice like approaching thunder. He moved around his desk with the agility of a cat, or *gato*, as he liked to say, and embraced Kenny in a bear hug.

"It's really good to see you, Kenny. I hear that you have recovered well from your last mission. Are you ready for another one?" He still held Kenny's shoulders and searched his face.

"Yes, sir."

"Sir? The door's closed, Uncle Kenny. Don't you think you could call me Dick? Just don't call me Dickie like you did when I was little."

"I'm not sure I remember you ever being little, Dick, and I never called you Dickie. That was Rick. How's your mom?"

General Williams walked over to a straight chair and sat down. Kenny sat in a chair near him and waited.

"Mom is doing well, as well as can be expected. She misses Dad terribly. We all do. But she is doing well, busy at church and at the scholarship committee at school. She would love to see you, Uncle Kenny. You are like a brother to her and Dad." He paused a moment and looked out the window at the landscape. When he looked back, he asked, "So, how is Rick doing? I saw him last night and, frankly, I'm worried."

"Rick is here, already?"

"He is. Rick came down last night and we had a chat. Is he as fit as you are?"

Kenny paused before answering, "I trust Rick with my life."

"I know, I know, Kenny. Well, here it is. We have a mission for you, and it will demand everything you've got, both you and Rick. The survival of Green Bay through the summer may well depend on this mission."

'Green Bay…,' Kenny thought. He took a long look at his friend. Only now did he see the worry, the fear even, behind his eyes. "When do we start, sir?"

"You go into isolation today. I'll meet you at Line Camp for dinner." Kenny rose to go, but General Williams stopped him. "There's somebody I need you to meet before you go." He motioned toward another door.

Kenny followed the general into the private chamber, a library of sorts, where a familiar figure sat. Kenny's stomach lurched. He recalled the counsel of his spiritual teacher some years earlier. When Kenny told him about a kind of nausea experienced while visiting a famous tourist area out west, the teacher explained that the feeling was an alert to the presence of evil. That was the feeling in Kenny's gut now.

The familiar figure was a former Wisconsin governor. Kenny had heard that he was involved in one of those companies providing private protection on government contract, Samson Security. Kenny referred to such companies as *Manitowish,* meaning Bad Spirit. He couldn't tell if his gut reaction was to spiritual reality of evil in the room or if it was just political memory. His distrust and dislike for this man bordered upon hate, and Kenny detested that feeling, too. The figure rose to shake Kenny's hand, his fine expensive suit hanging on his almost shapeless body. As their palms connected, a wave of nausea crashed over Kenny.

"The governor has brought me some intelligence that requires immediate action." General Williams gave Kenny a look that told him to just listen. "You are that action."

The governor puffed up and started, "We've got solid intel that a large group of foreign nationals is coming through Canada to join the Unholy Alliance this summer."

"That's where you come in, LG," General Williams interrupted. Turning his attention to the governor, he said, "Governor, this is the man I told you about, LG Kenneth Brewster. He and his partner are being assigned this mission today."

"Good," was the governor's response. "That's good." He seemed quite pleased with himself although Kenny was sure that was a perpetual condition.

General Williams ushered Kenny out of the private chambers with an arm across his shoulders. At the office door, he leaned in and attempted to whisper, "I'll see you for dinner, Uncle."

0910 Hours, 17 May

Nausea followed Kenny into the lobby but faded quickly as he noticed Ms. Anderson watching him. He paused while she put a few things away, locked her desk, logged out of her computer, and came around to meet him. He thought she was avoiding eye contact now. 'Strange.'

She allowed a small, sad smile and walked toward the door. As he held it for her, he caught a subtle, familiar fragrance that stirred something deep inside. 'What have I done?' Kenny asked himself. 'What have I done with all those pieces of my life lived but not remembered? Who is this woman to me?'

"Where are we going, Chief?" Kenny finally asked.

"Oh, how about a picnic?" She flashed a smile that allowed him to feel that some of what they shared must have been good.

"A picnic brunch? Sure. Why not?" Kenny answered. Then he thought, 'Someplace private, I'll bet. I guess I'll find out soon enough what she's up to.'

She unlocked the doors to a classic pale green Ford Bronco with a white metal top. Kenny ran his eyes over the machine like it was a work of art—which it was, in a way. It was absolutely original and as simple as the one Kenny bought in 1973.

"I know, Kenny, you had one very much like it when you were...," She trailed off and looked straight ahead as they buckled in.

"Young," Kenny finished for her, confirming with a little smile of understanding.

"This was my father's, and he worked on it all the time. He never tried to improve it, just kept it original. Then he gave it to me," she said with raised eyebrows and a shake of her head. "He didn't leave it to me in a will, he just gave it to me one day. That was almost ten years ago." She seemed to drift into a sad memory.

Kenny felt the discomfort of knowing, somehow, that he had heard this before, like he was living some kind of Groundhog Day, only....

"It's okay, LG. It's not your fault you don't remember. It's the patch—and the cocktail."

'Cocktail?' Kenny didn't know about the cocktail. He was sure she intended to say more but stopped herself.

They drove through the green Wisconsin countryside that looked all too normal for the troubles in the cities. But, looks were not deceiving Kenny today. There were signs of abnormality in unworked fields, in abandoned farms, and in the young people milling around the small towns. Soon, he realized they had reached the reservation. She turned onto a dirt road, then a two-track trail, and finally stopped in a turn-out.

Ms. Anderson opened the tailgate. She set out a table and two lawn chairs while Kenny watched. Opening a wicker picnic basket, she produced a blue tablecloth and placed it with care, sweeping out the wrinkles. She laid out two settings with plates, silverware, coffee mugs, and stemmed glasses. She motioned for Kenny to sit. He sat.

She served cold sparkling water in the glasses, hot coffee in the mugs, and asparagus quiche on the plates. Before she sat down, she set out a fruit plate and two candles. She handed a lighter to Kenny, and he obliged, speechless.

They ate slowly and politely at first, attempting small talk about weather and clouds, the terrain, and fishing. Kenny began to enjoy waiting for her to say what was on her mind. Age offers the opportunity for patience, or at least an appreciation of it. He stared her straight in the eye, her right eye, much the way his Labrador Retriever used to do when she thought it was time for her treat.

Lois squeezed a broad, tight smile. "Okay, Kenny. This is it. We are worried about you and Rick."

He stopped her right there with an outstretched hand. "Please tell me who we are—not the we you mean, the we sitting right here."

She dropped her head a bit. "I'm sorry, Kenny. I'm usually better at this, but right now something is very wrong. Okay, you are an LG and I am your liaison officer."

"Really?" Kenny raised his eyebrows, but she did not react.

"I am your connection to the Army National Guard while you are on missions, in recovery, etc. I manage your file."

"You're my handler," Kenny suggested.

"Okay, I'm your handler, and we are really worried about both of you."

"You're Rick's handler, too."

"No, that would be my friend, Sammi." Kenny felt a keen interest in the way she said friend.

"Ah, the other part of we."

"What? Oh, yeah. We, Sammi and I, are worried about you both.

"Well, Chief, how about...,"

"Ken!" She cut him off. "Sorry, Kenny, will you please call me Lois?"

"Sure, Lois. Maybe you could sort of lay it all out for me, because, in this jigsaw puzzle of my mind, I'm just not getting it."

"Kenny, Rick didn't come back from the last mission with you." Kenny felt his eyes widen and his breath quicken. He noticed Lois reading his body language before she hastily continued, "He came back, just not with you. He didn't come back for almost three weeks, and when he did, he refused to go to the VA. Sammi had to work with him for another week before he checked in. Then he refused medication and left against medical advice."

"I know, Lois. We talked yesterday."

"You remember yesterday?" Lois sat wide-eyed, jaw slack.

"Yes, I do."

Her eyes welled up and her lips drew thinner and turned a paler pink. "What did he say? About the last mission, I mean?"

"Look, Chief, I'm skating on thin ice here, and I never did skate well." Kenny gave a nervous little laugh. "Rick spoke to me in confidence. I presume your friend has spoken to you in confidence. Are you telling me that she doesn't know? That Rick didn't tell her?"

"Rick told her, but she couldn't tell me the specifics because of confidentiality. If Rick told you, then I'm the only one left out, I guess."

"You guess?" Kenny paused for several moments, a skill of patience developed through years of teaching teenagers. If he waited long enough, they got nervous and actually risked sounding stupid by offering an answer.

"I don't know if General Williams knows," she said. "Sammi didn't tell him."

"Okay, let's see if I get this. There are two parts—no, three. One, do I know what Rick told Sammi? Two, did Rick tell General Williams? Three, would somebody please tell you so you can handle me?" He paused to think about what he just said.

"Well?" She interrupted his private conversation.

"Well, well. One, I think so. Two, I don't know, but I'll ask. And three, oh hell, I don't know, Lois. It's really not up to me at this point. What are you doing later tonight?"

Lois looked at him, then down at her lap and into his eyes again. "Kenny, we all stay together at Line Camp until you and Rick are ready to leave, however long that takes."

"Really? That's interesting."

"Oh, yes, Kenny, it is most certainly interesting."

1053 Hours, 17 May

Lois and Kenny packed the picnic and drove back to the dirt road where she turned right instead of left. She glanced toward Kenny. He noticed, but showed no sign of it. After some time, she turned left onto another small trail, following that for perhaps a mile. Then she just pulled into an opening in the trees, down a ravine, and stopped. She got out, put all the picnic items in a backpack, left the chairs and table in the Bronco, and headed off into the woods. Kenny followed.

He began to get a strange sensation, like he was living in The Notebook, only he was the one with memory gaps, and she wasn't reading to him. She was showing him. 'Okay,' he decided, 'she seems to think I'm going to remember something pretty soon. But the patch is a permanent amnesiac, if not complete. I hope she's right.'

They walked on through the woods for nearly an hour before they entered a clearing and approached a strange scene, only it did not feel strange at all to Kenny. There was a wigwam nestled in an aspen grove with a small sweat lodge off to its southwest. East of the sweat lodge and south of the wigwam was a large fire pit with a small, almost smokeless campfire. There sat Rick with another woman in camouflage uniform.

Lois stopped and watched Kenny. "Line Camp," she said. "You know Rick, and that is Sergeant Howell, Sammi, with him. You'll like her. Everybody likes Sammi." Lois paused and studied Kenny. "Ken, she's my best friend, and she's very fragile, especially now. Please?"

Kenny nodded slowly. "Okay." He added, "Why do you call it Line Camp?"

"You know how General Williams is about words. He comes up with terms for everything, and they usually have multiple meanings, you know, like Little Guerrillas for LGs, or his infamous *Lobo Gatos*. His official meaning for this Line Camp is 'line of embarkation,' but I really think this is his 'line in the sand'."

"I like it." Kenny affirmed. "I like them both. This is where we draw the line."

"Yes, we do, Ken."

Kenny walked into camp as though he were going into a familiar, old church. He knew what was behind the wigwam, precisely where the stream flowed beyond the little hill to the southeast, and where General Williams stood watching them at this moment. With no greeting, he sat on the west side of the fire directly facing Rick. Lois took the place on the south side facing Sammi.

Rick was a bigger man than Kenny, solid and hard looking with a short but full beard that refused to turn completely gray despite his age. Like Kenny, he wore commercial camouflage hunting clothes. He looked up now and made eye contact with Kenny. Kenny looked toward Sammi, noticing her reddened eyes, and back at Rick. Rick looked into the fire. Lois was already staring at the flames. Sammi sat fidgeting her long, lean frame in no defined way, her light blonde hair pulled behind a delicate, pale face.

Sammi spoke first, "Hi, Lo."

"Hi, Sammi, Rick," Lois answered.

Rick just nodded, eyes fixed on the fire.

Kenny looked over at Sammi again, "Hi Sammi." She tried to smile back.

Lois attempted conversation. "I wonder how the general will come in today, and when."

"He's already here," Kenny advised.

"He's been here awhile," Rick added. "I think he wanted to watch you two come in." The fire became very important to all of them.

Sammi asked, "Lo, should we get started on dinner, or…?"

"I don't know Sammi. I don't know. How about some tea, first?"

"No," Rick declared simply, "we'll smudge, first."

"Then drum a bit," Kenny added.

Sammi and Lois rose almost in unison and went into the wigwam. Each returned with two drums, about a foot across, a round one in the left hand and an octagon one in the right. The rims were made of unfinished wood and the skins of thick elk rawhide. The beaters were tanned leather bags packed with animal hair and tied to natural sticks. Lois gave Kenny the octagon drum with one large cougar print painted on the rawhide in rich, brown tones. Her round drum was a medium fawn color with some elk hair remaining in little patches. The octagon drum Sammi gave Rick bore two black wolf prints. Her round drum skin was almost pure white.

They carefully placed the drums on the dry ground outside the fire pit. Sammi reached into a pocket and offered

Rick a bundle of sage folded with dry cedar greens, pieces of tobacco leaves, and strands of sweet grass tied with red cotton yarn. He picked up a glowing coal from the fire with a pair of green sticks, almost chopstick style, and placed it on a large river clam shell, then carefully set the smudge bundle on the coal. Lois offered a wing feather from a great horned owl to Rick, and he fanned the smoking bundle. When he passed the feather back to Lois, she stood up while Sammi took the shell with the smoking bundle in both hands and rose.

As the women moved behind Rick, both men stood. Lois fanned the smoke toward Rick as Sammi moved the bundle from his feet to his head and back. He turned around and they repeated, pausing while Rick drew some smoke up and around his head with his hands. He nodded, and the women repeated the procedure with Kenny. When they were finished, the process was reversed, Kenny holding the smudge and Rick fanning. Rick replaced the spent coal in the fire and drew a few fresh ones to the side of the fire pit. He placed the smudge bundle on those coals and all four returned to their places.

Kenny looked over at Rick and smiled with a slight nod. "Rick, Lois wants to know what I know about what you and Sammi know and if Dick knows."

"I know," Rick said.

Lois pivoted her head toward Kenny, who pretended to ignore her, then over to Rick, who said, "Lois, I promise it will soon become clearer."

She seemed to relax a bit and gave Kenny a softer look. Sammi fidgeted until Kenny started drumming. Rick, Lois, and Sammi all picked up their drums and beaters. Kenny developed a steady, slow rhythm: Bum, bum, bum, bum. Rick picked up the beat, keeping it soft. Lois and Sammi joined in ever so softly. They continued for some time—until time no longer mattered. Kenny began a second beat between the beats of basic rhythm. Soon, Lois interposed her own. It seemed to take a long time before Sammi added her drum voice. Rick kept the basic rhythm as all four held the beats soft.

Distinctions between individual beats and drums melted away. Other drum voices seemed to join the four, overtones or something else. They began to build in volume, intensity, and variety, but no one was leading. They improvised without violating each other. Kenny perspired, Rick breathed in rhythm, Lois danced from the hips up, and Sammi drained tears and fears down her cheeks. They faded, softened, and slowed. Kenny gave a series of seven sets of four beats: BUM, bum, bum, bum. All stopped.

Chapter Two

High Sun, 17 May

Silence seemed to echo from the surrounding forest and reverberate inside Kenny's heart. He felt the peace of acceptance, not that all things were as they should be or he wished them to be, but that it was okay the way things were. It didn't really make sense to him, but he was grateful for the feeling.

The sun had climbed to its zenith and begun descending. Their four shadows were short, just slightly east of true north. In a clearing among the aspen, they sat absorbing the heat, air as still as their drums. Even insects seemed to be in *siesta*. Like lovers in an afterglow, they were slow to awaken an awareness of reality beyond their own minds.

Rick gazed off to the southwest at the puffy white clouds forming, then at Kenny. "Well, Windy, it looks like you might have brought some storms with you again." The women looked at Rick and then at the clouds, but said nothing.

Kenny simply nodded, gradually becoming aware that he was quite warm. "I think I'll cool off in the stream." Lois and Sammi got up to put the drums away while Rick and Kenny walked to the little creek, took off their boots and shirts, and splashed their faces, heads, and necks. Rick sat on the near bank while Kenny crossed the stream. The women joined them but kept their shirts on, Lois beside Kenny and Sammi by Rick. The four sat there dangling their feet ankle deep in the cool water in the shade of a cottonwood tree just soaking in the day.

Rick exchanged looks with Sammi and focused on Lois as he spoke. "I remember our last mission. I removed my patch before I left the hospital. That's why I didn't need the cocktail here. So I remember everything from before we arrived at Line Camp. I know what happened and I remember. Knowing and remembering is better than knowing and not remembering. Not remembering does not equal not knowing, and that is where we miscalculated."

Kenny couldn't discern if what he saw in Sammi was fear, anger, sadness, or all three. Lois was stone-faced. 'Denial.'

Kenny responded, "It seems a noble attempt to prevent the tragic casualties of combat post traumatic stress by inducing amnesia, but something isn't working. I see evidence of PTSD all around whether people are using the patch or not. Maybe they're just reading signs of the times. No, we know something inside, we just don't know how or why we know it."

"That's it, Kenny," Rick said. "We know—you and I anyway—we know enough about the human mind to realize that we don't know enough about the mind to predict the emotional consequences of conscious sedation. I mean, we were there, for chrise sake. We just don't have conscious memory. We still have some kind of emotional memory. We just can't process it consciously. What the hell good is that?" Rick rubbed the Cape buffalo tattoo on his right forearm.

Lois leaned against Kenny just a touch and asked, her voice small and trembling with innocence, "What are you going to do?"

"We're going to do our duty, Lo," Kenny answered, "but no more patches, and no damned cocktail, whatever that is. They don't work anyway. When Rick told me his memory of our last mission, I was not surprised. I was sick to my stomach, but not surprised. It was like, yeah, I guess I knew that, at some level, anyway."

He hesitated while considering the recent changes in The Dream, the American faces. "I just wasn't letting it penetrate my conscious mind. It's another form of denial—denial by medication."

Lois looked right at Kenny, brow furrowed up and lips curled down. "What about the last mission, Kenny?"

"They were kids, Lo," Kenny responded as a reflex. "We killed kids, some no older than my daughter, Amy, when she died in Desert Storm. We thought we could help keep some of our kids from getting hurt by doing part of the job for them, and we end up killing kids, ourselves."

Kenny waded in his own silence, remembering what had just flooded out of him, wondering why he had opened up like that and why he had called Ms. Anderson, Lo, although it felt so natural. Now he noticed the silence of the others. Sammi leaned on Rick's right arm and Lois waited for the sky to reveal its secrets. "Ms. Anderson?" Kenny asked, "how about a little walk?"

"Sure, Kenny," Lois answered as she came back to Earth. She lifted her feet out of the stream and dried them off with her hands. Kenny did the same. They waited a few minutes without saying anything while they air dried, then put on their socks and boots.

Kenny slipped his shirt on and headed upstream with Lois beside him. They walked slowly away from Sammi and Rick, still not talking, pretending to notice the terrain until they were out of sight of Line Camp. Kenny paused, surveying the forest as Lois watched him. He turned toward her with a boyish little grin in his eyes and directed his gaze uphill a few yards toward a patch of brambles under the open scrub oaks. Lois followed his eyes with hers and searched. There, under the blackberry bush, lay a fawn as still as stone. Instinctively, they both panned the area for the doe, but she was not in sight. They looked at each other as though they both knew, or felt, that things were going to be okay.

They walked on in silence until they came to a spring area beside the stream and found another large cottonwood tree for shade. Kenny sat down slowly, his legs flexed out in front and his back against the tree. Lois sat cross-legged close by, facing him. This time she waited for him to answer her unspoken questions.

"You know my daughter, Amy, was killed in Dhahran, Saudi Arabia, during Desert Storm," he began. Lois waited. "It wasn't news at that time because she was not officially in country at all. I think that whole thing killed my wife. She was Amy's stepmom, but she loved her like a daughter. I know the cancer took Vicky, but I believe her grief made it impossible for her to fight the cancer, even from the beginning.

"Then, the second time around, our ears and hearts were full of Lori Piestewa and Jessica Lynch." He paused for a few moments while Lois waited. "One evening I was watching Tom Brokaw when he showed a picture of a Marine in dress blues, and I said, 'I know him.' I still saw him as the high school freshman I had taught years before and now he was dead in Iraq. I was so tired of kids getting killed and hurt. We cried for Lori and her children. We cried for Jessica even after she got home, again. Or maybe I just cried for Amy, or for myself. Rick cried with me, Lo. Always there was Rick, and now it seems there is only Rick."

He paused and came back to this warm beautiful day, noticing Lois wiping her eyes and nose. She gave him a look of compassionate understanding and began to reach out to him with her hands but stopped herself. She sat back, placing her hands at rest in front of her. "I knew the facts, Kenny, but I never heard you say it before."

Kenny gave a nod. "So Lois, what's your story? I suppose you've told me before, but this time I might remember."

"My story? Oh, wow. Can I get back to you on that?"

"When?" Kenny said.

"Yeah, when? Well, I joined the National Guard to pay for college, and I...," She looked at Kenny and stopped. "Oh, that's not what you mean, is it?" Kenny gave the slightest little shake of his head.

"I don't know what to say, Kenny. I mean, I'm not supposed to say much. That's my job, to know all about you but keep myself outside of it."

"How's that going, Lo?"

She gave a helpless little laugh. "Not so good."

"How's it going with Sammi? Are you staying outside of her problems too?"

Lois gave him a fried ice cream look, only inside out—sort of cold on the outside but warm on the inside. "Sammi and I have been friends for so long, much like you and Rick. I feel everything she's feeling, but she couldn't tell me everything she was thinking. It hasn't been much fun, Ken."

'She called me Ken, again. Interesting.' Then he asked, "Lo, is that my fault?"

"Ah, hmmm. Maybe I've been blaming you, Kenny. I'm sorry. No, it's not your fault. 'That is the way things are.' That's your quote."

"Not really. That's Chief Dan George's quote, or actually, Old Lodge Skins in Little Big Man."

"But, it's yours too. You told me about that one walking vision quest you did."

"Oh, I did? I must trust you, Chief."

"Well, I hope so, because, here goes." She inhaled and exhaled, looking into Kenny's eyes. "How about Rick? Is he okay? Are you okay? Without the patch, I mean?"

"We're not okay with the patch, Lo. Without it, I don't know, but with it I know that we are not okay." He sat, inspecting his thoughts. "Hey, look, one of the reasons—the big reason I think—that we do this, I mean Rick and I, is because we don't have much to lose. I mean, we're not kids. We don't have our whole lives ahead of us. Realistically, how much life do we have to lose? One year? Five? Ten, maybe, in some old farts' home? We're just a couple of tired old men. Neither of us leaves anyone to grieve...."

Lois stopped him with another ice cream look, only this one wasn't so warm on the inside. "First, Kenneth Luke Brewster, LG, you are not going to leave. Second, there are people right here, right now, who grieve the very thought of you leaving."

It sounded like a long speech that ran out of wind and just ended abruptly. Kenny looked at her as though he had never really seen her before. 'Why?' he asked himself.

"Because, you are one of the most interesting...,"

"I'm interesting?" he interrupted.

"And exasperating, and gentle, and real—yeah, real—human beings I have ever met. Besides, you saved my life, remember?"

"No, Lois, I really do not remember, but maybe that's a story for another time. It looks like Rick was right, again." Kenny nodded his head toward the billowing thunderclouds forming in the southwest.

"Is that why he calls you Windy?"

"Sure, that's it."

Lois looked at him with a grin of amusement mixed with frustration and shook her head several times. Kenny rose carefully, stretching the kinks out, and they headed back downstream.

Early Afternoon, 17 May

As they approached camp, Kenny noticed Rick dragging some coals from the fire. He picked them up on a piece of bark and carried them into the wigwam. The thunderclouds had formed a dark towering thunderhead with a spreading anvil top, and it was headed right for them. Kenny walked around the wigwam to the east side and stooped to enter through the open door.

When Lois came in, Rick was arranging coals and Sammi stacking a few small oak pieces near the fire pit. Lois looked around and asked, "Where's General Williams? He's going to get soaked."

Rick looked up at Kenny and then at Lois, "He left soon after you got here."

Lois started to form some word with her mouth, but it didn't come out. She raised her eyebrows, blinked slowly, and nodded her head as if to say, 'oh, yeah.'

Sammi looked up and smiled at her, "Hi, Lo."

Lois and Kenny both took a look at Sammi and then at each other. Kenny observed to himself, 'Well, her mood sure has improved.' Without turning his head, he shifted his eyes from Sammi back to Lois. 'Well, so has hers,' he answered himself.

Even inside the wigwam they could see that it had gotten much darker. Rick ducked outside and looked around. Kenny followed, then the women. There was a hush over the forest again only very different from the *siesta*. It was like the pause between breaths, after the exhale, before the inhale. Not a bird was on the wing.

The wind came cold and straight, and the sky was almost as dark as night. Sammi reached for Lois and pulled her back inside the wigwam. Rick simply looked at Kenny and shook his head. Kenny stood erect, looking off toward the west, tilted his head back, and took a large deliberate breath. As he exhaled audibly, he lowered his arms and head, then he knelt to touch the Earth.

Rick stepped into the wigwam, and Kenny soon followed. The wind velocity rose as the first rain fell followed by the hail. Sammi sat near the little fire next to Lois, still clinging to her arm. Rick sat next to Sammi, but Kenny kept his eyes on the weather as he knelt by the door. The ground was already nearly covered with hailstones as large as hen's eggs. Leaves and small branches littered the ground. As the hail stopped, it began to rain in earnest, like it was July. Kenny backed away from the door and sat next to Lois where they could all see outside.

Curtains of rain blew across camp, but the wind came from the west and their door was in the east. Rick had almost closed the smoke hole on top, so they stayed dry. Kenny looked around at the others. Lois was stoic as she patted Sammi's hand that gripped her arm. Sammi leaned in wide-eyed terror onto Lois's shoulder, but she did not utter a sound. Rick carefully tended the fire with small, dry pieces of oak. Still, it rained.

Lightning flashes brightened their whole camp, even inside the wigwam. Thunder clapped and rolled, sometimes directly overhead. Kenny counted to himself the time between flashes and thunder, almost twenty seconds. That meant the lightning was four miles away, but directly overhead, so tall was this thunderhead.

The rain diminished and the thunder rolled more distant in the east. It even seemed to be getting lighter. Rick looked directly at Kenny and said nothing. 'Tornado?' Kenny asked himself, and gave a raised eyebrow look to Rick. Lois watched their every movement, but Sammi was oblivious to everything except Lois's arm.

Distant thunder rolled in the west. 'Another cell is coming,' Kenny advised himself. Rick already knew, and nobody else needed to.

Rick took a look at Sammi, Kenny, and then Lois. "Lois, did Windy ever tell you about his history with storms on vision quests?"

"What?" She awakened to a reality with human voices again. "Oh, uh," she looked directly at Kenny, "no, he has not."

Kenny scooted around the fire pit to face them more directly, his back to the door. "The first time I did a vision quest on my own land, it rained. The second night I had a significant insight, a profound question which I felt compelled to answer, 'Do you love enough?' When I answered, 'I don't know,' it felt unacceptable, and I heard the question again in my mind. Only when I finally answered, 'Yes,' did the question no longer persist. Then I heard the rumble in the west. This was evening twilight and it rained all night. Cell after cell came by until my little valley was flowing with water several feet deep, but I was on a hill many feet above the water level. People still refer to it as a storm of the century because it washed out several roads, including mine. But I just sat there on the hill and watched it all night. It was awesome!"

"Weren't you afraid?" Sammi asked with a child's innocence.

"No, not really," Kenny answered. "I was much more afraid of the question, or my answer, actually, than I was of those storms. I don't think anybody got hurt in that storm at all. It just rained."

"Good," Sammi said.

"So, Kenny," Lois began, "can you elaborate on your answer to that question?"

"I don't really know, Lo." He paused. "I suppose my life is the elaboration, I mean the way I try to live every day." He stopped.

"Yeah, I think so, too," Lois said.

The thunder grew louder again and more rain fell, only without the wind and hail. Sammi let go of Lois's arm who gave it a little shake as if to check blood flow and nerve function.

The wigwam was fairly traditional, although more of a winter model, and well suited to withstand storms. Neither Kenny nor Rick was Native American, but they shared a love of living close to this land. The traditions and technologies of people indigenous to the area had evolved as adaptations to the regional climate and geography. It was also what they had learned in their shared wilderness survival school experiences.

Stout saplings had been staked into the ground in a circle about sixteen feet across. These saplings had been bent over in arcs and tied together forming a skeleton of a dome leaving a center opening on top. More sticks had been tied to these saplings, providing both strength and an anchor for still smaller sticks woven into place. Finer forest debris had been added and the entire structure shingled with bark slabs. They had even taken time to build an inner wall and insulate the space between the two. The east doorway and the center hole had mats woven of cattails and grass bundles tied onto frames with a kind of hinge made of cordage. It was a comfortable place, large enough to sleep all four on separate beds made of grass mats over leaf litter and still have some room to work on projects, cook, or just sit around and talk.

The air was fresher now, although not cold, as the second storm passed quickly. The ground was still covered with hail, a gift of nature that they accepted. Each grabbed a basket, some of woven vines and some bark, and went outside to pick up hail. Taking it into the cache, the underground pit like a root cellar out back, they deposited the hail into earthen crocks around the tiny cellar. This would save them work hauling water to keep their produce cool and fresh.

Midafternoon, 17 May

Sammi brought out a basket of romaine lettuce, celery, tomatoes, and green peppers. Rick retrieved two wooden cutting boards and a block of knives from the wigwam. Lois set a large wooden bowl on the ground along with a wooden condiment box. Kenny returned from the stream with a big bladder canteen full of filtered water. The four of them sat down, washing and cutting their produce for supper.

"Kenny," Lois hesitated. "I've never really heard how you and Rick met. You've both been kind of vague. Was it actually in Vietnam? I know your tours overlapped in time and place."

Sammi stiffened a bit as though she felt she had done something wrong. Kenny looked at Rick who gave a shrug as if to say it was okay with him.

Kenny shifted around in his position sitting on the ground. "We met at The Wall."

Lois continued to cut celery into the large bowl, focusing on her work. After a couple of minutes, she asked, "You wouldn't care to elaborate a bit more, would you Windy?"

Kenny felt a little right-sided smirk and glanced at Rick, who showed the slightest sign of amusement in his eyes. "It was 1984."

Lois stopped working, as if contemplating the significance of that elaboration, and raised an eyebrow with a kind of reverse nod, lifting her head in a way that told Kenny she had made a connection. "You went to the Vietnam Memorial during the time of your divorce."

Kenny gave Rick a look of smug understanding and said, "That's how she got this job, I'll bet. Brilliant powers of deduction. Need I say more?"

"Please," Lois said.

"Okay, Lo. It was right after Bonnie kicked me out of the house. K.J. was about fifteen and Amy twelve. I was angry and scared and I just woke up one morning that summer with a terrible hangover, loaded up my Goldwing, and ran away from home. I tried to run away from myself but that didn't work. I headed east and rode all day and night. The heat and humidity both approached a hundred during the day, and the night was clammy wet. I really didn't know, I mean at a conscious level—well, I wasn't all that conscious anyway—I didn't plan where I was going. I remember stopping in Bethesda to drink a large Gatorade. I was so dehydrated, I figure I drank a couple gallons on that trip and peed a pint.

"Anyway, I decided to head for downtown D.C. It seemed like I just followed some kind of flow until I saw the top of the Washington Monument, so I went there. By this time I was thinking about The Wall, so I picked up information and located parking nearby.

"As I walked toward it, I remember thinking two things. First, I thought, 'What happens if I don't feel anything?' The second thing I thought was, 'I probably smell about like most of these guys did when they died.'

"It just happened, I suppose, that I walked up on the short end of The Wall. I don't know, maybe they planned it that way, but anyway, the first name I saw was Brewer, and it triggered me to ask, 'Where should my name be?' I wandered around a bit, but I wanted to know where I belonged, so I asked a ranger, and he gave me the directory, or whatever, that showed the panels for my tour of duty. I found the names of those killed while I was in country. I only knew a few personally.

"Then I sat down. I just found a place in the grass back away from The Wall and sat. I suppose I was noticeable sitting there in corduroy jeans, cowboy boots, and long sleeve shirt on such a hot day, but I was glad to be wearing my dark riding glasses because the tears started flowing. Not a lot, but....

"I sat there awhile just watching people walk by, some looking over at me and others looking like me. I have never been any other place, not church, cemetery, not even Pearl Harbor, where people were more reverent. I watched young service men and women in beautiful summer dress uniforms pass by. At some time in there I remembered a line from The Green Berets where John Wayne holds up a weapon and says something like, 'It's a funny thing, a man carries one of these into combat and, by the grace of God, comes out in one piece, he carries a strange sense of guilt with him the rest of his life.' Then, I had my first real spiritual experience—at least, that I recall.

"I heard a voice, not outside, but inside my head, or heart maybe. It said, 'It's okay.' I sort of thought, 'What?' The voice answered, 'It's okay your name is not here.' I looked around to see, I don't know, if anybody else heard it, or if I was crazy or something. I sat there quietly and very relaxed now for some time, only it didn't seem to take any time.

"Then I heard the voice again, 'It's okay we died.' I wanted to scream, 'How can that be okay?' I didn't want to scream anymore. I think I knew it was okay, only I didn't know how I knew it. I still don't know how I accepted that, but I did.

"The voice spoke one more time. I had been angry, enraged even, at Nixon and Kissinger, and especially at Congress, for more than a decade already, only I hadn't always known it. Now the voice told me, 'It's okay it happened.' I'm still working on accepting that one. I know it's true, but I don't want to believe it yet."

Kenny stopped talking and looked around as though he had just gotten back from somewhere far away. Rick was watching Sammi season the salad with pepper and herbs. Lois was sprinkling nuts and craisins on top. She looked up with slow movement of her head. Kenny saw something in her eyes that he had never noticed before. He couldn't define it exactly, but he knew it was good.

"Was Rick there?" Lois asked.

"Oh, yeah. Rick turned around and looked at me. He had been looking at the names on the same panels from 1970, so I guessed we might have been there the same time. Something in his look invited me to get up. Besides, I was feeling lighter and cleaner now, so I just stepped forward and we both extended our hands. Somehow, it was like we were old friends.

"We found out we had been in different units but, not only in country much of the same time, we were in the same place part of that time but never met. We both participated in the Cambodian Invasion—excuse me, Incursion. Rick got wounded and I only got sick, in the head. *Dingky dow.* That's what the Vietnamese called us, *Dingky dow hoi ki,* or Sick Head Flower Flag, their way of saying crazy Americans.

"I suppose this is an understatement, but there is a bond of trust that goes way beyond camaraderie among people who have shared such experiences. I don't think it's just trust in someone protecting your life. I think it's a kind of trust in someone understanding how you feel and maybe why you are the way you are, especially the way you don't want to be.

"And that's all I have to say about that," Kenny said in his best Forrest Gump impression.

"Thank you, Kenny," Lois answered.

Chapter Three

Late Afternoon, 17 May

General Williams approached camp from behind the sweat lodge, attempting to sneak up without appearing to be stalking. Sammi heard a twig snap and turned her head to see him slowly moving among the trees. She looked at Rick who returned a direct glance that told her he already knew. Lois picked up on their interaction and observed the general walking directly toward them in his normal gait.

Kenny said, "He never quite gets that stalking is more about the mind than the feet."

"Lobo Gatos," The big man called, or rather commanded. Sammi stiffened significantly and Lois focused on her boss.

Rick greeted him, "Hey, Dick."

"Welcome," Kenny said, "I'm glad you're here. I'm getting hungry and running out of things to say."

"Shall we get ready for dinner?" Lois asked no one in particular.

"On your command, Chief," General Williams responded.

Lois and Sammi set the bowl of salad in the wigwam and proceeded to their latrine area out back. Kenny and Rick each found a tree, and the general walked to the stream to wash his face and hands. The ladies went directly from their latrine to the creek a little downstream from the general.

"Well, ladies," he began, "what is your assessment?"

Lois answered, "Sir, I'm not sure just what is going on, but I feel better than I did this morning."

"You do?" Sammi asked.

"Well, sure. This morning I had no idea what was wrong or who knew what."

"Oh, yeah," Sammi said. "Sorry, Lo."

"No, no, Sammi. You did what you had to do. You did the right thing, keeping the confidence." Lois said.

"Yes you did," General Williams affirmed. "You both did. Very professional. Nice job."

"Thank you, sir," Sammi said. Lois responded only with a frail smile.

As the three of them approached the fire pit, Rick and Kenny just sort of appeared with five personal size wooden bowls and forks.

"I suppose you both heard what we were talking about," Lois commented, looking first at Rick, then Kenny.

"Didn't need to," Kenny answered, "but, yes."

Early Evening, 17 May

The sun had lost much of its intensity, but the air remained warm and humid. As the shadows lengthened, a promise of a pleasant evening emerged. Kenny breathed it in slowly and deliberately and exhaled with intent.

Rick and Kenny brought small dry wood and coals from inside the wigwam while General Williams carried large armloads of oak chunks from the stack in the lean-to behind the sweat lodge. Together, they prepared for a nice big fire, but Rick kept it small for now. The women set the salad bowl and condiments on the ground and they each served themselves.

"It is beautiful out here," General Williams observed.

Sammi looked around as though this was something she had forgotten.

"Yes, it is," said Lois.

A pod of Blackhawk helicopters flew by to the southeast about then, and nobody said anything for several minutes.

"Green Bay is in turmoil right now," General Williams said, "as I expect you all know one way or another. I presume we are secure." He looked at Rick and Kenny. They both nodded. "The conflict between—well, among—the factions has spun out of control. It was the governor's assessment...," He paused as Kenny snapped a look at the general. "No, not him. The current governor's assessment is that citizens of Green Bay would be safer for now if we pulled the troops out because they were attracting all sorts of attacks, from all sides it seemed, and innocent people were being caught in the middle. There still are innocent people there." General Williams trailed off in uncharacteristic fashion. "The kinds of things we saw last summer in smaller cities around America has now found Wisconsin."

"Why Green Bay, Dick?" Kenny asked, "Why not Milwaukee or Madison?"

"That second question I do not ask," General Williams answered. "Why Green Bay I do ask, but I have no satisfactory answer, only so-called intelligence assessments." He stopped there and looked around the terrain outside their little circle. "But, it is what it is, and we are out for now. Officially, the blame is placed on this loose alliance among militant ethnic and ideological groups opposed to the Fight for Right people. I hate these names. They are so polarizing and inaccurate."

"I noticed you avoided that term the ex-governor used, Dick," Kenny said.

Lois snapped a look at Kenny, and Sammi sat wide eyed and open mouthed.

"I'll explain it all after dinner, Chief Anderson," the general said. "Right now I want to know how the four of you are doing. Are we ready for this mission?"

Kenny glanced at Lois who was watching Sammi. He turned to see Sammi fidgeting and contorting. Kenny didn't know if she were going to speak or scream.

Rick spoke, "Yes, sir."

Sammi shook her head and looked at Lois in fear.

"What is it, Sergeant Howell?" General Williams asked.

"Go ahead," Rick said quietly.

Kenny watched the general.

Sammi started, "Well…Rick…I mean, something is wrong.

Everyone waited.

Sammi went on, "Rick is different. He doesn't laugh anymore—ever, I think. He's so sad and depressed. I just wish...."

Lois reached over and placed a hand on Sammi's knee. Rick tended the fire. Kenny breathed deliberately.

General Williams waited patiently before asking, "What do you wish, Sammi?"

Sammi softened to hear her general call her by her first name. Lois nodded, and Sammi blurted, "I wish they would take their medicine."

Kenny nodded gently. Lois released a combined sigh and shrug. Rick tended the fire. General Williams said, "I do, too, but it's not my call. Is that all that's bothering you Sammi? Lois?"

"No, sir," Lois answered. "Green Bay is bothering us. The climate is bothering us. This election is bothering us." She paused and everyone waited for more.

In a child-like voice, Sammi added, "Turning forty is bothering us," then looked around in surprise as if to see who said that. Rick looked up at her. Kenny looked at Sammi and Rick and then met eyes with Lois.

"Hell, it's not so bad," General Williams offered as a tension release. "I can say from personal experience that there is life after forty. Good life, ladies."

Kenny flashed an attempted smile at Sammi, "There's life after sixty, Sammi," he said with a limping lilt in his voice.

Sammi looked at Rick, sighed, and waited. Rick finally responded. "It is okay, Sammi. One foot in front of the other, one day at a time. Tomorrow does not exist and may never exist for all we know. But tonight is here and it is beautiful." He paused before continuing. "Yesterday exists only in memories and today will cease to exist if we can't remember it. That's all. I don't want to lose any more todays because of those damned drugs and their amnesia. I want to remember today, here, with you, with all of you."

Sammi nodded tearfully, "I know, Rick, but you're so different now after that last mission without the patch. What? How…?"

"I was different before that mission, Sammi. You just didn't notice. I was hiding it, I suppose. But, I can do this mission. I need to do this mission. I need to be relevant, Sammi."

Sammi appeared ready to speak but bit her lip and nodded affirmation. Lois patted Sammi's knee. Kenny took a deep breath. Rick tended the fire. General Williams spoke softly, as softly as his voice allowed, "I love you people." Immediately, he gathered up his general bearing and commanded, "Let's get ready for the briefing."

Full Dark, 17 May

The briefing was a new experience for Kenny's conscious mind. In the past, he had already been on the patch at the VA before reporting for isolation. He sat in disbelief as Lois and Sammi returned from the wigwam with hand-held computers. They sat on either side of General Williams, Lois on his right and Sammi on his left. The blue-green light from their computer screens gave them each a ghostly glow. Rick looked at Kenny and shook his head.

"Okay, Sergeant Howell," the general said.

Sammi began, "Yes, sir. Our most recent intelligence assessment is that sizeable groups including foreign nationals will be converging on Northern Wisconsin soon, perhaps already. These are reported to be professional cadres prepared to recruit and train autonomous cells in the Green Bay area to disrupt the Fight for Right campaign of the National Freedom Party. They are expected to assemble in significant numbers, perhaps a few hundred, in a remote area of the Chequamegon-Nicolet National Forest where they will prepare for their assignments. This will be our only opportunity to interdict them as a group and disrupt their plans.

"They are expected to enter through Marquette and Escanaba, Michigan, and Duluth-Superior. The most convenient place to converge would be north of us, near the Wisconsin-Michigan border. The most opportune time to travel would be the few nights before and after the new moon when the roads are dark late for several hours. It is possible that they will move during this moon, but our assessment is that next month may help them to build momentum and affect the presidential election. However, we must be prepared for the contingency that the assembly has already begun.

"If our intelligence is sound, this is a dangerous group of professionals with significant capacity to kill using little or no visible weaponry. Conventional tactics are far too slow and cumbersome to find them, much less inflict any real damage because of their capacity to flee, blend in, live off the land and regroup at secondary or tertiary rendezvous points. That is why General Williams has chosen to use his favorite *Lobo Gatos*."

"Thank you, Sammi," General Williams said, "Chief Anderson?"

"Thank you, General Williams. Sammi gave you the best intelligence we have, so now I'm going to rough out the plan for you to develop. Our mission is to kill them, as many of them as possible, as quickly as possible. If this assessment is close to accurate, not only could Green Bay be in danger of collapsing completely this summer, but the presidential election could be usurped. It will depend entirely upon the two of you.

"First, you must find them without being detected. Then you must determine the location for the greatest assembly, tag it effectively, and get away undetected before the ordinance arrives. We will be using Rolling Thunder so that civilians will be less likely to recognize the explosions and so that the bodies will remain intact. The tags you will use are very small and inside fishing bobbers. LGs, you are going fishing.

"One more thing. If these intelligence reports are accurate, the assembly will break up very soon after the new moon. We may have a few weeks, but we may have much less, guys."

"Thank you, Lois," General Williams said. "Guys, you are not just my best LGs, you are my friends, my honorary uncles. At the very least, your success will likely decide the future of the Army's LG program. You know how the brass hates this thing. At the worst, we lose Green Bay and the democratic process. Of course, I might lose my job, which is nothing compared to what you could lose. Any questions?"

"Yes, sir," Lois asserted. "What ex-governor and what term?"

"Oh, right. An ex-governor, who shall remain nameless, helps to provide our intelligence." General Williams paused, apparently measuring his response. "He used a term today that Kenny didn't like referring to the groups that seem to be cooperating against the Fight for Right campaign." He paused again and Lois looked directly at him, waiting. "The governor calls them The Unholy Alliance."

"I see," was all Lois said.

"My turn, sir," Kenny said. "How far do we need to be from the tags, and how much time do we have from activation?"

"I expect you have never seen a demonstration of Rolling Thunder. It is a kind of neutron bomb, or timed cluster of bombs, that sounds like thunder and kills almost all life in a radius of four to five hundred meters, depending upon terrain and vegetation. That's more than a quarter mile, boys. The good news is you can set the time for the missile to arrive—except, it is important to keep that time as short as possible so the targeted people are still there when the missile hits. Are you in?"

"Are there other options?" Rick asked rhetorically, glancing at Kenny. "We're in."

"We need a date, time, and location," said Kenny. "We'd better get to work, Rick."

Rick looked to Sammi, "We'll sweat tomorrow night." Kenny nodded.

"Then we'll get to specifics right away," General Williams said. Sammi immediately rose to go, but Lois hesitated, looking to the general. "Stay, ladies," he said. "There'll be no need for cocktails tonight since there are no patches." He looked at Kenny. "The cocktail blocks the hypnotics in the patch. That's why you can remember the details of mission plans, but not the initial briefings. The effect wears off in a matter of hours, and the patch-induced amnesia sets in again so you do not remember the details and trauma of the actual mission."

Kenny affirmed, "Okay."

Rick added, "That's why we never remembered the girls. They left before cocktail hour. We only saw them while we were wearing patches, except for me last time, that is. That's when everybody knew I was off the patch."

"Okay, men," the general went on, "we need to get specific about time and place. I think this will actually work better with the ladies here. I think they can help."

"Yes, sir," Rick agreed.

"First question?" the general asked.

"When?" Kenny answered. "Time might be easier to identify by moon phase and planet alignment. How should we start, Rick?"

"Let's take a walk, separate sit meditations. Give us a drum call back when it feels right. Will you do that, Sammi?"

"I will." Sammi answered with mild surprise.

Rick and Kenny rose, stretched, and disappeared into the moonless, starlit night.

Wee Hours, 18 May

When the embers faded to black, General Williams stoked and fanned the fire to high flames and Sammi began to drum softly. Rick appeared by the vigorous fire almost immediately, as though he had been waiting for the call behind a nearby tree. Kenny walked in several minutes later. They both sat by the fire in quiet reverence while the others waited.

"Windy?" Rick said.

Kenny took a big breath and said, "I've got a problem. I focused on the action night, and all I saw was dark. I saw no moon, no stars, no planets, no reference. I couldn't even see any terrain features in my meditation, it was so dark. It was quiet, too. I think it was drizzling."

"Ahh," Rick said, "that would explain it. I got a whole lot of blackness, too. Kind of freaked me out, until I stopped analyzing and just watched. Lots of people, though."

"You saw people?" Kenny asked.

"Well, no, sensed, I guess. I saw nothing."

"Yeah," Kenny agreed, "but I sensed small groups of people moving toward a bigger group."

"Yeah," Rick said slowly. "Okay, we're going to need to try something. Let's do this again in the morning, in daylight, and try to get a sense of location."

"Okay," Kenny added, "and maybe we should look to time features for the night before the action when we might have to plant the tags. How many tags will we have, General?"

"How many do you want?" he asked.

"Four," Rick and Kenny said almost in unison.

"You shall have them," the general promised. "Shall we call it a night?

"No," Rick said. "Let's warm a bit then spread the fire and watch the embers for awhile."

"I like that," Sammi said, and settled in tight beside Rick.

Lois chanced a look toward Kenny, but he pretended not to notice and stirred the fire.

"I'll see you tomorrow for supper," General Williams said, and he walked off down a game trail. By the time the flames were gone, they heard his truck start and drive off. Stars came so bright the four could see the Milky Way overhead.

Kenny went to the wigwam first, his last thought before going to sleep being that there had been too many such nights erased from his memory. He felt the rage rising like a beast inside his chest. He tried the breathing and visualization techniques from his PTSD treatment, but the only thing that worked for him tonight was the sweet memory of Vicky and Amy playing like toddlers in the waves of Lake Michigan that week before she went off for active duty.

Breakfast Time, 18 May

Kenny first became aware of the smell of campfire coffee and hot cocoa, mixed he hoped. He looked over to see Lois's and Sammi's beds empty, but Sammi was curled up like a puppy in bed with Rick. He stretched the pains a bit and took his ditty bag to the latrine and stream. He noticed Lois sitting by the fire, but he took care of business first.

She watched him walk back from the stream and said, "Good morning, Ken."

"Good morning, Chief," he answered. "What's for breakfast?"

"Your favorite—mocha."

Kenny smiled all the way to the wigwam and back to the fire. He sat on a dry camp chair and she gave him a metal camp cup of hot coffee-cocoa mixed.

"Why the smiles this morning, Ken?"

"First, tell me why you call me Ken, sometimes, when nobody else is around." He thought he saw her blush just a bit.

"I call you Ken because that is the way I think of you. Do you mind?"

"No, not at all."

"Why do others call you Kenny? Have you always been Kenny?"

"I reckon people call me Kenny because that's how I introduce myself. I was Kenny as a kid and hated it, so I became Ken as an adolescent. When I grew up, about your age, I decided that what my mother called me was just fine. How do you introduce yourself, Lois?"

"I introduce myself to strangers as Lois, but I heard you call me Lo, sometimes."

"Well, I noticed that Sammi calls you Lo, so I figured you must like it."

"I do, but only when it is somebody I care about." The mocha became quite interesting to both of them.

"You still have the advantage on me," Kenny said. "You know my middle name, but I don't know what the J stands for in yours. Does duty prevent you from sharing that with me?"

"No," she said, hesitating. "The J is in honor of my father, as the Luke is in honor of yours...." She paused as Kenny looked intently at her. "I have seen all of your records—background, family." Kenny waited. "My father's name was Gerald, but my parents were kind enough to name me Jeri." She paused again. "Both my parents were killed four years ago in a car accident."

"I'm sorry, Lois Jeri." They looked at each other for a few moments.

"Well?" She asked.

"Well? You mean you know I love mocha but don't know what's funny about it?"

"Yeah huh."

"I loved to mix coffee, cocoa, and creamer when I was in the Army. It was my favorite in the field in the morning. Well, the first time I was in combat, we were attacked while I was having my morning mocha, and I hit the ground so fast I spilled it on me."

"What's funny about that?" she asked.

"What's funny is, when I felt the hot stuff on my leg, I thought I had been wounded."

"I didn't know that one, Kenny," she smiled. "Thanks for sharing." She looked to the wigwam. "Any signs of life in there?"

"Well, I'm not sure what the hell they're doing, but it appears to be living. What's up with that, Lo?"

"I'm not sure anybody knows, Ken. Beautiful morning though, don't you think?"

"Yeah, it is. I like the hazy mornings, and the dew. At least it's pleasantly cool. I think it's going to be muggy again today, damn near like Vietnam." He paused and looked at her. It occurred to him that that was not at all what she was talking about. 'What is she talking about?' he wondered.

Sammi stepped out, almost staggering, and headed toward the latrine area. Lois took off after her. Rick came out, scratched a couple of places, and headed elsewhere, so Kenny decided it was time for a trip of his own. He finished his mocha and headed to the woods.

Late Morning, 18 May

"Welcome back," Lois said as Kenny walked into camp. "Rick's been here for a couple of hours already."

"I don't think so," Kenny answered.

"A couple bowls of breakfast soup, though," Rick said. That's what he called coffee with anything in it.

Kenny noticed that Sammi wasn't hanging on Rick's arm but sitting next to Lois and working on her computer. "Well, partner?" Kenny asked.

"I drew something out. The girls are looking for it on the software."

"Good idea. What did you draw, place or time?"

"Both."

"Okay, Rick. I'll do the same."

"Here." Rick tossed him a small pack. Kenny sat down, pulled a pad and pencil out, and started drawing. First he sketched a kind of map with roads that bounded the area he had visualized. Then he sketched the southeast skyline with one planet and another close by, below on the left, and Mars, maybe, even lower and further east.

By the time he was nearly finished, Lois was looking over his shoulder. "Well, the sky looks nothing like Rick's. And what is that map?" she asked.

"Did he draw another road map?" Rick asked.

"Yeah," she answered slowly.

"Damn, boy, I wish you had a little infantry training," Rick chided.

"I draws what I sees, you crusty old fart," Kenny answered.

"Well, what does you sees?" Rick asked.

"Roads. I think I know the area where we should start."

Rick got up and came for a look. "Oh that must be, what? A hundred square miles?"

"Hey, if you're looking for a needle in a haystack, it helps if you can find the haystack, first," Kenny said.

"You are right, Windy. It will narrow their computer search," Rick answered.

"Is that what they're doing?" Kenny asked.

"Yep," Lois answered. "It's what we always do, but we usually do it behind the curtain. Hey, I think this might actually help. Look at this, Sammi."

Kenny and Rick followed her, kind of excited because they had never been able to work this way before. Sammi studied Kenny's map awhile and narrowed her search on the topographic computer map. Meanwhile, Kenny took a look at Rick's topographic sketch. Rick turned it so north was up.

"Rick," Kenny started slowly, "I think I know this place. It's isolated within a wilderness area—no machines allowed, so, foot travel only." He looked on the computer screen. "Zoom out a bit, Sammi. I think it's over here."

"There it is!" Sammi yelled. "Isn't it?"

"Yes, it is," Rick said.

"How sure are we, guys?" Lois asked.

"Not sure at all, yet," Rick answered. "We might need a group meditation this afternoon."

"A pipe ceremony this evening," Kenny suggested. "Then, there's the sweat lodge tonight," he added.

"Okay," Lois went on, "we'll work on the time fix."

"Their drawings don't match at all, Lo," Sammi said.

Lois asked, "Well, what about direction? Kenny marked southeast, and Rick's is sunset, waxing crescent moon with Venus above, and another planet, so...."

"West-southwest," Rick answered.

"Oh, okay," Sammi said, "And probably different times. Let's take a look."

"How does that work?" Kenny asked.

"Well," Lois answered, "we start today and run a sky program for the location you gave forward in time and stop it when we find a match. That is our date and time."

"How long will that take?" Kenny asked.

"That depends on how far it is into the future," Lois answered, "how much time we have to run the program beyond today."

"I think I'll take a nap," Rick said.

"Alone?" Kenny asked.

Lois's mouth dropped open and Sammi crawled inside her computer screen. Rick stopped and turned back to face them. "Yeah, I think that would be best," he said, and he grabbed a poncho from the wigwam and headed to the woods.

"I think I'll snooze right here," Kenny said and laid a poncho on the ground by the fire pit. "Wake me when you have something."

"Wake up," Sammi said almost immediately. Lois and Kenny stared at her. "I've got something that matches on May 23rd." The three looked at each other in disbelief.

"Five days?" Lois asked. Sammi started to cry, quietly, and that feeling of dread that Kenny hated came back in his gut. Lois swallowed hard and asked hoarsely, "Should we tell Rick?"

"No," Kenny said, "something tells me he already knows."

Chapter Four

Lunch Time, 18 May

Sammi jumped up at Rick's appearance but sat back down and waited for him to sit by the fire. She was still running the program to see if there was another date that matched their sketches, but she could find none.

"What's up?" Rick asked.

"Time, partner," Kenny answered. "Our date is May 23rd. We be hitchin' up and movin' out."

Rick just nodded. "I figured. What's for lunch?"

"Lunch?" Sammi jumped up.

But, Lois was ready. "Soup," she said. "The water is hot and we have dry soup." She went to the cache and came back with an assortment of individual packets. "Care to have your own or do a kettle dump?"

"I feel like a kettle dump," Sammi said.

"Fine with me," Kenny said. "Any fruit in that cache?"

"Oh, yeah," Lois answered. "Sorry guys, I should have thought of that."

"I'll get it," Kenny offered. Lois went with him.

When they got behind the wigwam by the cache, Lois asked, "Ken? How do you feel about this mission?"

"Feel?" Kenny asked. "I feel like something really big and loud and not so good is going to happen, and that it must happen, and that is the way things are."

"Ken? Will you come back?" She looked away and shook her head. "I'm sorry, Kenny, it's not my place to ask such a thing."

"Lois, what is your place?"

"I have no fucking idea, LG."

Kenny winced his head back to hear such language from her. 'I guess she's angry.'

She looked him straight in the eye, just one eye this time, "Yes, I am angry, but not at you, I don't think…maybe, shit. Well, when you come back, I'll be around," and she ducked into the cache. Kenny followed.

"I will keep that in mind." He grabbed a bag of oranges and looked over to see Lois with a bright smile holding one red apple in her hand stretched out for him.

"Cute, Chief, but my age of innocence was gone long before you were born." As soon as he said it, he regretted it. That delightfully wicked smile wilted into the saddest face he had seen since he last looked at Sammi. So, he stepped over and took a bite of apple right out of her hand. "Let's eat. We have work to do, Ms. Anderson."

When they got back to the fire, Sammi was kneeling at Rick's side. When she saw them, she jumped up, brushed herself off, and got real busy with the soup. Rick was just sitting peacefully, as though he had not a care in the world.

"Rick," Lois said, "Kenny says we have work to do. What's next?"

"Well, sister, you can help write our operation plan."

"You want to write it?" Lois asked. Her brow furrowed up with head tilted slightly forward in query.

"Figuratively, Lo," Kenny answered. "Help us think it all through before Dick gets back, then we can be ready for a good sweat."

"Where do we start?" Lois asked. "We never worked this part before."

"We start at May 23rd and work back to now," Rick answered. "The bottom line is we leave tomorrow."

"Before lunch," Kenny added. "We can get some real food on the road."

Lois feigned sticking her tongue out at him, lips firmly together. "Don't you have to make out a wish list for the mission?" she asked.

"Sure," Rick answered. "Don't you have the list from last time? Do like that, only for fishing."

"It's already done, Rick," Sammi said. "Damn it. It's in the general's truck."

Rick gave Lois a curious look, but she ignored him.

Kenny looked at Lois and smiled inside, 'That girl has a little more spunk than I gave her credit for. They both do, really.'

Midafternoon, 18 May

General Williams didn't even try to stalk in today, he just walked up the game trail. "*Lobo Gatos,*" he called.

"No hables," Rick answered.

General Williams walked in, set his backpack down, and sat in a camp chair. He glanced at the fire pit and saw the wood and rocks for the sweat lodge fire already in place. He then surveyed Rick, Kenny, Lois, and Sammi, in that order. "You have news for me," he concluded.

"We sweat tonight," Rick said, "and if everything checks out, we leave tomorrow before lunch. Would you like a briefing?"

"We can do that," Lois answered.

"Yes, you can do that later. Right now I would like to have a chat while we prepare an early dinner. I brought something for the occasion."

"Nothing naughty I hope, Dickie," Rick said. "We want to eat light before a sweat."

"Veggie subs," he answered. "Light enough?"

"Perfect," Kenny answered.

"Good," the general said. "Let's chat, then we can eat. Sammi, how are you doing?" Sammi didn't say a word. "That good, eh? Lois?"

"A little better than Sammi, sir."

"I love honesty," General Williams said. "Kenny?"

"Well, Dick, I really don't want to talk about how I feel. I believe we have the time and location, and I am ready to get this job done. If you have the money, honey, I have the time."

"Rick?"

"Okay, General, I know that something is not quite right here, and I also know that what you ask is what you believe must be done. Therefore, it is my sole purpose in life to see that it gets done. That is how I feel."

"Thank you, all," General Williams said.

"General Williams?" Lois asked, "how do you feel?"

"I feel like the luckiest man in the world to be working with you. I have a knot in my stomach the size of a basketball, a headache that won't quit, and a weird kind of certainty that we are doing the right thing. How's that for honesty?"

"Sir," Sammi started, "thank you. I feel really scared, everything is changing so fast. I just hope I do a good job for you."

"You already have, Sammi. Do you have any coffee around?"

"How about a ginger ale, General?" Lois asked.

"You have ginger ale out here?"

"No, sir, but I have ginger tea and some water that's still hot. It might help that stomach."

"I'd like some," Rick said. They all looked at him, the stoic, peaceful one.

"Ginger tea all around," General Williams commanded.

Early Evening Twilight, 18 May

The air was still, warm, and heavy with moisture, and the darkening forest was enchanting. Kenny brought out his ceremonial pipe given to him by a Native American friend, and Rick got up and began putting chairs away. The others followed his lead.

While Kenny laid out a folded blanket and carefully placed the pipe, a wooden tobacco bowl, tongs, pow wow tobacco mix, and a smudge stick in a clam shell upon the blanket, Rick prepared a small teepee fire at the outer edge of the fire pit. Lois and Sammi watched with intent interest, especially when Rick, Kenny, and even General Williams stripped to the waist.

"That won't be necessary, ladies," General Williams told them. "Only remove your headgear, shoes and socks."

Rick pulled a hand drill and fire board from a bag, fluffed up some dry cedar inner bark for tinder, and started a fire the old-fashioned way. Kenny now sat in the east position of the circle and began to describe the symbolism of the pipe and its ceremony. He became reverent as he picked up the pipestone bowl and cedar stem, joined them, and presented them skyward for all to see. Then he placed the joined pipe on two forked sticks secure in the ground. "Now we speak only of spiritual matters when the pipe is alive, joined. It is a good day."

While Kenny stirred some tobacco blend in the bowl, Rick smudged the circle and each individual, then, took his place again at Kenny's right hand. Kenny packed the pipe bowl one pinch of tobacco at a time, each one dedicated to some part of Creation including the air, rocks, green brothers, four legged, winged and finned. When ready, he simply asked, "May I have fire?" and Rick held a small coal on the packed tobacco with the wooden tongs. Kenny drew several times until the pipe was well lit.

The ceremony he presented was what he called Seven Arrows, honoring The Creator, Earth, each of the Four Directions, and The Creator, again. Kenny passed the pipe as he had described to them, first to Lois on his left. She drew smoke, exhaled, and passed it to the general who passed it to Sammi, then to Rick, and back to Kenny, who returned the pipe to the forked sticks and spoke, "We are blessed to be here together in this now. And, we are blessed with the memories we are making today. Life is a journey that always leads to death. We are on that journey. I have spoken."

Kenny looked at Lois, and she stared at him, clearing her throat, "I feel so alive right now. I wish I could feel this way forever. It is a beautiful world. I have spoken."

There was no thunder from the general tonight, for his voice was a hoarse whisper. "We are each little pieces in a great

Creation. Not one of us can understand the whole of that Creation, but tonight I understand my little part. I am grateful to be on this journey with you—all of you," and he looked at Sammi. "I have spoken."

Sammi sat tall in her lean frame, her pale face reflecting the flickers of the little fire. "Tonight I am brave. I don't understand it. It is new to me, but I feel a courage I have never known. I hope I can feel this tomorrow, and all of my tomorrows. I have spoken."

Rick began, "Windy is a great friend, Dick has been a joy as a nephew and as a commander, Lois is quite fun to tease, and Sammi…Sammi warms my cold heart. Today I am relevant, I have an important job to do. How can any old man ask for more than this? I am blessed to be a part of this little team. I have spoken."

In silence, Kenny separated the pipe stem from its bowl, laid the pieces on the blanket, got up and walked away. Sammi looked at Rick, and Lois watched Kenny go.

"Well?" General Williams thundered, "Shall we light this fire?"

Rick picked up the tongs and passed them to Sammi. "Just place a live coal under that tinder bundle," and he pointed to an opening in the big stack of wood and rocks. Sammi did as Rick instructed, and it began to smoke. "Now, give it life with your breath, Sammi," he coached. She drew a breath and blew on the tinder and glowing coal, and it erupted into flame. The small slivers of cedar began to burn quickly, and soon the forest was alive with light and shadows from the roaring fire.

"Lois," Rick said, "Why don't you go find Kenny? He's right over there under that spruce tree." In a moment she was gone.

Full Dark, 18 May

When she found Kenny, Lois simply sat down next to him and that is how they remained. The fire danced for a long time already and was beginning to die down, but the two still sat in silence without touching. They could see some activity in camp now as Rick began to carry glowing rocks from the fire to the sweat lodge. Kenny rose with care and reached a hand out to Lois. She took his hand eagerly and stood without effort.

They began to walk back to camp when Kenny stopped. He slowly pulled Lois toward him and hugged her tight. As he backed away, her lips sought his, but he pulled her head down and kissed her on the forehead. He put an arm on her shoulders as they turned toward camp. He dropped his arm and they continued walking in silence without touching.

There was more ginger tea in camp as they hydrated before the sweat. General Williams took a long look at Kenny and Lois but went about the task of settling the fire down. Sammi watched the two come in and smiled. Rick dropped the blanket over the sweat lodge door and said, "The rocks are in. It should be hot in an hour or so. Drink some tea."

The camp chairs were back, and the group sat quietly waiting for the lodge. "What do we wear?" Lois asked.

"Nothing, traditionally," Rick answered, pausing for effect. "But for shy white ladies, we usually wear something like a swimming suit."

Lois looked at Sammi, and they both headed for the wigwam. Rick took a long look at Kenny but said nothing.

Finally, General Williams asked, "What ceremony are you going to do, Rick?"

"The lodge will decide, sir," he answered, and they went back to the quiet.

General Williams went to his bag and pulled out a traditional cedar flute.

"You know that's a courting flute in some societies, Dick," Rick said.

"Would you like to play it?" he asked Rick and then gave Kenny a look. They both shook their heads. The general played the flute so softly and delicately that it muddled the mind to hear these sounds coming from that huge man. Both ladies emerged from the wigwam and drifted back to the fire pit. The tones and melodies seemed to belong to the woods so completely that a breeze came up to make the trees dance in rhythm.

Music has an effect on time, and the sweat lodge was hot already.

They entered, Rick first, Sammi, General Williams, Lois, and Kenny last as the hot rocks glowed. Here they shared a secret ceremony.

The little group exited to a steady drenching rain with camp so dark that they could only navigate by feel. Inside the wigwam, Rick lighted a candle with a match and then a small fire. There was nothing left to say as they dried off and crawled into sleeping bags. Tonight, General Williams stayed with them, borrowing Sammi's bed.

Dawn, 19 May

The birds were singing of spring and hope when Kenny awoke surprisingly full of energy. Sweat lodges do that sometimes. The smell of coffee and the sound of General

Williams's voice greeted him. Sammi was curled up next to Rick again, and Kenny grabbed his ditty bag and headed for the woods and stream. He could hear Lois and the general talking in low tones. He thought about stalking in but decided they didn't deserve that.

"Good morning, Kenny," General Williams said. Lois said nothing except with her eyes. She handed him a cup of mocha just to see him smile one more time.

"Top o' the mornin' to ya," Kenny answered.

Rick soon emerged and Lois almost ran to the wigwam to get Sammi.

When everyone was seated in the camp chairs around the morning fire, General Williams straightened up. "Sammi, you will ride back with Lois. I'll bring your car. LGs will take my truck and leave it at the Forest Service parking area. When you're gone, I'll walk the guys out. Ladies, get your stuff ready."

"Yes, sir," Lois and Sammi both replied. There was nothing else to say, and Sammi went to get her keys for the general. Lois went with her, and they hastily threw things into their bags. There were no tears this morning.

Rick and Sammi took a little walk, but Kenny stayed in camp. Sammi soon came back alone and looked around. Lois grabbed her bag, then set it down, and bold as brass walked up to Kenny and kissed him on the lips before he could move.

'Another memory,' he told himself, but he backed away before giving her a fatherly hug. Just like that the women walked away.

They were barely out of sight when Rick came back. He walked briskly into camp, took one look at Kenny, and said "Let's *di di mow,*" polite Vietnamese for get the hell out of here.

They grabbed a few things while the general dowsed the fire, then they walked out to his truck. There, General Williams opened a locked box in the back and pulled out trays of equipment. Kenny and Rick started packing for their fishing trip. When they got to the fishing gear, the general stopped them. He pulled out four bobbers and gave them each two. He showed them how to set and activate the tags, which were functionally similar to other tags they had used for marking targets.

There were no weapons, unless you count heavy fishing line, steel leaders and filet knives. When they were all ready and waiting for the general to give them the keys, he held out two credit card-sized cell phones instead.

"You want us to phone home?" Kenny asked.

"I wish," General Williams replied. "Tags for phase two."

"Phase two?" Kenny asked.

"After Rolling Thunder, you will place these tags on two bodies where you think helicopters might land." He pulled out two sports watches. "Tag remotes. If anybody—I mean anybody—shows up in helicopters, activate those tags and a missile will arrive in twelve minutes max." He paused to let it sink in.

"Phase two," Rick replied.

"More Rolling Thunder?" Kenny asked.

"No. This will be a big bang, shock and awe." When they just looked at him, he continued, "Hell, it takes Pentagon approval to get Rolling Thunder. This is my own ordinance. Any questions?"

There was a brief moment of searching each other's faces.

"Effective range?" Kenny asked.

"Uncles," General Williams answered, "if you are unprotected within a quarter mile of the active tag, you will be in a world of hurt. Dig a hole, climb in, and pull it in after you."

"Yes, sir," Rick said.

"We'll git 'er done, sir," Kenny added.

General Williams pulled them both into one merciless bear hug and then turned and walked away.

'This is getting hinky,' Kenny told himself.

"Yep," Rick said, "let's go fishin', buddy."

Chapter Five

1142 Hours, 19 May

At the ranger station, they purchased fishing licenses, maps and a parking permit. As they drove down the gravel road through the beautiful green forest, Kenny said, "It sure is strange to see all the leaves so big this early in May." Rick turned his head from his driving to look at Kenny a moment. They found the parking area empty, pulled the truck in so the permit showed, and walked down the road to a trail.

They began walking toward a small lake in the wilderness area and worked clockwise all the way around it, Kenny within sight of the lake and Rick a hundred yards into the forest. When they were satisfied they were alone for now, they set up camp on a little hill above the lake near the outlet stream and went fishing, without bobbers of course. Their camp soon looked and smelled like an authentic fishing camp.

After lunch of a few bluegills, they studied the maps carefully for a likely scout camp location isolated from trails, lakes, and other attractions but easy enough to navigate to in tough times. They found the first area was way too exposed by a newer trail not on the map, and the second lacked camouflage materials. But at the third site they found room for two scout pits and two caches separated enough to protect one from discovery of the other.

For the next two days they took turns preparing their pits and caches while the other stood guard. Of course, it took several trips, each by a different route, back to the fishing camp and truck for supplies, hauling soil out of the pits and dispersing it, and keeping up appearances in their fish camp. A few final touches of camouflage, and their scout camp was ready.

They returned to fish camp to enjoy a few more bluegills as the sun dropped below the trees. When they had completed the packing, they lay back on the ponchos to rest until the evening twilight. A pair of common loons whistled overhead on their way home from a hard day of fishing. Coyotes called out their intentions. Whippoorwills greeted the darkening wood.

Full Dark, 21 May

Rick gave Kenny a little shake, and he stretched himself awake. Without talking, they started walking down the trail by the starlight. Rick led silently as Kenny followed almost out of sight of him. They came to the logging grade that led them to the river ford. They had been feeling their way along the grade for more than an hour by the time they heard the waterfall and Rick stopped. Kenny felt uneasy. They flowed into the woods like water into sand and disappeared. A few feet off the grade and not much more from the ATV trail ahead, they lay in wait.

Two dark, silent shadows—no, forms less distinct than shadows—moved up the ATV trail from their left, crossed the logging grade, and melted into the woods several yards up the trail. Before those two were settled, a second pair appeared, turned right and traveled back up the logging grade Rick and Kenny had just vacated. The third pair turned left on the grade and forded the river. They were followed by a main body of twenty some more.

A significant distance behind the main body came another pair that crossed the river. Next to leave were the two from the logging grade. The last were the first two who arrived, the ones on the ATV trail across the grade. 'Sound tactics,' Kenny commented to himself. 'These guys are pretty good.'

Rick and Kenny lay there until dawn faded into full light. When it seemed believable that fishermen might be walking in to set up camp, they got up and ready to go. As they crossed the river, Rick said aloud, "Have you fished this river above the falls?"

"No," Kenny said, "But I heard it's pretty good."

"Let's go upstream a bit and camp," Rick said all the while he was reading the tracks on the grade.

"Sounds good. I'm more into fishing than hiking anyway."

"Okay, you set up camp, then. I'm going to hike up this grade a ways. You know me, always wanting to see what's around the corner and over the next hill."

Kenny gave Rick a look like, 'Are you sure?' Rick nodded, so Kenny turned right and headed upstream a hundred yards or so above the falls where they would be insulated from the grade by the sound of the water. There he set up camp, laid a line in the water and tried to nap while he waited for Rick.

Kenny alerted to nothing in particular and sat up, taking interest in his fishing line. 'Don't most fishermen carry a shooter in case of bears?' He sure wished he had his .357 magnum right now. He looked down the hill to see Rick following his trail into camp.

Rick walked to the edge of the river and out onto a large boulder, peering into the water. "I believe there are more fish here than we thought," he told Kenny.

"Are they still moving upstream?"

"Seems like it. We should catch our limit."

Sunset, 22 May

Kenny and Rick left their camp set up and stuffed a few fishing items in day packs and headed for the logging grade. They turned right and followed it south like they were walking to town. When Rick stopped, Kenny knew this was as far as Rick had gone this morning, the spot he had shown him on the map where the grade intersected with another logging road. From here they would scout-walk after a brief wait.

They tightened their packs and stalked through the woods to the crossroad about a hundred yards west of the grade. Rick lay down and rolled across the road, emulating a raccoon walking, and Kenny followed the same way. They blended into the forest and headed back to the east onto the grade again and proceeded south toward the spot Rick had previously noted on the map as an observation post.

They crossed a stream and continued up a hill, then quickly down again. Rick turned right into a beaked hazelnut thicket. He crawled along a deer trail until they began to climb out of it. They got high enough on that little horseshoe shaped hill so they could see toward the grade, but low enough so they could sink behind the bushes.

It was a great plan, but there was one problem. Nobody came tonight.

Dawn found them looking at each other. Kenny gave Rick an inquisitive look and motioned his head downgrade, south. Rick nodded and they became fishermen again—tired, hungry, thirsty old fishermen.

Sunrise, 23 May

Rick and Kenny crawled out of the thicket and onto the grade. They were less than a mile from the place they had envisioned in their meditations at Line Camp as the rally point for these cadres, at least the point on the map that looked like their envisionings. Tomorrow was the day they had expected to activate the tags. They had to get close today. They had to.

They walked down the grade like Sunday fishermen. 'Hey, is it Sunday?' Kenny asked himself. 'No, Saturday, because it was Sunday when I left the VA on the 17th. Okay, Saturday fishermen.'

Kenny saw Rick's head turn, and he noticed the tracks heading west off the grade up a game trail. They noticed several more trails, eleven Kenny counted, along the grade all heading west. They had traveled about a half mile past the envisioned rally point when they crossed a promising stream. This one, they knew, flowed northwest right through that expected camp.

"Let's go fishing," Rick said.

"Already on it. Look at this," Kenny called quietly, "a nice brookie."

"Well, get a couple more, and let's eat," Rick answered, busy pumping some river water through a filter into a canteen.

"Okay, boss," Kenny said. "Hey, Rick, ever done any serious night fishing for trout?"

Rick looked up at him with keen interest. "No, I haven't. How does it work?"

"Well," Kenny started, "I'm not too sure. I only read about it. You feel your way along the bank, playing your line out downstream in front of you. But, I heard you can use bobbers without spooking the big ones at night."

"Sounds like fun, partner. Let's sleep the day away and have some fun tonight."

Sunset, 23 May

Kenny wrapped his shirt, pants, and boots inside his poncho and tied the package high and tight to the trunk of a fir tree. He wore only his tight, camouflage insect-proof long underwear and socks. He put his full daypack on backwards, so it hung in front of him, with his fishing gear in the outer pocket. He went to the cold fire, picked up a charred ember, and blackened his face and hands. He avoided ashes for the final touch, though, because the water might turn them to a kind of lye and burn his skin. He looked up to see Rick raise a finger to his lips and sink to the ground. Two people in olive drab walked silently by heading north along the grade. Rick nodded to Kenny and they slipped away into the woods to the west.

Step by step, they worked their way through the woods until the stream turned north and meandered east a bit. Rick motioned to a rock outcrop ahead, and they inched their way to the crest. Slowly, in the fading sunlight, they began to see movement through the woods ahead. There, in a broad natural amphitheater, was a large gathering of people, maybe a hundred or more. They could make out the stream flowing toward the camp and through the marsh meadow. They watched as groups of people moved about the area, apparently getting ready for something.

Rick grabbed Kenny's shoulder to get his attention. He motioned with his fingers to indicate walking to the stream, swimming or wading downstream and releasing something.

'The bobbers,' Kenny thought.

Rick continued his hand mime of working their way back to this spot. Then he opened his eyes wide, ducked down behind the hill, and shook himself and Kenny along with him. Kenny understood Rick's instructions to get back here and hunker down.

Inch by inch, they crept back downhill to the stream. One large boulder protruding into the stream would be their landmark. Rick tapped it to confirm to Kenny where they would return. The waxing crescent moon would set soon after the sun so it would be a dark night, but there was light from torches at the assembly. Once at the stream, they went fishing, for real. Rick actually caught a large trout that he released.

Step by step they moved downstream, Kenny following Rick until they could hear the assembly ahead. They were speaking English and singing gospel music. Near the edge of the open meadow, Rick tied on a bobber tag and activated it and Kenny did the same. They let them out as far as they could, then cut the lines. They each tied on and activated another, only this time they tied the lines to stout shrubs.

As soon as they finished, Kenny turned around and began water stalking, diagonally side to side, back upstream. They had set the tags for forty minutes, hopefully allowing them time to wait out any passing guards. It seemed like hours before they reached that rock, but the assembly was still going, the music giving way to oratory.

Kenny bumped into the rock and turned to motion Rick. Immediately, they climbed out of the stream and crawled back up the slope, staying below the crest of the rock outcrop. They were about halfway when the thunder started, only it was much louder than Kenny had expected. There were lightning-like flashes and more thunder that seemed to vibrate the trees above them. Kenny hugged the ground and prayed for peace. 'How inconsistent is that?' he asked himself.

Thunder ceased, and Rick began to rise, but Kenny pulled him back down. 'What's the hurry?' Kenny asked himself. Rick settled down. Another wave of thunder rolled. And Rick patted Kenny's head in thanks.

They expected to hear yelling and weeping and screaming, but it was eerily silent except for a deer alerting behind them with a whistle/snort that sounded like "whew". Kenny wondered about the outposts like the two guys they had seen, but they could hear nothing. They waited.

Rick motioned uphill, and Kenny began moving ahead. They crawled up and over the rock outcrop where they could see the torches of the assembly scattered below. Even in the starlight, they could see two dark blotches on the ground a few yards ahead. Kenny crawled within a few feet when he smelled it. 'Shit,' he said to himself, but he continued. There, within a hundred yards of where they had waited, but on the other side of the rock outcrop exposed to the thunder, lay two bodies, one of those outposts.

They each crawled to a body because, well, that's what a soldier does, even a reluctant soldier. There is intelligence on those bodies. Kenny turned the body over and reached for the neck. No pulse, but a chain, and on that chain, a cross. 'This is hinky,' he told himself. He checked the shirt pockets and felt breasts—small, firm, young breasts.

Kenny vomited.

Rick came over to him, maybe to quiet him down. Kenny took Rick's hand and gave him the cross, then placed it on a breast. Rick moaned like a dying animal.

Rick stood up straight and walked down the hill into the amphitheater assembly area. Kenny looked around, got up, and followed him twenty or thirty yards behind. There were bodies everywhere. Rick found one about his size and removed his clothes. Kenny did the same. Within minutes, they were dressed head to toe in dark olive nylon uniform camping gear.

Standing in what Kenny estimated to be the center of mayhem, in the marsh meadow, they made their decisions. Rick pointed to a thick stand of aspen re-growth south of the amphitheater and west of the meadow. "I'll be in there," he said out loud and walked off.

Kenny stood there a moment, trying unsuccessfully to process what his senses were providing—and to feel his intuition. He watched as Rick knelt down at a body, took something out of his pocket, and placed it under the body. 'The tag!' Kenny reminded himself, and he looked at his watch.

0136 Hours, 24 May

Kenny turned and headed northeast toward a hill on the other side of the stream. He stopped at a body and placed his tag inside the shirt pocket, crossed the stream, and walked to the other edge of the meadow. He walked with caution into the forest and up a hill where he could see the whole area. 'If any outposts return, it will likely be through here,' he convinced himself. He sat down, leaned against a sugar maple tree and wept.

The torches below had all burned themselves out when Kenny stopped crying. 'This is messed up, but I'm in it now, and there's no going back. If somebody drops in here tomorrow morning, they are going to hell in a hurry. Spider hole! I need a spider hole.'

Kenny worked his way uphill further away from the scene and picked a spot right below the crest. 'Too close? I'd better make a good spider hole.' He pulled the small entrenching tool out of his bag and started digging. Suddenly, he stopped and looked around. 'Oh, good, a downed limb.' He went back to digging like his life depended on it.

Kenny grabbed the fallen oak limb and carried it over to camouflage his spider hole. He broke some twigs to weave a quick cover and crawled in, trying his best to pull the hole in after him.

Dawn, 24 May

Dawn stalked in as dawn does, increasing light so gradually as to defy awareness of its coming. Kenny reminded himself to stay alert as he sat motionless, trance-like, in wide angle vision. He took notice of the movement of the mist—not really fog, just a humid summer morning haze—as it drifted, apparition like, among the old growth whiskers and the younger trees. As the light increased, colors gradually emerged, first the dark greens of the pine and spruce, then the lighter translucent greens of the scattered undergrowth, oaks, and the distant meadow.

As the sun rose above the horizon, streams of light filtered through the treetops, creating a transparent curtain or veil that danced ever so gently with the forest shadows. Pure sunlight began painting the open meadow to the west a brilliant green with speckles of rusty brown on the bracken ferns and sparkling off the top of the fog shrouding the stream valley below. Kenny drew a deep breath in awe and gratitude for the scene in which he participated, that joyous warm feeling rising in his chest colliding with the horror of the bodies strewn about the forest floor. His mind could not manage the conflict, the dissonance, between the pristine beauty and the grotesque evil.

He paused his mind. 'Where are the birds?' Dawn usually invites a parade of birds singing and flitting, moving through the trees. 'Behind me? Yes. They are not coming in here.' Kenny had a compelling urge to fly away with the birds, but he kept his post. The mission was to ambush whoever arrived on this site, to kill them, any and all of them. So, he waited to do his duty, but his mind still wrestled with the emotional conflict.

Rick had positioned himself to the southwest in the thick aspen growth near the open meadow but across the stream and up the next hill. They waited hours trapped in this absurdity. Still, they waited. Kenny alternated his field of vision from the whole scene to the lone body at the far edge of the clearing that concealed the tag Rick had placed.

The helicopters approached fast, low, angry. One sleek gray Cobra varoomed past, then one more. They took distant mobile defensive postures, zigzagging and circling their protection in a frenetic dance. The big, lumbering, twin rotor Chinook approached and descended, blasting its hot wind onto the meadow as it landed. Immediately, some 30 armed troopers in black battle dress uniforms, helmets, and armored vests ran to establish a close, hasty perimeter around the landing zone. Two placed a mortar near the rear of the

Chinook while four more set up two machine gun positions on opposite sides of the crown of the meadow.

'*Manitowish*? Why are those mercenaries here?'

He heard the approach of another helicopter, neither Chinook nor Cobra, nor any combat machine. It sounded like an observation helicopter, or like one of those civilian units hospitals use. Yes, there it was, a commercial medevac.

It landed far away from the Chinook and the bodies with the tags, way on this side of the meadow close to Kenny, but no medical personnel emerged. Instead, two large suits, men in their 20s or 30s, stepped out, then an older man, a familiar man. 'Son of a bitch!' Kenny drew a breath so sudden he darted his eyes about to see if anyone had heard. Of course not, for he was a couple hundred yards away from the ex-governor. 'That son of a bitch,' Kenny thought again. 'He manipulated this whole thing with his so-called intelligence.'

Kenny perceived a movement across the stream to the southwest, an olive drab figure stumbling and limping toward the perimeter from the outside. 'Someone is alive there?' he wondered. Two troopers approached the figure with weapons pointed, but he stumbled and fell. They picked him up and helped him walk. Kenny sat in disbelief as he recognized, even with the limping and stumbling, a familiar pattern of foot placement. 'Rick! What are you doing?' he thought.

Rick dropped to his knees as they approached the body that concealed his tag. He appeared to be sobbing as he clutched the body. Kenny watched in horror as Rick drew his hand from under the body and deftly slipped something into his shirt. 'Did he take the tag?'

Ever so slowly, Kenny rotated his wrist to look at his watch. It had switched to stop watch mode, meaning the tag had already been activated. It read 8:43, 8:44, 8:45... The missile was on its way, almost here. 'Three minutes? Maybe less!' Kenny's mind raced. Rick stood up, straighter now, head erect, and walked directly toward the medevac—and closer to Kenny.

Rick started talking to the son of a bitch, coming closer and closer to him, and to Kenny. 'Too close!' Kenny realized. For a few surreal moments, everybody froze as Rick approached, then the two suits yelled and the troopers who had been helping Rick lunged toward him.

Kenny sank as low as possible but could not look away. He did not see the missile. He did not hear it. There was a brilliant, silent flash and a terrible bang—then, nothing.

Chapter Six

Daylight, Unknown Date

Kenny's nothing was disturbed first by the odor, a dirty, septic kind of smell. He stirred slightly in the spider hole and sniffed. 'Oooh, man,' he paused. The memory of the missile emerged and his eyes opened wide in the near darkness of the hole. 'Damn, did I shit my pants?' He wondered if he had been so close to dying that his sphincter had relaxed.

He poked the spider hole door open ever so slightly. The smell seemed to be coming from outside. That was a relief. Kenny searched for an explanation. 'Bear,' he recognized. His mind raced for action, but he was trapped in that tiny hole. Then it occurred to him that the bear meant there probably were no live people around. 'Good.' He waited and listened.

Nothing. He heard nothing. Kenny could not hear a sound, not even the ringing in his ears. He was in total silence. He had no reaction to that realization.

With the door lifted slightly, he caught sight of a black bear boar ambling toward the stream. Kenny strained to take in the scene in the fog. 'No, wait, the sun is shining, short shadows, my side—it's afternoon. What time is it? Shit, what day is it? Why is there fog in the sunshine? Smoke?'

Kenny sniffed. 'Not smoke.' He looked at the tree only a few feet away. It was cloudy too. Reluctantly he accepted that the fog was really cloudy vision. 'Retina burn.'

He took a deep breath and let it go. Awareness was his most valuable survival skill, and now that awareness would have to be almost entirely intuitive rather than physical. He would have to "think his way" out of this situation. 'Tonight,' he concluded. 'What is the moon phase? It was only new moon plus two days when Rick planted the missile.' Kenny knew the moon would set a couple hours or more after the sun, and the phase would tell him the day. He relaxed into his little hole and waited for the moon.

Deep Darkness, Unknown Date

The moon evaded Kenny as he sat in the spider hole, not because he missed the set, but because it was hidden by the clouds. A rain had begun falling, a warm gentle rain that was little more than mist. Kenny was in luck tonight.

He slowly worked his way out of the spider hole and sat. He removed his borrowed boots and uniform, leaving only his bug underwear and socks. Better to arouse suspicion found in underwear than in the stolen uniform. Besides, he could feel his way through the woods better this way.

Kenny tucked his glasses into the case in what was left of his daypack. He had one pemmican bar, a water filter, an empty water bladder, his entrenching tool, some fishing gear, and an extra pair of socks. Rick, the infantryman, always stressed taking care of your feet. It was time to head for scout camp.

As he rose slowly to his feet, struggling against the stiffness and aching in his body, he became aware of another problem—his balance. He settled back onto his protesting knees. Kenny's mind turned like the spinning he had just felt. 'Inactivity, or was there an inner ear problem?' He probed the forest floor for a walking stick within reach, but found none. 'Okay, I'll crawl,' he determined.

It was dark as a coal mine, but Kenny knew the orientation of his spider hole, so he started crawling to the right, diagonally across and down the hill, which he figured was north by northwest. He could find the stream north of the marsh meadow and follow it to the river.

Kenny didn't mind the crawling on his hands, especially on the soft, wet Earth, and he was hoping to find a walking stick anyway, but his knees hated it. They weren't fond of much activity, but this was near torture. His knees celebrated with his mind when he found a stout maple branch. It was crooked, but so was he. It would do.

With his stick, he could walk on his feet, almost upright, and work his way downhill. His knees protested, but Kenny explained the necessity of the situation to them. Suddenly, his bowel explained another urgency to his mind, and he had to relieve it. Evil sometimes did that to him. 'Where did all this evil come from?' he thought, recalling The Thin Red Line.

As he neared what felt like the bottom of the slope, he paused to look around. Of course, his eyes didn't really see anything, but his mind did. He thought back to his wilderness awareness training and focused on the white spot in his mind that seemed to point the way. He followed that faithfully, and he was soon stepping into the stream.

It is a blessed thing, how the mind works. In a situation of dire need, minor pains and distractions seem to dissipate. He knew the water was cold, but his focus on navigating was so intense, that he didn't notice. His body would provide all the needed energy—for awhile. Then he would need rest and warmth. 'The bivy above the falls,' he told himself. 'I can make that.'

Kenny loved the forest, day or night, and there was something mysterious and magical about the woods in a slow, warm rain like this. It was like being in the womb again. He felt nurtured and protected, and he slowly progressed downstream.

The rain seemed to stop, but the vegetation kept Kenny wet so he wasn't sure. As the stream seemed to be making another right turn, his white spot was trying to lead him away to the left. 'The logical mind or the intuitive mind? Which do I trust tonight?' Kenny crawled out of the stream and followed the white spot.

After traveling a significant distance through open forest, he crested a sizeable hill, and he thought he detected movement ahead. He could see or hear nothing, and his gut gave him no alarm, but he felt something. Putting his ear on the damp ground, he thought he felt some vibrations. 'The waterfall?'

Kenny stalked forward and half left until his right foot touched an erect bivy. 'Damn,' he thought, as he felt around on hands and knees. 'I made it already.' He began to shiver just a bit, and his bivy was so inviting, but he had a tight feeling in his belly now. He couldn't stay here.

Kenny felt around for the fire stirring stick he knew was in this camp and found it. He rolled his bivy up tight and strapped it onto his daypack. Pulling the pack as high as he could on his shoulders, he grabbed the hiking stick in his right hand and fire stirring stick in his left. He stepped into the river.

He began to shiver more now, and he knew if he fell, he could have a painful ride down the falls—well, cascade, really, but it would hurt. 'Don't even think about it.' He concentrated on planting each foot, one after the other, bracing against the current with his sticks.

The water reached his waist a couple of times, threatening to send him downstream, but he made it to the bank. Crawling out, he would have loved to lie on the bank for a few seconds, but the rocks were so jagged and uncomfortable they forced him on. Besides, he had a plan now. He would make his way north until he crossed that ATV trail above the grade at the ford—shouldn't be but a few hundred yards. Once across that, he could seek some shelter, maybe a young fir stand, and crawl in his bivy. But, he was shivering now.

When he reached the trail, he rolled across like before. Anybody watching would see movement like an animal, raccoon or mink perhaps, rather than human. He was moving quicker now, because of the shivers. He made his way blindly up and over another hill before finding a fallen hemlock tree. 'This will do.' He crawled under and pulled his bivy sack up and around him. He kept a stocking cap mask in his bivy as well as more extra socks. With the stocking cap on his head and dry socks on his hands and feet, he pulled the bag tight around him and breathed.

First Color, Date Uncertain

Kenny awoke from a dream of beautiful nature music. There are rare times when nature treats us with a synergy of place and time so extraordinary as to appear magical. His dream was a memory of one of those times.

It was a July years ago in the Pine Barrens of New Jersey when the first color of dawn arrived with a symphony of bird calls. They began as the light, with subtle softness. Specie after specie, bird after bird, joined in until a chorus of full harmony spread through the forest like sunlight itself. Kenny and Rick were there, walking around with their mouths open, looking at each other. Within minutes the birds stopped.

Kenny peered out of the bag to see the first green color appear on the ferns, and he suspected this was such a magical morning—but he could hear nothing. He could see birds of many feathers flitting from shrub to shrub and tree to tree, and he could even see them singing in the branches, but all he heard was in his memory. Still, he accepted the magic of today, 'What day is it?'

He began to believe he might live, although he still wasn't sure he wanted to. This is a Kenny paradox, to be so despondent to wish for death and still endure cold, hunger, thirst, pain, and torment of heart just to try to stay alive. 'I need to get to my scout pit. At least if I die there, I'm already in a grave.' PTSD depression is like that.

For some strange reason, he felt that kiss again, the one Lois had sneaked upon him. He thought of mocha and smiled—inside, anyway. He thought of Rick, and then he saw Sammi's sad, sad face. 'I need to get to my scout pit.'

He stuffed everything away and started walking as best he could. He needed a few hundred yards with indistinct trail before he could take a break. He found that opportunity in a young aspen grove where he could hide and yet see out. There he ate his bar and drank his fill. Thankfully, his bowel was still working.

The sun was rising and he had some distance to go. He put on his stocking cap and tied the extra socks around his neck. 'I must be a sight. I'm probably pretty safe, because if anybody sees me, they'll run the other way. If Lois could see me now, she wouldn't want whatever she thinks she wants from me. What does she want?'

'This is my Quest,' he told himself, 'maybe my Final Quest.' He had heard about different levels of Vision Quests, one being silence. 'Okay, I'll do a Silent Quest until I find out what The Creator wants me to do next.' He trudged on.

Mid Morning, Day One

Kenny recognized the terrain now as he approached scout camp. He hated entering camp in daylight, but he really needed to get into that scout pit. His balance was much improved—well, most of the time—and his eyes seemed to be a little clearer. His ears heard nothing. He was still using the walking stick because, well, it didn't hurt so much when he walked, but he tossed it aside now in a blackberry bramble. He would leave less track without it.

Over protests from his knees and back, both lower and middle, he made the sun-wise circle around the area searching for sign. Satisfied he was alone, he walked as nonchalantly as he could into camp and stopped at the reference tree, a small red oak. From there, he chose his direction toward the happy little white pine and counted his paces to locate his cache. He removed the bag and closed and concealed the cache. He then retraced his steps, walking backwards to the reference tree, chose another direction toward the bent aspen, and found the door to his scout pit.

Carefully removing the door lid, he placed the cache bag and his day bag inside and slipped in himself. Sitting in the pit, he carefully arranged the camouflage debris around the opening, looked around one more time, then lay down, reached up and set the door in place. 'Home,' he sighed.

A scout pit is dark, shaped like a grave, dug only a couple feet deep with a foot or so of logs and soil on top. Rick used to shake his head at Kenny's pit because it was too big. Kenny was mildly claustrophobic. Besides, he needed room to flex his knees and stretch his back. It was probably just the right size for General Williams, but Kenny was grateful for the space today.

Kenny had also stuck a couple of reeds through the roof on either side of the door. He said the light helped him keep track of time, but it really gave him the feeling that he could breathe better. Anyway, his pit was not as completely dark as Rick's during the day. Kenny was grateful for that, too, today.

There was one more task before he rested. Well, two. He used rocks to count the days, so he took the first one from the stack on the right side where his hand could reach, rolled to his left, and placed it in the little bowl he had prepared. 'Day One.' Then he prayed. He rambled, but he kept circling back to the question about the next step in this life. Finally, he curled up on his left side in a modified fetal position on his wool blanket, wrapped it around him and changed consciousness.

Chapter Seven

Darkness, Day One

Kenny thought he awoke, but he could see or hear nothing. He could, however, smell the earth and knew he was home in his scout pit. He found his little sump latrine and urinated, more out of habit than necessity. He grabbed a handful of earth from the pile and scattered it on top to keep the smell down. He was grateful for an empty bowel.

He could not be certain of the time or date, but he did not believe he had missed an entire long May day.

One of the interesting things about vision quests is they seldom go as expected. They are, after all, sort of spiritual holograms of life. Kenny expected his mind to fixate on Rick and the past few days, but he knew better than to rely on expectations. He found himself instead a teenager back on his grandfather's dairy farm. He remembered putting up hay in July. His favorite part was loading the bales on the wagon behind the baler because there was a rhythm to it and a challenge to keep up with the baler while engineering and building the perfect stack that would stand the bumpy ride up that hill to the barn. And he was helping Grandpa. Kenny was a man, small but strapping, pulling his own weight, but it was hot.

Kenny didn't like heat. He didn't like cold either, but he was getting warm now and tossed the blanket aside. He remembered the heat of the farm work fondly only because of his love and respect for his grandfather. What a man. What a life he lived.

'I'm sorry, Grandpa, I wasted my life. I never wanted to be like my father, such a mean drunk, but I guess I was pretty much the same. I can't fault Bonnie for kicking me out or Kenny Jr. for never speaking to me again. I never wanted to speak to my dad either—until it was too late.

'The only good thing I did surviving Vietnam was Amy, and I wasted that, too, or we did, society. I wonder how many Amys I just killed.

'I'm sorry, Grandpa. I know you and Grandma tried so hard, and I still ended up like this....'

"It's not the end." Kenny heard that voice in his head, not his own. He thought, but did not say anything in words, not even in his mind. He looked around the blackness and realized the absurdity of his action.

'Okay, if it's not the end, what is next?' There was no answer at this time.

Kenny stirred a bit, trying to stretch and loosen up. He noticed his feet were sore, so he wiggled around where he could draw one knee up and feel his foot, then the other. Walking barefoot and in socks had wounded them, and they needed a little attention. Actually, Kenny's mind welcomed the distraction.

He felt around in his cache pack for the first aid kit. He found some little packets and felt the textures. He took two that felt like alcohol swabs and one that might be antibiotic. He tore open the first and smelled it, 'Yep, alcohol,' and wiped his left foot.

'Ooh, well, I'm still alive.' When he finished the right foot with the other alcohol swab, he smeared some antibiotic around the sore spots on each foot. Then he put on some clean socks.

He dug his other pair of moccasin boots out of the cache pack and put them behind his neck. He lay back with arms crossed on his chest, like in a coffin, and slept.

Daylight, Day Two

Kenny awoke with the awareness of light, ever so faint, at the top of the reeds and with the sensation that his arms were still asleep. The pressure on his ulnar nerves had made his lower arms and little finger sides of his hands go numb. It took a lot of wiggling, but they came around.

The reed that dipped toward the east seemed brighter than the west one, so he guessed it was morning. He checked his rock bowl and found one, so he reached for the little pile and placed the second rock in the bowl for day two. He liked day two—something significant was likely to happen, at least that had been his limited experience. Maybe it did, but if so, he made no notice of it. It was a long day.

Vision quests in the woods usually provide some entertainment, even if it's only the dancing of the leaves in the trees or a few clouds moving by. He would even welcome a spider crawling on him right now, anything. But, there he was, and he felt very alone. Immediately, he felt Lois's kiss again. 'Weird.'

Darkness, Day Two

Kenny awoke with a start, not from a dream or any physical stimulus, just a feeling. It was totally dark again, except he thought he could see something down by his feet, a figure off in the distance, obviously in his mind. He lay his head down, but was compelled to pick it up again. There was a figure off in the darkness, a familiar figure, but he could not recognize him—he thought it was a him.

"How can you forgive anyone else, if you don't first forgive yourself?"

'That voice again. Interesting question, though. I don't know,' Kenny answered in his mind in a tired, resigned sort of way. He lay back for what seemed a long time, but when he looked up, the figure was still there. 'You're not going away, are you?' Kenny asked. No response.

'Okay, what was the question? Oh, yeah, if I don't forgive myself....' That seemed so, selfish, egocentric, grandiose. 'Who am I to forgive myself?'

A quick and terse response, "Who are you to judge?"

'Good one. Alright, so not forgiving anyone, including myself, is a form of judgment, and judgment is not my business, so not forgiving is not my business.' Kenny looked and looked but the figure was gone. 'Ah, Day Two,' he thought.

Suddenly, his mind went back to Bonnie. She had been such a happy young mother, a really nice woman, but in the end she was angry and bitter like, well, like his own mother.

His thoughts turned to his father and there was no anger there anymore. Well, maybe there was. 'Forgive myself first?'

Kenny knew that Bonnie's bitterness was because of him, but back then, nobody knew what was in the mind of a Vietnam Vet. 'How could they? We wouldn't tell them. We were ashamed of our own thoughts.' An idea suddenly formed in his mind, like spontaneous combustion: 'Maybe Dad had similar thoughts.'

Kenny cried himself to sleep without many tears, sort of like dry heaving.

Daylight, Day Three

Day Three was Kenny's least favorite of a four day quest, probably because expectations get tangled with ideas that Day Two was the big insight. He knew better than to allow expectations, but at his age, he still had an adolescent mind in some ways. At least that was the way he saw himself. 'Judgment?'

He remembered something he had heard an elder say once about pushy people in a crowded supermarket, "That's just people living life." This same person had once talked about reaching out to a pathetic tortured soul and later asking himself, "If you can forgive that miserable person, why can't you forgive yourself? You're no better or worse than he is."

'Yes,' Kenny thought, 'I am no better or worse than my father—or anybody else, really. We're all just living life with our own handicaps.'

Immediately, he felt cleaner—no, not comparatively, he felt really clean. "Thank you, Grandfather," Kenny whispered aloud to The Creator, at least he thought it was aloud. He followed with "Thank you, Dad," and lay back in peace with thoughts of Vicky. My, how that woman had loved him back to some kind of health. 'Heaven must have been built for women like that who can love men like us.'

He saw Lois's face, the smiling one at her desk, and felt a little guilty like he was contaminating Vicky's memory. 'Silly boy,' he thought and then realized such words were not at all like him. Obviously, judgment had become a habit with Kenny. Fortunately, it was only Day Three.

Daylight, Day Four

Sometimes Day Three is like that, many hours of boredom inside your own mind. For many questers, it is quitter's day because it brings a person face to face with the ugliest beast in Creation, himself. Fortunately for Kenny, he had faced himself many times, and he was feeling clean now. Day Four is often a day of acceptance, like 'I can make it one more day.' Unfortunately, that attitude that you can make it leads to trouble. Kenny was accepting today. He was genuinely ready to die or to live as The Creator chose. That is an amazing feeling of freedom.

Breathe in, breathe out, a drink of water, a little pee. If you ever think a day is too short to accomplish anything meaningful, try a vision quest. Kenny's back and legs still hurt, but he didn't care. He still felt confusion about this mission, but it was okay. Amy, Vicky, and Dad were still dead, but that was just the way things were. He was still dissatisfied with his life, but he wasn't dead yet. And he still wondered what Lois wanted from him, and that was okay, too.

It was sometime in this day, light or dark, Kenny didn't know, when the soldier came. The best Kenny could discern was that it was the spirit of a fallen young man. He didn't know the uniform, time period, or even the nation. There was no verbal communication in Kenny's mind this time, just a feeling: Live. That's all there was, but Kenny knew that the question he had thought so important that God Almighty had to answer it, the one about what he should do next, was answered in one four letter word. To Kenny, it meant he should go home, to his own area not that far from here, and live free off the land until he figured out something else to do. He was going to live again.

First Light, Birth Day

Some tribes refer to a vision quest as a little death, and completing one is like being reborn. Kenny emerged from the scout pit, the grave which had become a womb, and felt like beginning life anew. After collecting supplies from the cache, eating, and drinking, he gathered up his things and walked to the nearest stream where he bathed and washed his clothes. He and his clothes dried in the sun before he started his trek back home. There was no mission, no time line, no expectation, no thought of reporting back to the VA.

He still couldn't hear, but his eyes were as good as last week, and all body parts that he needed were working. What did he need from the VA? The brass would only want to debrief him, and he had had enough of that. Besides, he couldn't hear their questions, anyway. Only his lips felt like they were missing something.

When he approached the highway, he settled down in a hidden spot to observe. He saw more traffic than he expected, some of it official looking, and it finally occurred to him that going home right now might not be such a good idea. Of course that horrible scene had been found, and local and state officials would have all kinds of questions. Those with privilege to know his role would have a lot more questions.

The assembly had not been the cadre of professionals and foreign nationals opposed to Fight for Right as the son of a bitch had reported. They had been Christians, many of them young, and they were probably on their way to Green Bay to help the Fight for Right Campaign. Kenny did not judge if they were good guys or bad guys, but they certainly were not what the intelligence reports had led them to believe.

Then there was the matter of Samson Security and their ex-governor captain. That was bound to confuse people all the way to D.C. Those mercenaries weren't confused, though. Some of them may very well have been close enough to the son of a bitch to know Kenny's identity. They would be out for blood, and blood was their profession.

The Fight for Right people might well be out for blood too, although he doubted they would know about him—unless they were close to the son of a bitch or Samson Security, and that didn't make any sense at all. In fact, none of it made sense to Kenny except that his gut had been right, that there had been something terribly wrong. In hindsight, it was clear that General Williams also had known that things were not as they seemed.

'General Williams!' Kenny thought. He must be of great interest to lots of people about now. That shock and awe was his ordinance. How was he going to explain that part of the mission? Would the son of a bitch's presence at the scene be enough to justify that action? Certainly the ex-governor's intelligence credibility was destroyed, and maybe that of Samson Security, probably some other complicit parties, but....

Kenny decided to go home anyway, well, almost home. He had some real caches on his land that he wanted in his hands. He could set up camp a little distance away on county land, out in the swamp where nobody went except in hunting season, and make a few clandestine trips to his home to get some tools. So, that was his plan, but now he was hungry. He took his cache bag, backtracked to a public campsite, made a fire, and had his first hot food in too long. He would go back and cross the road in the late dark.

Sunset, Birth Day

Kenny watched the southeastern sky with eagerness, but the trees were in the way. It appeared to be going to stay clear, and the moon would tell him the day. 'Let's see, new moon was on the twenty second, so the first quarter would be the twenty ninth. That means the full moon would be about June fourth or fifth'.

With that thought, he made haste to the road where he could get a look at the sky to the south. And, there it was, high moon in a precise first quarter. Today was only the twenty ninth of May. He hadn't lost any time. No wonder nobody had been around that place yet when he crawled out of his spider hole. Good, maybe his injuries weren't that bad. Maybe his hearing would return. Maybe.

Kenny started walking home right down the trail to the south, but he chose to take another to the east before he got to the highway. He had an idea he could cross at the little-used gravel crossroad at the crest of a hill. That way he could spot headlights of approaching vehicles on the tree tops before they could see him on the road, and it wasn't really out of the way. Besides, he was in no hurry. He had the rest of his life to get there. Such freedom!

Kenny remembered Janice Joplin singing, "Freedom's just another word for nothin' left to lose." Maybe that was it. Amy was gone, Vicky was gone, and now Rick, his friend for so many years, was gone. What did he have left to lose? 'Today,' Kenny answered his thought. 'Life.' Besides, just because Kris Kristofferson wrote it, that didn't make it true.

There was something more to this feeling of freedom. It wasn't that he no longer feared death. He had faced that many years ago. It wasn't that he didn't care if he lived or died. He did. He wanted to live. Maybe he just didn't have anything to prove anymore—well, at least, today. Maybe that was it.

He walked down the gravel road and across the highway as though he were the only person left alive on Earth. Everybody was home early today. 'What day of the week is it? The seventeenth was Sunday so the twenty fourth was Sunday and today is Friday. Everybody went out for fish and either went home early or is busy partying.'

Just then he turned around to see car lights in the treetops on the highway behind him and he melted into the woods. He was close to the county land now, but he didn't know his way in from this direction well. He decided to stay in the woods and rest until everybody went home.

Moonset, 29 May

The moon beat some of those people home, but Kenny waited a little longer. The starlight would be fine for navigating. He just needed to find that other logging road, and then he could make his way into his area. After waiting another hour or so with no cars coming down this little road, Kenny returned to it and preceded another mile or so until he crossed a little stream. He couldn't hear or see it, but he could feel the cool dampness and knew he was on a valley floor between two hills. He found the logging road right where he expected, before the crest of the next hill.

Walking logging roads by starlight is interesting. For one thing, man is not the only critter that does that. One can bump into all kinds of hairy things. Kenny decided to whistle. He figured if any people were out here in the dark, they would be as interested in avoiding a crazy person as a bear would. He started singing, but couldn't hear what he sounded like, so went back to whistling.

He wasn't at all sure where he was, now, but he knew he was on the right road. Besides, he couldn't be lost because he had no particular place to go and no particular time to get there. He decided to rest in the woods until he could see a little better.

First Light, 30 May

Waiting in the dark woods, Kenny wondered if he should keep a calendar. Then he wondered why he had cared what calendar day it was, anyway. He decided he didn't want to think about it anymore and caught a few winks. First light found him back on the logging road heading east. He needed to find another old logging road, just a trail that hadn't been used in many years. This would be his way into county land. Well, maybe ATVs used it, but they weren't supposed to.

It turned out he hadn't traveled as far on the logging road as he had thought last night, and he didn't find his trail to the south until the sun was up into the trees. But, when he found it, he began to feel at home. He also began to get an uneasy feeling, much like that little voice in his head that said, 'Don't do it,' just before he sliced the tip of his finger off opening a bag of salad mix with a filet knife. He decided to get real careful about his approach and left the trail, heading southwest into the woods. He also decided to make a primitive camp way out in the cedar swamp where humans only go during hunting season, if then.

Kenny had been taught that primitive survival living could be as effective in spiritual renewal and finding direction for life as a vision quest, although he personally put more faith in the quest. The best, though, was to follow the quest with survival living, and that is exactly what he planned to do. For the first time in his long life, he could enter a full survival situation with no fixed end time. He would stay as long as it felt right.

High Sun, 30 May

Kenny considered cedar swamps sacred places and entered them with reverence. He loved them even though they could be dangerous. He had one personal experience making his way through a swamp keeping dry ankles for long distances only to suddenly have one leg disappear completely into water. He had learned to move from tree root to tree root as much as possible.

Probably the best time to enjoy a cedar swamp is at the beginning of a heavy snowfall. It is like living in one of those little glass balls people used to have—quite surreal. There is a sense of unlimited time and space, partly because it is so easy to lose all sense of direction. Kenny had spent many hours in such bliss when he was pretending to be hunting.

The second best time to be in a cedar swamp is whenever possible to get in one. Kenny was feeling truly blessed to be so free today to be here, and he was quite unconcerned about finding his way. Crocodile Dundee had explained how his aborigine friend found his way in the dark. "He thinks his way." Well, Kenny actually agreed, only it isn't the kind of thinking industrial society uses. It is an intuitive thinking with another part of the mind connected directly to the gut. That's what he was doing now, and he soon stepped onto the island.

He knew this place well. Deep in this large swamp was a little hill shaped roughly like a raindrop with the small end pointing toward Kenny's land. He felt deeply connected here, and the red oak trees provided excellent material for building and insulating a debris hut. Kenny sat down under one and finished the last of his rations from the cache and drank his fill. Then he went to work.

Chapter Eight

Sunrise

The survival camp was beautiful, at least to the experienced eye. The debris hut was a work of art, not oversized as was Kenny's habit. A pile of forest debris is what it was, sticks, leaves and grasses piled on a framework of larger ribs of sticks leaning on one ridge pole. Kenny had used a rock about thirty inches high as the foundation for the ridge pole, leaving him a very small opening on the east end to enter, feet first, of course. Beside the rock, the roof continued a couple of feet, leaving a small area for Kenny to work or keep his important stuff. The rest of the hut was packed full of debris so it became a sleeping bag. Beautiful in functional simplicity, it served as shelter without being very noticeable to anybody who might wander by.

Kenny really didn't know how long he had been here—he had chosen to keep no calendar, or, more honestly, refused to make a choice, so he had none. He fed himself with trapping, fishing, some hunting, and an occasional good fortune of finding a sizeable turtle or snake. The one whitetail deer he shot with his survival bow fed him several days and provided jerky for many more. He even had a rawhide bag now and some brain-tanned buckskin he might use for a shirt. He let the bear go.

Black bears were of special significance to Kenny, sort of a totem representing spiritual power and healing. They also reminded him of his old spiritual teacher and advisor. His deal with bears was that if they stayed out of his camp, he would stay out of their business. He even made a point to share some of his bounty with them but always a few hundred yards from his little island. So, when the adolescent male came a little too close and huffed at him, Kenny wasted an arrow in a tree beside the young bear's head, just to send a message, which was well received. The bear left in a hurry. Besides, shooting bears with a flint-tipped cedar arrow is risky because it tends to piss them off.

The past few days, Kenny had noticed a little ringing in his right ear. His left ear started ringing soon after he got here, and he thought he could hear some low pitches now, like the commuter plane that came over every evening, and sometimes the ravens. He began to wonder if the VA could do anything for him.

His few excursions toward his land soon after he had made camp were always aborted. Sometimes it was activity on the road which seemed suspicious. Sometimes it was that uneasy feeling. Once he got to his neighbor's place and thought he saw a state vehicle there.

The little stream provided all the water he needed, and there was food enough to sustain him. In fact, he imagined himself to be gaining weight, which he needed. So he lived his simple little life the way he thought The Creator was telling him to do.

High First Quarter Moon

Kenny knew by the berries that he was well into June, maybe even July. He began to think about time again, and he remembered that there was supposed to be a partial lunar eclipse around the Fourth of July because he remembered thinking that it was an interesting coincidence, if there were such things. That evening he sat very quiet and thought about drumming again. Oh, how he missed that, but it was just too noisy for his private little island. He remembered that warm afternoon with Rick, Lois, and Sammi. 'God, that was a long time ago.'

The next evening he thought he heard drumming again—four loud, separated beats, then a long pause, then four more. It reminded him of the blind drum stalk that helped him learn how to walk almost naked through the dark woods. Was he hearing this in his mind or in his slightly improving left ear? Maybe it was The Creator calling him home. The odd thing is that it seemed to be coming from the direction his little island pointed, toward his Lonesome Pines.

The following evening, Kenny worked his way in the slow rain to the edge of the swamp to the southeast, then over the large glacial hill on his neighbor's land. He stopped below the crest facing his property, not much more than a quarter mile from his home. For a time he heard nothing, but soon after the rain stopped, he heard drumming. 'Yes, it is real.' He paused and wondered, 'Did I say that out loud? No, you didn't.'

This time he could hear softer, more complex drumming between those loud calling beats. It was an interesting rhythm that sounded familiar, 'No, not Rick.' He sat there and enjoyed the concert. Tears flowed slowly, but he had no idea why. It was a sad concert. 'The moon will rise later tomorrow, in early waxing gibbous.' He decided he might get close enough to trust his eyes.

Rising Waxing Gibbous Moon

By the time the moon rose into the trees, the twilight was fading in the forest and Kenny was walking softly on his own property. The concert had not yet begun, so he paused near his northwest corner. He loved this place. It was like his heart was tied to it by invisible strings, or maybe an umbilical cord. The place loved him, too. He could feel that. Strangely, there was no uneasy feeling tonight, only uneasy thoughts of the conscious mind and the twisted perceptions of a combat veteran.

He heard activity at the neighbors' cabin as though they were arriving for a long Fourth of July holiday. He decided to move cautiously into a thick stand of balsam fir and wait until things quieted down, but he didn't wait long. Instead, he kept stalking through the thick high swamp perched on the ancient black bedrock, toward his favorite place in the world to sit, a little rock outcrop not accidently overlooking the road to his camp and spirited by a particularly friendly soul. There he could wait in patience.

The first drum beats startled him because they were so loud, almost desperate. Maybe they were. He wondered why the neighbors didn't complain, but then the fireworks around the lake started, and he figured they were just minding their own business. Soon the soft concert began, again, plaintive, pleading, calling him. He resisted.

It wasn't the drummer he resisted, whoever that might be. It was the VA, the brass, and those damned suits that would show up from who knows where. He had even had nightmares about them. After the drumming stopped and the fireworks seemed to end for the night, Kenny stalked toward his cabin.

The moon was descending now, and moon shadows blessed the road he traveled.

In camp, the moon illuminated one vehicle in front of his little dome cabin. It was a small, boxy shape that appeared to have a white top, but he chose to get no closer, thinking there might be a dog or some other alarm system. He melted back into the woods on the west side, settled in where he could see the vehicle, and waited. He knew he had boxed himself in where he could not get back to his island without crossing at least three logging roads in daylight, but he was compelled to see his drummer.

Dawn

Kenny had managed a little sleep, but the early light aroused his awareness. Soon after the dark greens of the leaves emerged, he could see that the vehicle was green and white. A little more light and Kenny could not deny that it was Lois's Bronco, but 'Who was driving it?' PTSD is like that, always expecting trouble.

He waited, checking again that the forest would shade him from the rising sun. Before the sun rose above the far treetops, Lois walked out in jeans and denim shirt, hair just sort of flopping around. She made a kind of circle around camp, peering into the woods like she was looking for something, rubbing her eyes from time to time. One time she looked directly at Kenny but moved on.

She fueled the campfire and put a coffeepot on the grate, and it wasn't long before Kenny could smell coffee and hot chocolate. Lois poured herself a mug and set a second one on the little table between two chairs. Kenny could take no more.

He rose very slowly and stalked away, peering both ways before walking sideways across his road that led to the neighbor's place and into the thickets of his high swamp. Once he was back on county land, he wandered about in no particular direction until he found himself back in the swamp far from his camp. He decided to stay right there and sleep on soft, dry moss.

Sunset

Distant thunder woke Kenny and he looked around. Coming toward him through the swamp less than a hundred yards away was a huge black bear, not some frisky adolescent, and he appeared to have no idea Kenny was there. Forty or fifty yards closer their eyes met and Kenny dropped his stare, keeping track of the big fella with his peripheral vision. Perhaps the bear did not know Kenny was human, but more likely he sensed that there was no threat.

This was not Kenny's camp, and the bear was not an intruder. Kenny was not an intruder either, but he gave room to the big bear, a sign of respect, by averting his eyes. The bear veered to his right and kept on walking on a course that would stay some fifty yards from Kenny. As the bear began to walk further away, he turned to look back as if to say this swamp is big enough for both of us if you mind your own business. It was not until the first loud clap of thunder that the bear broke into a lope.

Kenny immediately got up and started heading north to his little island. The rain was coming down hard by the time he got home, the wind was blowing in gusts, and thunder and lightning were big and frequent. Kenny celebrated what he could hear and wondered about Sammi. Was she with Lois, and was she scared?

He was totally drenched, so he shed his clothes and crawled feet first into his debris hut. 'This is a very satisfactory way to live,' he told himself, 'but tomorrow I break camp.'

Sunrise

The storm went on and on, but Kenny slept soundly. He did not hear the rushing water, but he knew what happened in cedar swamps. He was now on an island in a big shallow lake. Since he was awake and it was still raining, he decided to take a shower. He pulled the ditty bag he hadn't used in a moon and lathered himself from top to bottom, washed his hair, cleaned his fingernails, and scrubbed his clothes. In the first aid kit, he found scissors and a razor, so he cut and shaved his thin shaggy beard. He tasseled his wet hair and decided against cutting it, especially without a mirror.

It didn't matter that everything was wet. He had a wet trip ahead of him anyway. When all his man-made stuff was packed, he moved it out of camp. He scattered ashes and covered the fire pit with earth. He tore down the spit, the debris wall by the fire, and the debris hut, scattering sticks and debris at random. He was not destroying anything, just returning it to a more natural state and erasing his tracks. Then he dressed in wet clothes and began cautiously wading out of the swamp.

It finally stopped raining about the time he made it to high ground. Wet but not cold, because of the exertion, he practically collapsed in the needles below a big old white pine and slept. He was shivering slightly when he awoke, but he noticed a sunny spot at the edge of the pine needles and crawled there and slept some more.

Sunset

Kenny awoke groggy but almost dry. He decided to find the logging road and walk for awhile. His knees were really hurting today. 'Some homecoming,' he thought. He was stiff and tired and not very alert, but he doubted if many people would be out tonight, so he took it very slowly, leaning on his bow almost like a cane.

Right now he wished he knew the date. He would really like to be home for the full moon in case he could see some of the eclipse. Anything else drawing him on was still being denied, except the drum, which seemed to be losing all hope.

He managed to find his one pair of dry socks wrapped in that old bivy and put them on. For the rest of his clothes, he had slept and walked himself dry. 'It didn't seem so far last time,' he told himself. He answered, 'Quit your whining,' and so, he did.

The moon was high already when Kenny reached his favorite sitting rock. He was home now. His cabin was just down the road, but this rock was his home. The spirit he called Summer Moon came to give him a backrub. He had never told anybody about her, not even Rick. He always invited people to sit on the rock. Those who accepted either felt welcome there or chose to sit somewhere else. Summer Moon was not friendly to everybody.

He wondered if he had told Lois about Summer Moon and not remembered. He started to feel that anger again about his stolen memories but took notice of the moon rising above the spruce, fir and pine. It was big, but maybe not quite full, and just a bit early ascending. He decided to watch it, anyway, in case the eclipse was tonight. Besides, he had nothing else to do. He was certainly not going to go to the cabin door in the middle of the night.

Chapter Nine

Dawn

Kenny sat in the camp chair wrapped in a wool blanket from his shed, stirring the fire with a long stick. He sat so that he could watch both doors on the geodesic dome, one on the southeast, and the other on the southwest. The sun was kissing the tops of the trees on the west side of camp when the southwest patio door opened and Lois stepped out. She did not see him immediately because she was looking into the woods to the west.

When she turned around, she startled, put both shaking hands to her mouth and quivered all over so that Kenny was seriously afraid she might pee her pants.

"Good morning, Lois," he said, and she jumped and quivered again before running over and touching him, his arms, his chest, as if to see if he were real. Then she grabbed him and buried her face in his skinny little chest and squeezed. He patted her shoulders.

When she finally let go, she grabbed his face and started talking, at least it looked like she was talking. "Lo!" Kenny said. "Lois, I cannot hear you. My ears are broke." He was aware that probably sounded dumb, but he didn't care, today. Then he smiled and asked, "Got any mocha?"

She opened her mouth to speak, then closed it again, and shook her head forward and back, as if to say "Uh, huh."

She started for the door, but came back to pull Kenny along, but he resisted. "Why don't you just bring the stuff out here? I'm not quite ready to go in, yet," motioning to his clothes.

Lois shrugged like, "So, what?" Then she mouthed, "Okay," and ran to the door.

She was back in a flash but had to make a second trip for the cocoa. Kenny filled the coffee pot from the hand pump and put it on the grate, and just like that he was back in his old world. When Lois came out a second time, he motioned for her to sit in the chair beside him.

Kenny asked, "Is anybody else here?"

She shook her head, "No."

"Lois, Rick is gone. He's dead." She recoiled and teared up, but she also nodded as though she had expected that. "I want you to know that it was his choice, and he chose to make certain he accomplished this mission. In any other war, he would get the Medal of Honor."

Lois pointed at Kenny with question on her face and mouthed, "You?"

"I was too close, and I couldn't look away, so I lost my hearing, but it's coming back…a little. I heard your drum."

With that she beamed, shivered again, and touched his arms all over.

As the coffee started to boil, Lois got busy preparing the mugs with cocoa and creamer and just sort of fussing. 'I wonder what's on her mind,' Kenny thought, so he said, "Lois, what's on your mind?" She looked at him with tears in her eyes, and what looked like a flash of anger, and mouthed something. He wasn't sure, but one of the words looked like 'hell'. She put her hands on her hips and said something, then cried and hugged him again. 'Oh, this is going to be interesting,' Kenny told himself.

Lois poured the coffee through a filter into the mugs and stirred. She stirred one some more and handed it to Kenny sitting in the chair. Then, she put one finger in the air, like she had an idea, and ran in the house. In a couple of minutes she was back with a pen and pad of paper. She pulled the other chair up next to him and sat close, wrote on the tablet and showed it to him, "Where the hell have you been?"

"I've been wandering around, bumping into trees and bears, mostly."

She shook her head in all kinds of directions, smiled, cried, inhaled, and sighed. Finally, she nodded her head, "Yes," and patted his hand. Then, she wrote, "I'm glad you're home. What can you tell me?"

"Maybe you can tell me a few things. First, what kind of trouble am I in?"

She looked at him with confusion, then a sign of possible understanding. She wrote, "I'm not sure. What are you worried about?"

"Well, this mission didn't go exactly as planned. I'm worried about the suits and brass. And, what about the *Manitowish*?"

She wrote, "*Mannitoish*?"

"The private Samson Security people that the son of a bitch owned."

"What son of a bitch?" she wrote.

"The ex-governor."

Now she had a concerned look, writing, "The ex-governor is missing."

"Yeah, he's missing all right, in the same flash-bang with Rick. Rick took the son of a bitch out. You didn't know?"

"No," she mouthed, shaking her head.

Kenny thought a moment. "How's Dick?"

"General Williams retired," she wrote. "Suits and brass all over. They accepted his resignation."

"Where is he, Lo?"

She shook her head.

"You can't, Lo, or won't?"

"He asked me not to tell," she wrote.

"Okay, okay, where's Sammi?"

"Her mom's. Retired too," she wrote.

"What about you?"

"I'm here," she mouthed, but Kenny gave her a sad serious look, and she wrote, "I got promoted," and shrugged, then added, "I have a job to finish," and tapped her finger on his sternum. After a pause, she wrote, "Will you go to the VA?"

"Not today," he answered.

"Oh no," she mouthed, and wrote, "Today July 4th...next Tuesday?"

"Maybe. We'll see Monday." He looked deep in her eyes and asked, "Do you think they can help me?" and pointed to his right ear.

Her look said, "Maybe, I don't know, I hope so." She reached both hands over and put them on his thigh just above his knee, nodding her head.

She grabbed the pen again, "What about the Samson Security?"

He didn't know what she knew about the second part to the mission, and if the general had kept her out of it, there was a reason, so he pondered his reply. "The damned *Manitowish*—that means bad spirit—were there after the, I mean, to look at the carnage or something. The son of a bitch was there with them. They died." He looked away. "Everybody died but me." He swallowed.

She waited a long time before writing, "Why son of a bitch?"

"I never did like him. I could smell evil, and he proved me right."

"How?" she wrote.

Kenny looked at her in disbelief. 'How could someone so close to General Williams not know?'

"Chief, what does the intelligence report say about our mission?"

She wrote, "223 professional cadre including foreign nationals killed."

"Bullshit!" Kenny spit. "They weren't professional cadre, and they weren't foreign nationals. They were Christian kids."

"What?" she mouthed.

"The first body I came to had a cross and small round tits."

"Oh, my God!" she mouthed. He could read those lips.

"That son of a bitch set this whole thing up. That so-called intelligence is bullshit. They were singing Gospel songs when we blew them up. I don't know what is going on, but I'm sure Dick has his suspicions."

"Oh, my God," she mouthed again, "oh, my God."

"Care to tell me where Dick is now?"

She shook her head. "I gave my word," she wrote.

Kenny nodded in resignation. "I think I'll take a bath and get some clean clothes."

"Wait," Lois signaled with her hands, and pointed a finger at herself. She wrote, "Let me get it ready. Haircut?"

"Haircut, bath, nap," he said.

Midmorning, 4 July

Kenny languished in the bathtub, dozing on and off. He could sense Lois moving about and see her shadow go under the closed bathroom door. One time his peripheral vision caught her peek in and leave again, but he ignored it. Finally, it seemed she could stand it no more, and she waved the towel, literally, through the door.

"Okay, okay," he said and grabbed the towel. He already had one on the rack, but she seemed to think this one was better, so he took it. He toweled dry—what an interesting procedure—and dressed in the clothes she had put on the vanity. They were his clothes, hanging loosely on his thin frame now, and he dared a look in the mirror. He tried not to articulate any thought. He could smell the cooking eggs, onions, mushrooms, maybe, and…broccoli?

Lois was smiling when she turned around, but that faded when she looked at him. She covered the pan on the stove and came over to him, brushing her hands on his chest, tears in her eyes. She snatched the pad from the table and wrote, "So thin."

"You been peeking?" he asked. She actually blushed a bit and nodded.

It was a cozy little cabin, although with many strange corners. A ten-sided geodesic dome is like that, but it was the closest thing to a wigwam Kenny could manage. The bath was on a northwest wall, the small bedroom in the northeast with the fireplace between and in front of the closet/hall that connected the two. The back door was southeast, by the closet and stairway to the loft. An open kitchen overlooked his stream valley to the south. The southwest space was a small sitting area in front of the patio door and deck looking down the stream valley, Kenny's favorite view. In the center of the house was a round table where Kenny sat down.

Kenny slowly drank the tall glass of sweet, tangy orange juice like it was the grandest nectar in the world. He tried eating everything Lois put in front of him, but the woman never seemed to stop. "I can't gain it all back in one day, Lo," he said. She smiled beautifully at him, probably just to hear him say her name again, he thought.

On the pad, she wrote, "I made the bed for you."

It suddenly occurred to him that she had probably been sleeping there and he was moving her out. Only now did he see the sheets and blankets by the sofa. Lois noticed his gaze and nodded a rather forceful, "Yes."

He thought about that nice, soft bed and her soft hands and decided not to think about it anymore. "Tell me about Dick."

She sat down next to him with the pad—so close he could smell that subtle fragrance—and wrote, "Dick is working on something. He is OK."

Kenny looked deep in her eyes, both of them, one at a time, and nodded. Then he said, "Tell me about Sammi." Lois began to tear, smiled weakly, and suddenly showed signs of an idea. She raised an index finger and went behind the couch, bringing back a bag.

She pulled out an envelope, opened it and removed a folded piece of paper which she handed to Kenny. When he opened it, she pointed to the date.

FAREWELL

by Samantha Howell - 24 May

Oh, Rick, my Rick, why do I weep?
You drift across my frozen heart,
Apparition of Reality,
Flickering light within the dark,

You drift across my frozen heart,
When first I chance upon your light,
Flickering light within the dark,
In cold dark place I call myself,

When first I chance upon your light,
Consummate souls without Eros,
In cold dark place I call myself,
Within the prison of my pain,

Consummate souls without Eros,
One tiny bud of hope and trust,
Within the prison of my pain,
Lightly blushing promised growth,

One tiny bud of hope and trust,
In fear and somber spirit dread,
Lightly blushing promised growth,
Aroused in lucid fitful sleep,

In fear of somber spirit dread,
Oh, Rick, my Rick, why do I weep?
Aroused in lucid fitful sleep,
Apparition of Reality.

Kenny looked at Lois, and she mouthed, "She knew."

"She knew," Kenny said. "I think somehow we all knew by May 17th, we just kept denying it. Or, we knew the feelings but not the who or how." Lois nodded.

When she went to do dishes, he noticed that she wasn't getting much water. He also saw that she was not using the light over the counter. "Why don't you turn the light on?" he asked. She walked over and with one hand on her hip, flipped a switch up, down, and up again. He walked over and looked at a panel on the closet by the stairs, opened the door and pushed a button. The light came on. Her strange look of curiosity, mouthing, "How?" tried to make him smile.

"Inverter," he said, pointing at the closet, and, "solar panels," pointing at the roof.

She now had an incredulous look that succeeded in producing a big grin. "Can you hear the pump running?" he asked. She nodded. "The pump will fill the tank and you'll have more water soon."

Lois's face suddenly jumped to reveal a big idea and ran away. 'She's getting pretty good at this mime, stuff,' he thought. 'She could have been a silent movie star.'

She came back with her little computer, an AC plug in her hand, and a question on her face. "Sure," he said, "it's true sine wave," and she was off working. He was off to take a nap.

Sunset, 4 July

Magic is seldom repeated, but for the second time since Kenny had found Lonesome Pines, he was privileged to watch the stream valley fill up completely with a layer of dense fog a few feet high. Only once before had he seen it this dense at the same time that a full moon rose into the treetops across the valley to the southeast. As the moon rose, with pine boughs silhouetted against the almost perfect disk, light sparkled off the surface of the fog like tiny diamonds.

The first time he had been blessed with this sight was the week he bought the land, and he had wept not only for the sheer beauty, but for the loneliness of no one there to share it with him. Vicky had been home working that week.

Kenny and Lois sat at the dark fire pit now, side by side in the camp chairs, and she reached her right hand over and took his left. He did not pull away, but even gave hers a slight squeeze. Such moments deserve to be shared. Silently, he wept again.

They watched the moon move perceptively skyward until it cleared the trees, and then it seemed to linger. When Kenny felt nothing could be better, a thin cloud drifted eastward across the face of the moon like a veil covering a shy face. Kenny looked at Lois to see her mouthing something he thought might be "Wow," and he could see sparkles of tears on her cheeks. Something warm began to fill an empty space in the center of his being.

"Yeah, I'll go to the VA." He thought he spoke so quietly that he looked to see if Lois had heard. Her squeeze of his hand let him know she had. 'Nice grip,' he thought.

Before the moon approached its zenith, it appeared to lose its luster. A shadow of dusky red seemed to darken and diminish it. They were privileged to see a partial eclipse that was all too brief. But, they were getting cold anyway in this fresher, drier air today, so Kenny built a small fire and they lingered.

Before Moonset, 5 July

Kenny was wide awake and fully dressed as the moon sank down the valley in the southwest. He had an idea, so he woke Lois from sleeping on the couch. "Lo, there is something else I'd like you to see." He handed her a hooded sweatshirt and jacket. Slowly, she got the idea.

When she was ready, he took her hand and led her out the patio door, off the deck, and down the little trail into the woods. He made his way to an elevated hunting/viewing platform overlooking his valley and the forest to the west. Kenny dropped a folded blanket onto the damp floor, then wrapped the two of them in another blanket. Lois snuggled against him and they waited.

The sun began to chase the darkness left by the sinking moon, and they watched as color slowly emerged. Thin fog remained in places above the warm water of the stream and remnant of the beaver pond, but the air was clear above it. The greens appeared first, and soon Kenny and Lois could make out different textures of various trees at the forest edge. Kenny imagined the birds were singing, but he couldn't hear them this morning, and he wondered if he ever would.

Suddenly, it seemed, the tallest trees changed color as the sun rose above the horizon behind them and lit the treetops like candles. As a painter adding watercolor to an ink sketch, the sun colored the trees, top to bottom, in all the various hues of green, brown, white, grey, black, and, at the end, even a few yellows on the grasses and ferns. Lois looked up into Kenny's eyes and mouthed, "Thank you."

"Lo, you have got to see this in autumn." She kissed the tender spot below his ear.

Sunrise, 7 July

Kenny carried his bag to Lois's Bronco and threw it in the passenger seat. Lois, in dress uniform with her brand new CWO 4 insignia, packed the remainder of her things carefully in the back. It had been a couple of silent days.

As the sun had come up that other day, July 5th, Kenny's mood had gone down. Sometimes he called it the black coyote, his melancholy. He had tried busying himself around camp and talking to Lois. He had tried sitting on his rock, and he had tried reading. Lois, he thought, had tried everything she could imagine, but it was of no use. PTSD is like that, too.

He had been afraid that he might decide not to go to the VA this morning, but if there was any chance to hear the birds again, he wanted to try. Besides, he knew Lois had made all the arrangements. So, he was going.

Maybe he was afraid to hear—no, to read—that there was nothing they could do for him. Maybe he was afraid the suits and brass were coming. Maybe he was worried about Dick. Maybe he was afraid of who he was now that he could no longer be an LG. Maybe he just knew that something bad was going to happen, but not what or when. Maybe....

Lois waited for Kenny to get in, satchel in his lap, and then she got behind the wheel. She reached over and patted his knee. He acknowledged and said, "Thanks, Lois, sorry for...." She slapped his knee and started the Bronco. It was a quiet ride to the VA less than an hour away.

They took him through the admission process, but each new person seemed to have trouble understanding that Kenny could not hear, even though it was on the admission forms, so Lois was busy with pad and pen. They put him in a room with another guy, and Lois disappeared for what seemed to Kenny like a week and a half. When she came back, she gave him a piece of paper with a complete timeline.

"Thanks, Chief," is all he said. The audiologist would see him tomorrow. 'Pretty quick,' he told himself. 'This Chief must have a little clout.'

Lois sat in a chair beside his bed and wrote. "Have to go Madison. Can do more for you there. Be back for surgery."

"Thanks, Chief." Her look told him she was really tired of hearing that. "Thanks, Lo." She smiled and left.

'So, she thinks they'll do surgery. God bless optimists.'

He took a look at his roommate rustling around and was thankful that he couldn't hear right now. Just when he was wondering what he was supposed to do until tomorrow, people arrived and started poking and prodding him with all sorts of cold, hard devices. One baby-faced doctor even looked in his ears. 'No wonder people hate hospitals.'

Then, for some other strange reason, when it got dark and he thought he might actually sleep, probably with the help of their modern medicine, more people came in, turned the ceiling lights on, and started pushing buttons and turning knobs and writing secrets in little notebooks. For a soul who has killed people, off and on for decades, it was hard to just lie there. 'Now is when I need amnesia,' he thought.

Chapter Ten

0547 Hours, 8 July

Somebody came in before breakfast and wrote on a pad, "Scan." He didn't know what kind and didn't really care. After breakfast they took him someplace else for an MRI, or something, and X-rays. He was really getting his head examined and wondered when the shrink would show up. Before noon he was sorry for the thought.

The good thing about shrinks is they don't know what to do with you if you can't hear them. They like to pretend that you do all the talking, but their egos require their questions to be more important than your answers. He loved messing with their minds. After all, he had taught psychology as well as history and government. He also expected he knew more about the boundary of sanity and insanity than most of them ever would. This one sulked away in a few minutes.

It was the middle of the afternoon when the surgeon came in. Kenny was pretty sure he was a surgeon from his scrubs. Besides, he acted like a surgeon—cocksure. Kenny liked surgeons that way.

His sidekick wrote on a pad, "Any questions?"

"Yeah," Kenny said, "can you help me?"

The surgeon nodded, and the sidekick wrote, "We think so."

"When?"

"Tomorrow morning," the nice assistant wrote.

'Damn,' Kenny thought, 'I wonder who Chief knows in D.C. Maybe I better be nicer to her.' Kenny looked hard at the surgeon and asked, "What are my chances?"

"For what?" the surgeon mouthed.

"What are my chances to hear again?"

The surgeon took the pad and wrote, "75%."

"I'll take that," Kenny answered. "What are my chances of surviving?"

"90%," the surgeon wrote.

"I'll take that, too," Kenny said. It wasn't like he hadn't considered the scenarios. "Where do I sign?"

"Read this," the surgeon wrote, and his assistant gave Kenny a booklet and release forms. Kenny motioned for a pen, but the surgeon patted the book and mouthed, "Read this."

Kenny flipped through the papers and tossed them on the table. He knew somebody would be around for his signature, probably in a big hurry. He wondered what time tomorrow, but it didn't really matter. He wondered where Lois was, and that did matter. He wondered why he wasn't depressed anymore.

0522 Hours, 9 July

Kenny first became aware of a feeling of goodness beside him, and when he opened his eyes, Lois was there sleeping in a chair in her uniform. He was really beginning to admire this woman, professionally as well as personally. "Good morning, Chief," he said.

She answered something, and Kenny was pretty sure from her look that he was glad he couldn't hear. He smiled, thinking maybe he wouldn't call her that anymore.

"Lo, do you know what time the surgery is scheduled?"

She wrote, "Good morning you grumpy old fart." (That's pretty much what he thought she had said.) "It was 0600, but there was an emergency, so maybe about 1000."

"Thanks, Lo."

"Are you sure about this?" she wrote.

"Yes, I am, but thank you for asking. And, Lo, thanks for everything."

She nodded and patted his hand. He really liked that pat.

"Say, Lo, just who do you know in high places to get this done so quickly?"

She smiled slyly at him and wrote, "I'll tell you all about him when you come to dinner at my place and can listen to me."

"Yeah." He lay back. 'Him?'

The surgeon must have had quick hands or some important lunch date, because they came for his prep before eight, and he was gone before nine. On the way down that hall, lying flat on his back in another drug induced stupor, he noticed similarities and differences between facing surgery and facing combat. He might not come out alive, but at least today he wouldn't try to kill anybody. He was comfortable with that.

Surgery

Kenny was aware that he was hallucinating, or he thought he was. He was also convinced that these narcotic induced hallucinations were interwoven with Vision. 'Don't analyze,' he reminded himself, 'observe.'

The white light was seductive. No, that's not the right word, enthralling, maybe, and he moved toward it. He walked easily at first but then began to feel as though he were walking into a stiff wind. He turned around to notice he was dragging something dark. He thought of his anger about those hypnotic drugs and the amnesia and the days, weeks, months taken out of his life. He accepted that "they" were trying to help him, so he let the anger go, really let it go this time, and he walked easier, closer to the light.

Again he felt the head wind, and he thought about all those years of rage at their failure, his failure, in Vietnam. He remembered his day at The Wall when he met Rick, the voices and their message, and he decided—he chose—to let this rage go too, and he walked easier, closer and closer to the light.

When he felt the wind again, he was thinking about Bonnie and Kenny Jr. This was not a rage he was holding onto, but something even harder to abandon, his guilt and remorse. 'It is not up to them to let go,' he told himself. 'It is my baggage,' and for the first time he let that go, too, and he walked easier and closer to the light.

It was attracting him like a magnet now, and he was feeling something wonderful. It was not exactly thrill, but it was beyond all excitement, yet sublimely peaceful at the same time. When he thought he could reach out and touch the light—so unbelievably bright now, yet it did not hurt his eyes—just then, he felt the wind again, blowing him back, but his mind would think of no other guilt, remorse, anger, or rage that he could release.

Kenny knew, he was positive, that he was holding onto something, but it was not a bad something. Still it was like a sail that caught the wind and took him further and further away from that light. Deep inside, where the narcotics could not go, he was certain that he would go to that light, someday.

A question formed in his mind, but not in words, and he chose to turn around, to begin the long journey back to whatever it was that had a hold on him. No, that wasn't right. Nothing had a hold on him. He had a hold on something and was not yet willing to let it go.

1531 Hours, 9 July

Kenny could read the orientation board and clock when they wheeled him into his room, relieved to be back at all. Lois stood up, smiled, and gave him a thumbs up. Obviously, she knew more than he did, and that was fine. They got him back in bed and everything was good—until his head started to hurt. 'I was probably supposed to read about that,' he thought.

They set up tubes and machines and such. Then they gave him the button. He knew what that was for, the little button that would give him more pain medicine when he requested it, within time constraints, of course. He hated drugs but knew enough about pain to know that he had to stay ahead of it. Lois walked around the bed, Kenny following with his eyes. She picked up the button, sort of shaking it in front of his face. Kenny blinked a few times, took the button from her, and pushed it dramatically. 'Yes, Mommy,' he thought.

Lois went to the other side and sat in the hard straight chair by his side, holding his hand. Kenny lay there and accepted the attention. There wouldn't be much when he got home, he figured. He thought about asking when he might go home, but he didn't want to move his head. Come to think of it, they had him strapped down pretty good—like they didn't want him to move much at all. 'I probably should have read about that, too.'

He reached down to check if he still had a catheter in, which he did. One less thing to worry about. The bowel wouldn't be working for a day or two at best, he figured.

'What an ugly ceiling,' he noticed. 'Why don't they put hospital beds in the woods so you can watch birds and clouds and wind in the leaves?' That thought was so ridiculous, it amused him and he chuckled aloud, he thought, and maybe he heard it. He rolled his eyes toward Lois to catch her looking at him with concern. She saw his eyes and patted his hand again.

People swam in and out, he pushed the button and dozed, and Lois held his hand. He had a thought of nausea, but decided that wouldn't be good for his head, and kind of sloppy, not to mention dangerous, on his back like this, so he decided to meditate. He went to his Special Place and played with the animals. He went to Line Camp and drank some of Lois's ginger tea. He went to the UW campus like he used to do in high school when he watched the lady buds come out on that first really nice spring day, the coeds who bared as much as was legal and sometimes a little bit more. He went to church with Grandma and Grandpa again, and he ate pie and ice cream in the fellowship hall after the service. He watched the moon rise over fog at Lonesome Pines with Lois, and he went to sleep.

He woke up to pain and sound, both of which he welcomed. He pushed the button and looked around the best he could. Lois was standing, kind of hovering over him. She showed him the pad, "Did you say something?"

"Maybe," he said, and he was sure he heard that. "Lo, I think I heard my own voice."

"Well, don't talk so much, Windy," she said, bending over him, and she kissed him on the forehead. Somehow, his lips felt cheated, and that confused him. Oh, well, most everything confused him today.

He pointed an index finger into his open mouth, made a yuck face, and sort of spit, "Ptew."

She studied that a moment, and asked, "Bad taste?" He blinked three times. "Well, what do you want, ice? Tell me."

"Lo, you told me to shut up."

"Oh, for goodness sake. Are you yanking my chain?"

"As hard as I can, considering."

"I'll ask your nurse what we can do. Now, shut up."

0733 Hours, 10 July

A new doctor showed up and sat down beside him. "Good morning, LG. Can you hear me?" he asked in clear, distinct low frequency tones.

"Yes," Kenny smiled.

"Great. Your surgeon will be in later today to check his work, but I'll be your hearing specialist. We have great hope for more improvement."

Kenny beamed, "When can I go home?"

"We won't even talk about that for a few days," he looked at Lois and back. "You have to heal and rehab before we look at that."

"He will have a place to go home to with twenty-four hour care," Lois told the doctor. Kenny rolled his eyes to look at her.

"Well that could certainly make a difference. We'll talk about that later," he said as he left.

Kenny looked at Lois, waiting for an explanation. "I think I found a place for you to stay in Madison, near me.," she said, "and that's all I have to say about that, for now."

The surgeon came by that afternoon to admire his handiwork. Kenny couldn't be sure just what he was looking at, but he seemed pleased. Then he sat down, which worried Kenny.

"You gave us a scare, there, Kenny, but things look really good right now. We finished your right ear, and I think it will do pretty well, but we had to stop with the left. We thought we were losing you, but you came back. Your left ear seemed to be less injured and already healing, so we have hopes you will get more of your hearing back. But the right one may be almost back to where it was before the injury, depending on how things go. Any questions?"

"I almost died?"

"Let's just say your vitals alarmed us for a few minutes—a little more than a few minutes—even into recovery. Glad to see you back, Kenny."

"I thought so," Kenny said.

When he was gone, Kenny asked Lois, "Did you know?"

"Yes, Ken, I knew when you were still in recovery that they were worried. I'm glad to see you back, too." Kenny could see her mouth start to form words, but her teeth bit them right off.

'So much trouble for a used up old man,' Kenny thought. 'Being judgmental again. No wonder I get depressed.'

"Ken, I'm going home now."

"Back to Madison?"

"Yes, I have a lot of work to do, but I'll be checking up on you. If I can, I'll get back in a few days." She looked sorrowfully at him. "I'm sorry I can't stay."

"You go, Lo, take care of all that business. And thanks for all you did for me."

She walked around toward the door, but came back and kissed him on the lips. Then she was gone. Kenny didn't push that button again until almost dark.

1136 Hours, 11 July

It was a long day without Lois. Funny how he could be perfectly content in the woods without human companionship, but here in civilization, he almost always felt lonesome. His roommate was no help at all. Kenny hadn't realized until the night aide came in that he really couldn't hear all that well. He couldn't make out what she was saying. His roommate seemed to hear Kenny but never got the idea that he had to speak loudly and clearly. He was appreciative of everybody else's efforts to help him hear.

They had him up today and walking around. His strength was pretty good for an old man, but his balance was a bit off. Nobody seemed concerned about that. The pain was pretty low grade now, but they kept a close watch on his vitals. Lunch would be here soon.

1037 Hours, 14 July

Lois walked in! Kenny was amazed how excited he was, and she looked great. No uniform today, just a nice pair of tan slacks and a pale blue, short-sleeve blouse. "Hi, Kenny. How are you?"

"I'm ready to go home."

"Well, that's what we're going to talk about, today," she sat down next to him and took his hand.

"Are you handling me again, Ch…I mean, Lois?"

"Yes, I am. They want to keep you here another day or two, then a couple of weeks in rehab."

"Weeks? What rehab? How the hell do you rehab ears?"

"I think it might be a little more between the ears, Ken."

"Oh, shit." That's another thing about shrinks. Sometimes you think they have given up, but they're just planning a different bunch of questions. "What are my options?"

"I'm not sure, yet, Ken, but I don't really think you have any. You can't take care of yourself, and my friends won't take you against medical advice."

"Friends?"

"Well, yeah, some people I know in a co-op house down by campus."

"Oh, by campus? I like that." Kenny smiled.

"Yeah, they need a few bucks and will take good care of you but mind their own business at the same time, you know?"

"How do you know these people?"

"You're getting pretty worked up about this."

For the first time, Kenny began to wonder if he could really trust her—well, the second time. That business about her having so much work to do in Madison bugged him, too.

"Lo, can we go outside and talk?"

"Sure, Ken. I'll talk to your nurse." Lois seemed to brighten cautiously.

"They'll be glad to get rid of me." He rolled out of bed, put on his robe, and walked out, Lois following. "I'm going out," he told a nurse at the station, and they did.

Outside, they found a bench away from people and Kenny looked at Lois. She waited. "Lo, you know I don't know you nearly as well as you know me."

"I know, Ken." Lois gave him her professional face.

"I've really only known you for a few days—it feels like more, but not really."

"Is there something on your mind, Ken?"

"A couple of things. First, what are we to each other? I mean, how well, uh...."

"Maybe I can help," and she looked around. "Our relationship was always very professional until, well, until Rick didn't come back on time, the mission before last. That really shook us up, Sammi and me, and I realized something." She stopped and looked around while Kenny waited. "I realized I, uhm, wanted more than a professional relationship." She stopped.

"Have I," Ken started, "ever been...inappropriate?"

"Oh, no!" she assured him. "You've been a perfect gentleman, damn it." She smiled with moist eyes. "Ken, I had hopes of saying this in a different place and time." She paused, but he waited. "I'm in love with you." She looked vulnerable now, all professionalism gone.

Kenny blinked. "You think you're in love with me?"

"No, you, you frustrating.... I am in love with you. I'm not a kid. I know what love is," She stopped. He waited. "What was the second thing?"

"What?" Kenny asked, startled. "Oh, the second thing. I forgot. No, wait, how do I know I can trust you?" he blurted out. "Oh, shit. I don't mean it like that."

"How do you mean it?" She had that professional look again.

"Well, I don't really know, I guess. I'm just trying to make sense of your important work in Madison without Dick, and your important 'him' in high places."

"Ah, you're out of the loop. How does it feel?"

"You already know how it feels, Lois."

"Yes, I do, Ken, and I'm sorry, but I can't say any more, yet. Maybe when you come for dinner."

Kenny just looked away for awhile. When he looked back, he took her hands in his and said, "I do trust you, but I don't know about dinner at your place."

"Fair enough, Ken, for now."

0836 Hours, 30 July

Kenny hopped into the passenger seat of Lois's Bronco and sat impatiently while she got every little thing situated before she started it up. "Are you ready?" she asked.

"Yeah, already. Let's went," he answered. Lois looked over and shook her head with a smile. Kenny took a deep breath of free air and saluted goodbye to the VA for what he hoped was the last time. Oh, he knew better, but he hoped.

"I'm surprised they let you escape so soon," Lois said.

"Humph," Kenny answered. "I have the feeling you were keeping me in there. Is there something I should know?"

"Soon, Kenny, very soon. Still trust me?"

"Yes, Lois, I do, God help us both." Only then did he notice the little dents on her hood, "Hail damage?" he asked.

"Yes, it is."

"Is that from Line Camp?"

"Yes, it is."

"Why haven't you fixed it?" he asked.

"It reminded me of Line Camp. I was waiting for you to come home."

"Well, I'm home now, Lo."

"Not quite, Ken, but soon, I hope."

"I wonder why I didn't notice it before, on the way to the VA."

"Maybe because your head was too far up your ass."

Kenny chuckled, "I think you're right, Lo."

Chapter Eleven

High Waning Gibbous Moon, 6 August

Kenny couldn't sleep again, and he sat by the quiet shore of Lake Mendota at the end of the street where he lived in the co-op house. 'What am I waiting for?' he asked himself. 'I am ready to go home and take care of myself.' He couldn't go, though. It was like he was tethered to Madison, had staked himself out waiting to count *coups*.

Madison was still the only city Kenny ever loved, maybe because it was home, maybe because of the University, or maybe because of the ethnic diversity of international students and residents both. Probably it was all of this plus the four lakes in the region, and the green spaces. Kenny decided to take a walk to the arboretum.

He crossed the isthmus, pausing on State Street where the transients found some comfort, and on to Lake Monona. There he could watch the moon set over the bay before heading for Lake Wingra, the little lake by the zoo. Kenny paused by the spot where the round monkey house should have been, where he had learned something about body language and status such a long time ago.

He walked into the arboretum by starlight alone and somehow felt right again. This was a special place to him, a place modern man had preserved for scientific reasons, but in doing so, had protected some secret, ancient, sacred areas. He found one of them and prayed. He pulled out his personal pipe, the one-piece raven he had carved from a downed branch from his own red oak tree, and packed some powwow blend. He was aware that the sage might smell like another kind of herbal smoke, but he didn't care. Tolerance was still the theme in Madison; at least he hoped it was. Besides, what were they going to do to a broken little old man? He smiled a bit to think what their reaction might be when they identified his sage and had to release him. He almost hoped he would get arrested—almost.

It's a funny thing about prayers. They get answered. Kenny prayed gratitude for his life, and he asked for guidance to do the work of The Creator. Answers come in many forms and many means. This time he simply saw an unusually clear image of Green Bay burning. He had no idea what that meant, but he knew he could not go home to Lonesome Pines, yet.

Most people need help interpreting visions and other answers to prayers, and Kenny really missed Rick, tonight. There was only one person he knew whom he trusted, and sometimes he had his doubts about her. 'Yeah, what's that about, anyway?' he asked himself. Tonight he did not answer Kenny.

He had planned to stay until full light but stood up without knowing why and began walking back. The city was beginning to come alive, not with traffic and other signs of hurried, wasted life, but with street people moving from night places to day places. A small woman pulling a cheap, little red wagon, like Kenny's childhood toy, walked hunched over toward him, and he made way on the walk for her. She walked right up to him, stopped, peered into his face and spoke in a raspy, frail, but confident voice, "She loves you, you know," and walked on.

"Yeah, I know," Kenny answered, surprised at his own voice. He didn't think he had meant to say it aloud.

The lady turned around, slowly put the wagon handle down and rolled both palms up, shrugging her shoulders like, "Well, then?" Kenny waved acknowledgement and walked home to his co-op house.

Late Morning, 9 August

Lois spread the little cloth on the grassy hill in front of UW Bascom Hall, but off to the side towards North Hall. It was a simple picnic today, bread, cheese and whole berries, with sparkling water to finish. "Sorry there's no mocha, Ken."

Kenny grinned and pulled a thermos out of his bag. "Why don't we go out in the middle?" Kenny gestured.

"I don't want to wreck the statue," Lois answered.

Kenny chuckled at the old student myth that Abe Lincoln would stand up whenever a virgin walked in front of him. It made him think, though.

"Ken?" Lois began seriously, "why don't we date?"

He blinked and looked at her, "What are we doing, Lo?"

"Is this a date, Kenny?" and she kissed him for real. This time he kissed her back, but only a little. He looked around to see if anyone was noticing or going to tell them to get a room, but they were being ignored.

It felt like a contradiction that a shy guy like Kenny could feel at home here as a student, but he had. There are two ways of being alone, he figured—by yourself or in a crowd. He was always quite anonymous on campus.

He thought back to the changes he had watched here over the years. In the '60s of his high school days when he planned to study agriculture and help his grandpa, this was a place for hippy radicals and antiwar protests—shaggy people with little green bags and long hair. When he returned from Vietnam and came here to study history, education, and political science, intending to make sense of the world, it was a serious place with future yuppies clawing for success. 'Everything changed in 1970,' he reminded himself.

He had never read this theory of history, so he invented it. The bombing of Sterling Hall only a couple hundred yards away, the killing of students at Kent State, the conviction of Lt. Calley in a court martial, and the invasion of sovereign Cambodia in which he was complicit, all seemed to change this place as much as they had changed him. He wondered why nobody else seemed to notice that.

"Welcome back," Lois said. Kenny blinked at her and looked toward Old Abe. Kenny noticed a man over there who just didn't fit on campus, and for Madison, that was saying a lot. It was Sunday, though. Maybe he was a parent checking up on his daughter or something. Maybe.

"Lois, do you have a body guard?"

"Nooo, do I need one?"

He couldn't think of anything intelligent to say, so he said, "I think I can do that."

"Good," she said, "if it keeps you close to me. I never had a body guard before, and I certainly never dated one."

Evening, 19 August

They rested on a blanket, picnic put away, and waited for the concert to begin on Capitol Square. Kenny was comfortable in the crowds on campus, but this kind made him nervous. He lightly brushed the .380 in his left inside vest pocket. It was illegal as hell, but he had seen that same guy again last Sunday, and he thought, or imagined, that he was here tonight. Still, he really wanted to talk to Lois.

"Lo, there's something I've been wondering about."

"Yeah, me too," she said.

"What? What are you wondering about?"

"You first, Kenny."

He thought a moment. "No, Lo, you first. Really."

His serious, kind of hurt look convinced her. "Well, Ken, I was wondering when you were coming to my place for dinner."

"Oh, well, when is your birthday?"

"July 6th."

Kenny thought for more than a moment, remembering the silent days at his cabin when he was lost in his black coyote depression.

"Oh, I'm sorry Lo. Hmmm. I tell you what. You go on an adventure with me Saturday, and we'll set a date. Okay?"

"Where are we going, Ken?"

"My adventure, your dinner. Deal?"

"Sure. What are my options, anyway?" Lois asked.

He thought a moment and decided not to answer that. "I'll pick you up right here at 0545 Saturday, 22 August."

She blinked at him. "Pick me up? With what?"

"My adventure, Lo."

"I'll be here. What do I wear?"

"Jeans, boots, you know, Indiana Jones adventure clothes."

She looked hard at him but said nothing.

"Do you trust me, Lois?"

"Of course I do. I will be here."

0543 Hours, 22 August

Kenny circled the square on his new, used Honda XR650L, a big street/dirt combo bike, and saw Lois standing almost in the exact spot where they had listened to the concert. When he pulled up, he removed his helmet and waved. She came running over, and he handed her a helmet and jacket. "Have you ridden before?" he asked.

"Only a little, Ken," she answered.

"Well, sit still and trust me. I'm driving now. Don't handle me."

"Yes, dear," she answered in her weak June Cleaver imitation and climbed on behind him. Kenny looked around hard before putting his helmet on and taking off.

He rode carefully through the streets, making his way to the causeway and onto the beltline. He headed east and kept it legal until he crossed under the interstate and onto open road. Then, he opened it up. Lois held on so tight he had a little trouble breathing, but he still flew until the traffic heading toward Madison picked up a bit. He slowed down and followed the country roads for many miles and turns.

Just when Lois seemed to be relaxing, he turned onto a lane and rode slowly through an old farm yard and gravel pit. He cranked it again in lower gears through the field road. If anybody was still following him, he wanted them to hear where he went. He finally stopped by a pond and motioned for Lois to get off. He parked the bike in the tree line, pretending to hide it, and took off his helmet. Lois was staring at him, helmet in hand. "Grandpa's farm," he said, pointing up a huge hill. "It's okay, I called the owners for permission."

Kenny opened up one bike bag and removed a pack. He also clipped his .380 on his belt in front of his left hip.

"How long have you been carrying that?" Lois asked.

"Since I first got a good look at your tail." Lois brightened almost to a smile before the alarm went off.

"I've been followed?" she asked.

"Yes, dear, that's what I meant when I first asked about a bodyguard." He handed her the pack and pulled another bag out of the other side. He removed a folded rifle and set it up. He also grabbed some ear plugs and showed them to Lois, then dropped them in his shirt pocket. She didn't seem to have anything to say.

Kenny led her across a drainage ditch, through an abandoned field in the marsh, across another ditch and into the woods. He stopped, and asked her, "How are you with poison ivy?"

"Never had it," she answered with a question in her tone.

"Good. Don't touch the ground, and don't kiss my feet."

"Don't worry, Ken."

They climbed a big hill and sat on a couple of stumps by an old fire pit out in the open. Kenny pointed to something red and shiny in the rising sun. "The bike," he said. "Now, I've been wondering about something."

"No, shit," she said.

"Tell me about Sammi and Rick."

Lois pulled a thermos out of the bag and poured a cup of mocha to share. She took a sip and handed it to Kenny. "They fell in love."

"How did that happen?" Kenny asked. "Please, tell me something."

"Okay, Ken, I'll tell you what I know. Sammi had never had much to do with men. By the time she and her mom came to town, her father was already in prison—for abusing Sammi. She avoided boys as much as possible in school until she thought she fell in love in college. He raped her. Well, he probably didn't think it was rape, and she wasn't sure, either, at the time, but it was. After that, she avoided men altogether until Rick came along. She knew she could trust him, and he relied on her, especially after quitting the patch."

"He never told me," Kenny said.

"Well, there wasn't much to tell. They never did consummate. Sammi never even considered that—until she turned forty."

A tiny voice in Kenny's head tried to say something, but his hearing was impaired.

"When he didn't come back a second time, she went all to pieces. She is still really glad for what they had—at Line Camp, I mean. That was about the extent of their relationship."

Kenny got up and walked into the woods a ways and peed, mostly for something to do. He came back and sat down again. "Okay, Lo, tell me about you."

Lois squirmed and cleared her throat, but said nothing. She looked up at Kenny, helpless.

Kenny tried to help her out. "What do you want from me, Lo?"

"I'm not sure, Kenny, really," and she looked right at him, "I think I want all of you, whatever you have to share." They watched the sun paint the hill to the west and kept an eye on the bike. Lois shattered the silence first, "Ken, what do you want?"

"I guess I want to be sure you know what you're getting into."

"What are you worried about, Kenny?"

"Okay, Lo, I'm worried about what kind of man I am—in many ways, really. Hon, I have been celibate since before Vicky died. I don't know...."

Lois caressed his knees, both of them. "Only a good man would think about that."

"Yeah, right," he sneered. "A good man. Lo, I have been through all the stages of normal male sexuality, I think. As an adolescent, I didn't think at all, at least not with the big head. When I thought I was a man, I was grossly selfish, thinking only of my own pleasure and satisfaction. When I finally matured a little, I began to take some interest in pleasing a woman, well, Vicky. In the end, pleasing her was my pleasure, but, you know, Lo, that was selfish too. I was still feeding my ego by being 'The Man'. Then, that was gone too."

"Ken, it's okay. It really is. You can talk about it. I'm not threatened by your past. I am not threatened by you at all."

"Well, see, that's the thing, how unequal this relationship would be. You are open and honest, and I am scared of being a failure again, one more time, one more way."

There just didn't seem to be anything else to say on that subject until Kenny got philosophical. "Lo, would you like to hear my theory on marriage?"

"I think I would."

"Well, I think the healthiest thing is for everybody to marry three times." Lois gave him a disapproving look. "No, really, I'm serious. See, in youth, you should marry somebody in middle age. That way there is sexual compatibility, someone to help you learn, and a spouse to put you through school."

Her look was now disdain. "I'm telling you, I am serious. See, then in middle age you switch roles and marry somebody young." Lois shook her head. "Then, if you make it to old age, find somebody your own age to not have sex with." At that Lois had to chuckle a little.

"So, Brewster, are you saying I should find some young stud to teach and put through school?"

"I'm saying it would make a lot more sense than finding some old fool to not have sex with."

"So, that's your theory, huh? Want to hear my theory?"

"Not in the least," he answered.

"Well, you're going to, Kenneth Brewster."

"I knew that."

"My theory is you owe me one romantic dinner at my place and we'll let nature take its course, whatever that may be. Really," she added noticing his vulnerable look.

"Romantic?" Kenny asked quietly.

"Oh, yes, very romantic."

"Not your place though. It's probably bugged."

"Oh, shit," she said, looking him over. "Okay, but I pick the place."

"Fine, but no reservations," Kenny answered.

"Fine, but I drive." Lois insisted.

"Fine, but not your Bronco."

"Fine. When?"

"August 28th," he snapped.

"Why August 28th?"

"You were supposed to say fine. Why not August 28th? It just popped into my little head."

"Fine, August 28th, I'll pick you up at—what day is that?"

"Friday," he quipped. She gave him a little double take.

"I'll pick you up at 1545 at…?"

"How about meeting me at the truck stop by Lake Mills?" Kenny asked. "You know the one?" She nodded. "We can switch vehicles there," he added.

"I'm not driving that bike."

Kenny chuckled, "Damned right you're not, not with me riding behind. I'll have a rental."

"I'll drive."

"Fine."

Chapter Twelve

1540 Hours, 28 August

Kenny sat at the counter sipping coffee, dressed in old blue jeans, sleeveless plaid shirt, and a dirty cowboy hat. His back was uncharacteristically toward the door to the gas pumps where he could keep an eye on the parking lot to his right. He noticed Lois pull in, park her Bronco in the middle of the lot, and walk toward the door behind him wearing her camouflaged fatigues. He heard the door open, and she walked right up beside him to ask directions from the waitress.

"Can you tell me how to get to the Matt Kenseth Fan Club?" Lois asked.

"I can help you there, lady," Kenny said in a loud gruff voice that made her jump. "You just go on through town there, and take a half right 'cross the tracks, and follow that A on over to 18." Lois gave him a look that made him almost choke to keep from chortling. "I got a map in the truck out back, honey. I'll give you what you want."

"That won't be necessary," she spit, and the waitress gave her more specific directions. When she had the details clear, Lois sort of looked around, so Kenny helped her out again.

"The restrooms are back there, soldier lady" he almost barked, "by the back door and my truck."

She didn't even acknowledge him as she walked toward the restrooms.

"Guess I might as well get back on the road," Kenny told the waitress, and he walked stiffly out back to wait for Lois.

She was out in just a minute and watched him climb into the passenger seat of an old, red Ford Escape. Saying nothing, she opened the driver door, threw her cap and uniform blouse in back, and sat down in her soft, cream colored tank top. She found the keys in the ignition, looked around and started it up.

"Are you having fun, Brewster?" she asked without looking at him as she drove out of the parking lot.

"So far," he answered. At that she burst into laughter.

"You know, Miss," he started in a Larry the Cable Guy style, "some folks back there might suspect somethin'. I mean, we was a little over the top. They might think we bein' naughty."

"Are we?" she asked, taking a quick look at him.

"I'm feeling a little naughty."

"Hold that thought." She looked around the SUV and said, "This thing's kind of old to be a rental."

"Well, I bought it. Too many forms at a rental place, too many records, so I bought this." When she gave him a questioning look, he just asked, "What else am I supposed to do with my money, buy a casket and plot somewhere?"

Lois shook her head and patted his thigh. He could get used to that. He thought about asking where they were going and why she had no bags, but he figured the intrigue might be stimulating. Besides, she would be waiting for him to ask, and he really was feeling kind of naughty today.

Kenny began to think she was feeling naughty, too, because she didn't say a word about where they were going or why he wasn't asking. She just started talking about her favorite kinds of cats. When Kenny had enough of that, he asked, "Truce?"

"Peace," she said.

"Where are we going, Lo?"

"It's a secret. My adventure, don't ya know?" she challenged.

"Not for long, I hope."

"Not long, Ken."

"I would ask why you have no bag, but I suppose that's a secret too."

"Nah, that's no secret. Everything is ready for me there."

'Hmm,' he thought, 'that is intriguing.' She was right, though, because pretty soon they pulled into a driveway at a little old lake cottage, the kind he imagined Al Capone had stayed in, and probably that old.

"It belongs to friends," she said. "Don't worry, I haven't been here this week. I just asked my friend and she told me she would take care of everything.

Kenny grabbed his satchel and followed her to the door, but she handed him the key and waited while he unlocked it.

It was an old cottage with old cottage smells, sounds, and furniture. On the table was a vase of beautiful roses in many colors. There were carnations in the bathroom and candles in the bedroom on the stands beside the out-of-place modern bed and comforter. Kenny took a look in the refrigerator to find it well stocked, but for the life of him, he couldn't think what to do next. He hesitated and Lois kissed him.

"I'm going to take a shower," she announced. He felt like he was moving his mouth but nothing came out. "I'll be out in a few minutes," she said.

Of course it was more than a few minutes, but not that long, really. Her hair was up in a way he had never seen and she was wearing a deep teal cocktail dress, a modest string of pearls, and little strappy shoes—and she was wearing makeup and earrings! Kenny took a sniff to make sure it was her, but that turned into a hug and kiss.

"I'm going to cook, now," she announced as she tied on a lace-trimmed apron that had been hanging by the stove.

"I, um, I think I'll watch," and he sat at the table, but very soon he grabbed his satchel and took a shower, too.

By the time he got back, wearing his very best jeans and T-shirt, she was sitting at the table. "Welcome home, Ken," was all she said.

He nodded, "Yeah, welcome."

She smiled one of those smiles only women really in love can manage, and he melted into a chair at the table. He could smell something cooking and wondered why she wasn't fussing over it. He was kind of looking forward to watching that.

As if on cue, she got up, lifted the cover from the big pan, and stirred. "Are you hungry, hon?" she asked, looking back over her shoulder.

"Not really," he said, rather hoarsely.

She turned the fire down low and sat down. "Okay, we can talk a bit, then," and she patted his hand. He liked that almost as much as when she patted his knee. "Ken, what would you like to know?"

"What? Oh, those questions? What were they?" he stammered.

"Well, one was something about who I knew in high places."

"Oh, yeah, who puts the power to the strings you pull?"

"Well, have you heard the name, Brad Dickenson?" she asked

"Senator Brad Dickenson?"

"Yes, Ken. You see, he asked me to marry him almost twenty years ago."

"And you didn't?"

"Turned him down flat." She sat there, smug, waiting for a reaction.

"Why?"

"Well, at the time, I thought it was because I just didn't love him. He was—and is—a really nice man. Now I think it's because I was waiting for you."

"And somehow, in his undying gratitude for your rejection, he does favors for you now?"

"Something like that. Actually, this is the only favor I ever asked of him, but we have always been good friends. Anything else about that?"

"Is there anything else?" Kenny asked cautiously.

"Nope."

"Case closed then, Lo. I remember another question, though. Did I really save your life?"

"You did." She paused, and Kenny raised his eyebrows. "It was not on a mission like you might think. We were in Line Camp, you and Rick were out doing your meditation thing in the early evening, and I decided to wander away from camp by myself. I hadn't been gone very long when I heard a 'Huff, huff' kind of sound in the thick stuff ahead of me."

"Bear," Kenny said.

"Bear. I just froze, and he—you said it was a he, later, an adolescent male—he stood up and kind of growled or something. I couldn't move. He went down all fours and sort of charged toward me. Then he stood up again, waiving his arms around with big black claws." She paused.

Kenny asked, "And then what happened?"

"You just seemed to appear behind him. You walked softly right up close and asked him 'What the hell are you doing?' He went down an all fours again and turned toward you, then raised up and stared at you." She paused again.

"So help me, Lo, if this is a joke, I'm going to spank your butt."

"Oooh," she said, "I wish I had a punch line. It's true, Ken, I swear. You had a stick in your hand, like a small baseball bat, and you threw it at him, backwards sort of, like this," and she swung an overhead backhand motion. "Honest to God, Ken, the stick hit him, and he sort of grunted and took off running."

Kenny laughed, "I didn't really save your life. He was just bullying you."

"I think you did. Besides, you saved my dignity." He looked quizzically at her.

"You completely ignored the fact that I peed my pants—it's a wonder that's all I did—and you let Sammi know so she could help me be less conspicuous."

"And, you fell in love with me right then."

"No," she said, "and then you watched him run away...," she was giggling so much now, she could hardly talk, "...watched him run away and you said, 'Damned kids. They're all alike. If you don't stand up to them, they'll bully the hell out of you.' I swear, if I hadn't already peed my pants, that would have done it. I started laughing hysterically and couldn't stop."

"That's when you fell in love with me."

"No, I told you, Ken, I think I have always been in love with you, and I was just waiting for you to arrive in my life. Are you hungry yet?"

"Well, yes, but there is one more question. Where is Dick?"

"I really don't want to talk about that tonight, hon. I really don't. I promise I'll tell you all I know tomorrow morning after breakfast."

"I'm staying for breakfast?"

"Oh, yeah, you're staying. Aren't you?"

"Oh, I certainly hope so, Lo."

Waning Twilight, 28 August

Lois walked past Kenny to the night stand on the left side of the bed and lit a candle. As she walked around the other side to light another candle, Kenny stood by the bed and watched her put the lighter down and turn off the light. Kenny slipped out of his clothes quickly and lay back on the bed in his briefs. Lois was much more deliberate. Standing in the soft candle light, she unbuttoned her little cocktail dress one button at a time and let it fall away to the floor as she faced Kenny on the bed. He watched in some kind of disbelief. 'Am I really doing this?' he asked himself. 'Am I up for this?' He nearly chuckled aloud at his accidental pun.

She slowly released her bra and allowed it to slip to the floor, revealing her firm breasts, nipples rigid with excitement. She turned around, slid her panties over her full hips and sat on the bed in a single fluid movement, as though she had thoroughly rehearsed it. The thought of that rehearsal aroused Kenny's mind and frightened him at the same time. 'It has been so long.'

She rolled toward him and snuggled onto his left shoulder. Kenny asked, "Did you hear about the old man who went to the doctor?"

She lifted her head to look at him. "Nooo."

"He went to see the doctor and asked, 'Doc, can you lower my sex drive a bit?' The doctor checked to see if he had heard right, 'Lower it?' 'Yeah,' the man responded, 'Lower it about three feet. Lately it seems to be mostly in my head.' "

Kenny waited. She snuggled her head back onto his shoulder and caressed his chest with her left hand. "Are you worried, Ken?"

"Oh, yeah."

"Don't be. This is all I need."

Kenny held her close, but he knew she was not telling the truth. He didn't know what the truth was, and he suspected she really didn't know either, at least not consciously. He didn't know what to say, so he asked, "Do you know how man was given fifty years of sex life?"

"Tell me later." She sought his lips and kissed him gently, briefly, without demand. "I love you, Ken. I really do."

Kenny's mind wasn't working too well at the moment, so he had no immediate response. Finally, he asked, "Do you have protection?"

"I don't need any protection," she hushed, her head on his shoulder again.

Kenny thought—or, something—for a moment. "Do you have any lubrication?"

She shook her head deliberately on his shoulder. "I don't need any lubrication either, Kenny." She paused and looked up into his eyes. "Care to see for yourself?"

Kenny began to sense that old, so old, feeling of arousal, and he liked it. He drew her close, and his right hand began a slow dance down her back, over her firm, round buttocks, and back along her thighs. Her body responded. His hand found its way and he aroused further as his fingers confirmed her offer.

"Just a minute," she whispered, as she rolled onto her back and slipped a pillow under her elevated hips. Kenny was acutely aware that such a position was used to enhance pleasure, and that completed his arousal. Much later, another reason for the position occurred to him.

Kenny had approached sex with gratitude for years before his abstinence, especially through Vicky's illnesses and treatments. He had traveled from eager youth seeking satiety to mature satisfaction in giving pleasure. He had known that one of the times would be his last, and he had consciously tried to make each one special, memorable. Now, he was really sure this could be his last, and he wished to savor it.

Savor it, he did. Lois gave all indications that she enjoyed it, too. They held each other for a long time after. Even their breathing seemed to be synchronized.

"Thank you, Ken."

He gave her a squeeze. "Thank you. Care to hear how man got fifty years of sex life?"

"I'd love to."

"Okay. Well, when God created the world, he gave the animals twenty years of normal sex life each. But, the monkey said, 'I don't need all that. Ten years would be sufficient.' Well, man jumped up and said, 'I'll take the other ten, God.' So God said, 'Okay.' Then the donkey said, 'I don't need more than ten years either.' Of course, man said, 'I'll take the other ten,' and God said 'Okay.' Finally, the lion said, courageously, 'Well, I sure don't need all twenty. I can get the job done in ten years or less.' God just looked at man and said, 'Okay.' And that explains why man has twenty years of normal sex life, ten years of monkeyin' around, ten years of making an ass out of himself, and ten years of lyin' about it."

Lois laughed, giggled, and laughed some more. Kenny laughed just to hear her. "Kenny, that is so stupid, and I've heard it before, but...," and she giggled some more.

"Lo, that's the first time I've heard you laugh like that."

"Well, that's the first time I've heard you laugh like that, too, Kenny." Soberly, she added, "That is the first time I've had such a good laugh in a long, long time."

"Well, sure, Lo. It's the first time you've been in bed with me," and they were both off laughing again. Today, the world made sense, at least, their little part of it. It was a good day to live, Kenny decided, before he slipped off to sleep.

Full Sun, 29 August

He must have slept unusually soundly for his first awareness was the smell of bacon frying. Stretching himself awake, he stalked toward the kitchen but noticed the fresh, clean smell of the bathroom and decided to take a quick shower. When he walked softly into the kitchen wrapped in a towel, Lois asked, "How do you like your eggs, Kenny?"

"Cold."

Lois turned and looked curiously at him, "Cold?"

"Lo, did you hear about the old guy who went to the doctor complaining about his sex life?"

"Oh, my God, Ken."

"Yeah, he said, 'Doc, I'm having a little trouble maintaining an erection.' The doctor asked, rather absently, 'Oh, really? And when did you first notice this?' The guy answered, 'Well, Doc, last night and then again this morning?'"

Lois stared blankly at Kenny until her entire face slowly lit up as the light came on. She looked at the bulge in his towel and said, "Cold it is." She turned off the stove, covered the pan, and moved it off the burner. "Ken? And, what stage of sex life are you in now?" she asked as she walked by, lightly brushing the bulging towel.

"I'll get back to you on that."

Kenny had developed a theory on sexual arousal with his vast experience of two wives. He figured the first time for a couple is always especially exciting because of the mix of desire and fear, anticipation and thrill. Now, he reckoned the first time in daylight might offer similar feelings. Besides, daylight enhanced the deeper intimacy of full eye contact at special moments. At least, that was Kenny's theory.

They didn't really eat the eggs cold, but they were a bit rubbery. As they chewed, Kenny asked, "So, Lo, do you know the three most important things to remember in old age?" She stopped chewing and looked at him in utter disbelief as Kenny continued, "Yeah, I heard it years ago, but it was really funny when Jack Nicholson said it in The Bucket List. One: Never pass up a latrine. Two: Never, ever trust a fart. And three: Never, ever, ever, waste an erection."

"Oh my God, Ken, are you serious?"

"What? No. Oh, hell no, I'm not serious. It's a joke or maybe just a comment on the recent past, like this morning."

"Oh, good, 'cause, I'm not twenty anymore either, or thirty something for that matter. So, just what stage of sex life are you in?"

"Well, Lo, I think it's Unicorn."

"Unicorn," she said flatly.

"Yeah, unicorn, you know, somewhere between mythical and extinct." Lois looked at him with sparkling eyes and trembling mouth in amused adoration as she started to chuckle.

"Does that mean you have another ten years of sex life?"

"I figure twenty. Unicorns don't reproduce."

Chapter Thirteen

Mid Day, 29 August

Kenny and Lois were lying on the bed doing nothing in particular but devoting attention to each other. Some might call it hugging. Biologists might call it grooming. They were just…living, really living, in the moment.

"Lois?"

"Yes, Ken."

"How long can we have this cottage?"

"As long as we want, I guess. All week, anyway. How long do you want to stay?"

"What about your work?"

"I'm on leave all week."

"All week," Kenny repeated as though pondering.

"Is it time I tell you about Dick?"

"This is going to be a downer, isn't it, Lo?"

"It's going to be a distraction."

"Can I do anything about it today?"

"God, I hope not. Stay with me today, Ken."

"Then, tell me about it tomorrow. I want to pretend today is forever."

"Let's not pretend. Let's make today forever."

"Nothing is forever, Lo."

"Love is. Love is forever."

"Well, I love Dick too. I think you better tell me, now. Let's go in the kitchen."

Lois sat across from him at the little table and held his hands. "General Williams made me promise not to tell anyone, and you in particular, where he was going and what he was doing. So, I'm going to tell you everything I know except that. Figure out what you can, but don't ask me to break my word."

"I won't ask again, Lo. I promise."

"He had suspicions about the intelligence, for sure. He never shared those with me until after he left."

"You're in contact with him?"

"I was up to last week. He broke it off for my safety." Kenny nodded. "He did have suspicions about the ex-governor, and he is sure somebody is manipulating things to deliberately provoke both sides. He doesn't know much more, yet, but I can tell he suspects some group." She looked at Kenny with pause. "Ken, do you have any ideas?"

"Yeah, well, Samson Security comes to mind. I mean, they worked for the son of a bitch. And, I suppose they could have an interest in causing trouble. It brings more private security contracts. Somebody there certainly knows those reports from the last mission are falsified."

"Yeah," she said, "I tried getting more information on their contracts but got a really weird reaction from my contacts, so I dropped it."

"Good girl. Are you working this alone, Lo?"

"Well, yeah."

"You're dead meat without a handler, kid. I suppose you can't promise me to quit."

"Can you promise me to quit, Ken?"

"I already have."

"Uh huh. And just what are you going to do when you figure something out?"

"I'm going to tell my handler. Can you do the same?"

"I can tell you."

"Okay, Lo, you are holding out on me, but, okay. Dick has his reasons, and maybe it's to protect him and/or his mission, so let's be really careful here."

"Hey, Ken, if I am being tailed, and if my place is bugged, maybe we can use that, somehow."

"Too late. They already know we know about the tail and suspect the bugs. I think the best thing to do is act what we are, scared, and stop poking around until we have a real lead. Hey, I'm going back to the VA next week for my post-op follow up. Maybe I can find out something from the other LGs there."

"Oh, Kenny, there are no more LGs. The program has been discontinued. The new powers gave up on what they called the Last Gaspers and pulled the plug."

"Maybe even better. There's bound to be some former LGs there, and if there's anything more dangerous than an LG, it's a really pissed off former LG."

Late Afternoon, 10 September

Kenny reached for the cottage doorknob with the key, but found it unlocked, so he just stepped in. Lois looked up from the kitchen counter with surprise, hair damp with sweat in a headband and wearing a T-shirt and running shorts. "Kenny," her face lit up. "You're home." She ran over to give him a hug, but backed off a bit. "Oh, I'm all sweaty. I just got back from a run and haven't showered yet."

Kenny gently pulled her in for a squeeze and a brief kiss.

She backed away again. "I didn't expect you for a couple of hours yet. I just put the vegetables in the roast. I need to take a shower, okay, Ken?"

"Sure, every crisis is an opportunity."

She looked a little puzzled and then brightened. "Oh, another first? Our first shower together?" She stepped back and looked carefully at his face and posture. "Kenny, you look really tired. Would you rather just lie down?"

"Oh, I don't think so, Lo. I want the shower first. How are you at foot rubs?"

"Well, that'll be another first, but I'd love to." She put the crock pot on low and led Kenny by the hand to the bathroom.

It was not that the shower was not erotic, but that something heavy was in there with them. Kenny could feel it. So, they emerged slightly aglow and somewhat refreshed, but not as eager as either might have imagined. Kenny put on some clean shorts and a T-shirt and Lois did the same. He lay back on the bed with his legs on two pillows in Lois's lap while she massaged his individual toes. Kenny was asleep before she finished the first foot.

The smell of the beef roast first aroused Kenny's awareness, and he stirred slightly. Lois lifted her head from his shoulder and looked into his eyes. With a sad little smile, Kenny pulled her close. "Lo, have you heard about the plan, Operation Earth Rescue?"

She shook her head, "No."

"I don't know if it's real, but I saw a couple of guys at the VA who had been in Green Bay. We found a quiet spot on the grounds and they opened up with me. They both heard, in separate interrogations, that there is a push by the Fight for

Right people, through the White House, for an international plan to alter the Earth's atmosphere, temporarily."

"Why, Ken?"

"They say it will reduce the greenhouse effect—something about precipitating or condensing—they didn't know—some of the greenhouse gases."

"You mean, reverse global warming?" Lois asked, rather skeptically.

"Well, that's the plan, Lo. I suppose most governments are looking for something or someone to blame for this global trend toward chaos. Summer heat, droughts, floods, crop disasters, etc. are as likely as anything. That's just my guess."

"Is that possible, Kenny? I mean, can our technology really reverse climate change?"

"I don't know about that, Lo. That's not what scares me."

Lois backed away wide-eyed. "Something scares you?"

Kenny looked deep into her eyes, maybe her soul. "Well, sure, Lo. Lots of things scare me. We scare me. But, this really scares the hell out of me. It gives me the quivering shivers." Lois backed away a little further and studied Kenny.

"Lois, have you ever read The Revelation of John the Divine?"

"You mean, Revelations in the Bible?"

"Yes. John referred to seeing the sun turn black upon the opening of the sixth seal, stars falling, and the moon turning blood red." Lois breathed a little quicker as she stared with a worried look.

Kenny continued, "Actually, a similar prophecy appears in the Old Testament in Joel, probably other places too, but I don't know." Kenny paused as Lois started to tear up. He held her close again.

"Rick and I heard a prophecy like it somewhere else. Maybe it's all the same one. The moon turns red before a major change in global culture, maybe a changing of worlds as the Hopi describe. I don't know." He paused as Lois sniffed. Kenny held her back a little so he could look at her. "What I believe, my dear, is that when the moon turns red, we have one year of relative peace and safety to prepare to enter the wilderness. After that, the world will descend into chaotic conflict from which very few people will survive—except those who live simply and in harmony with the laws of Nature. The nightmare will last ten years before a new human culture will emerge."

Lois tried to speak, "But…so…what...?"

"So, dear Lois, the rumor is that Operation Earth Rescue will turn the entire atmosphere a very unnatural red color for a few days." Lois just sort of collapsed into Kenny's chest, sobbing.

Kenny held her until she stopped sobbing before he went on. "I heard something else, Lo, from the Green Bay guys. Let's go to the table."

It was Kenny's turn to hold Lois's hands while he shared the bad news as he sat across from her. "Lois, these same guys swear that Samson Security is everywhere in Green Bay. They run the damned place, now. They are all over the Fight for Right campaign, bodyguards for the big wheels, and they seem to pass through other neighborhoods where our troops couldn't go. Everybody fights everybody, but nobody fights Samson. It's unnatural, they said. That was their word, unnatural.

"Lo, did you know that the Fight for Right campaign in Green Bay is a big cog in the national campaign?"

"I guess I knew that."

"Did you also know that the most powerful strategist in that campaign is a former teammate of Dick Williams?"

"No. Did you coach him, too, then?"

"Yes, I did," he paused. "I also heard one more thing. One of the guys swore he saw a big man that looked an awful lot like General Williams in black BDUs—Samson Security uniforms."

Lois's face went whiter than the tablecloth. "Ken?"

"Yes?"

Lois strained to regain composure, putting on her Chief mask again. Kenny watched her do it. "Ken, what is it you're looking for?"

Ken thought for longer than a moment. He knew she was distracting him, and he knew she had more information, but he had promised he would not ask her to break her confidence to Dick. Besides, he could probably do the math in a day or two. So, he answered with an honest distraction of his own.

"I'm looking for a place where…where life is like full survival living. I'm looking for my daggaboy water hole. Maybe it's not a place, but a time or a situation where there are no more expectations on me except those of God, Himself, and I am free to be me without judgment…without my own judgment, even.

"Ken, just what the hell is a daggaboy?"

"A daggaboy is a retired male cape buffalo in South Africa. He no longer lives with the herd, wandering all over. He just stays on his own little range by himself, or with a few other daggaboys, and wallows in the dagga—mud.

"Rick's tattoo?"

"Yup."

"Ken, you want to wander off by yourself and live alone?" She held a look somewhere between her chief mask and stark terror.

He waited as long as he could to answer. "Lo, I have this recurrent dream of shadows chasing me. Some, the little ones, have faces, but the big shadow I can't define. I want to find a place where that shadow cannot go."

Lois waited too, waiting even to breathe, it seemed.

"Lo, it's like Lonesome Pines. I knew it was out there, and I looked for it for twenty years before I found it. It asks nothing from me but love and respect, and it gives me all that and much more.

"I can't seem to find my other Lonesome Pines, Lo. I guess the one in my heart. Do you remember a comment I made about guilt from surviving combat?"

"You mean that John Wayne quote?" Lois wore no mask at all now.

"Yeah. We seem to think we owe somebody something really big because we survived and they didn't, or they got wounded, or are still in danger, or are lost, or.... You know what I mean?" Kenny's eyes revealed his fear of being misunderstood.

"I think I do," Lois assured, staring deep into his eyes.

"I'm looking for a place and time that is beyond all that. It's like somebody has a mortgage on my life, on my soul even, and I want that damned thing paid off, already."

Lois leaned forward across the table and looked at him, "Like somebody has got a marker out on you, a chit for your blood."

Kenny looked wide-eyed at her. "Exactly, a blood chit. It's like somebody has this...this note, and they don't even have to wave it, I just have to know they have it, and I feel obligated to do something to help them." He took a breath. "Lo, I'm looking for a place, a time, a life that is mortgage free, where nobody has a chit demanding me to kill or leave my home to help. You know?"

"I hope you find it, Ken, and I hope I'm right there with you."

"Yeah…me, too," but, at the same time, his mind searched for a way to help Dick, to stop the *Manitowish,* to save Green Bay, to stop that Earth Rescue shit, and….

"Ken? Do you think that is in Green Bay? That place, that freedom?"

Kenny looked out the window.

Chapter Fourteen

Dawn, 11 September

Kenny was sitting on the bench on the dock drinking his second cup of coffee from the thermos when the sun came up. Lois walked down and sat beside him, putting her hand in his and laying her head on his shoulder. He pulled her close. The shadows backed away from left to right as the sun rose, and they watched the movement in silence. Kenny knew what he had to do, and he suspected Lois knew, too, but nothing really does last forever—except maybe love.

Kenny really meant what he had told Lois yesterday about his dream, about being free from that feeling that he had to do something, but he wasn't there yet. And, he knew it wasn't in Green Bay. But maybe, just maybe, Green Bay was on his way there. Dick, Green Bay, the people of the whole world still held blood chits, and he had to do something to help. He was compelled to help.

"Lo"

"Don't say it, not yet, Ken."

Surface fog drifted, almost as if alive, around the lake. They heard a small outboard motor crank up and head out fishing. One great blue heron settled in and hunted the shallows down the shore. Life went on here as though Green Bay, or climate change, or political campaigns, or Dick's safety, were all quite irrelevant. Kenny wondered why he couldn't live like that. What was wrong with him?

Lois stood up. "What would you like for breakfast, hon?"

"I don't care."

She came back and gave him a hug around the neck and said, "Come on up and talk to me inside. Let's figure out what we're going to do."

"We, *Kimo Sabe*?" Kenny was a touch sarcastic.

"We, Tonto. You're only as alone as you choose to be."

On the way up the stairs to the cottage, Kenny said, "I'm sorry I get depressed. I don't mean to."

"I know, Ken. I'm sorry I get mad at you. I don't mean to."

"You get mad at me?" he asked with genuine surprise.

"Oh, my God. You don't know? I'm mad right now," and she went in the door.

"What are you mad about, now?"

"Where do I start? I'm mad because…no, we don't have time for this. Sit down here, Windy, and let's talk." She threw some biscuits and jam on the table, a jar of peanut butter, and a knife. "Breakfast, Mister I Don't Care."

"Lo, I'm going to Green Bay."

"Nooo." She dragged it out, shaking her head.

"If the prophecy comes true, and I didn't talk to Daniel—the campaign strategist, my student—I would never forgive myself."

"You're not so good at that anyway." As soon as she said it, she covered her mouth and waited.

Kenny laughed. "You are right, I'm not. That's why I have to go."

"But, Kenny, you hate cities." She was pleading now.

"Well, I hate killing, too, and this time I'm not going to kill, just talk. Will you help me prepare?"

"Of course. When will you be back?"

"If I succeed, I'll be back by October, I suppose."

"If you succeed? You mean, if you succeed in stopping Operation Earth Rescue, the plan of international scope? Who do you think you are?"

"Yes, that's what I mean." He ignored the last question, probably because he didn't know the answer.

"And, if you do not succeed?"

"I'm going home to Lonesome Pines."

"God, Ken. I'm going with you."

"No, you're not." Ken had his teacher face on, talking at the Chief.

"When are you leaving?" Lois asked without posture.

"When I'm ready." Kenny answered honestly free of sarcasm.

They ate a few biscuits and jam. Kenny had some with peanut butter, and they looked into each other's eyes.

"I love you, Lois."

"I know, Ken, and thank you for saying it. I love you, also. Would you like to cuddle?"

It was a quiet but complete cuddle. He tried to make this love last and she cooperated intuitively. There was that one moment so full of eternity that Kenny finally comprehended love lasting forever. If this would be his last time, it was alright with him. He just knew it didn't get any better.

Sunrise, 14 September

Kenny and Lois sat at the little table one more time, talking and not talking. They had spent days doing that, preparing for the inevitable. Lois watched as Kenny fidgeted, trying to say something and just not getting it out.

"Kenny, do you know the difference between a stubborn old man and a billy goat?"

Kenny looked at her in disbelief, thought a moment, and asked, "The billy goat smells better?"

"No, damn it, Kenny, you're funnier than I am."

"Doesn't take much." He said, deadpan.

"Brewster, are you going to play with me, or not?"

Kenny thought she was cute when she was so serious about being funny. "Okay, okay. No, I have no idea what the difference is between a gentle old man and a billy goat."

She glared at him. "You don't know the difference between a grumpy, stubborn, pigheaded old man and a billy goat?"

"No idea, ma'am."

"For the life of me, neither do I. Any chance you're ready to share with me now?"

"I've decided something, Lo." He watched her hold her breath. "I'm going back to Lonesome Pines no matter what happens in Green Bay."

"I knew that, Ken," she exhaled.

"Something else—I have no right to say it—I would love it if you could be there with me. Just in case, you know?"

She patted his hands again. "I promise you, I will be there as soon as possible. I do have some work to do, in case General Williams needs something. Besides, I still have a job you know."

"Okay, just so you know you're invited, but it is your call."

Lois watched him intently as his eyes darted about the little cottage and landed on his satchel by the door.

"Ken, I'll make this commitment to you. I will come to Lonesome Pines for my birthday, and I'd like something special from you, maybe something you make with your own hands. If you'll still have me then, I'll stay."

Ken's face brightened and relaxed. They stood in unison. He picked up his satchel and hugged her one more time, turned, and walked out the door.

First Light, 15 September

Kenny left the old Escape in an abandoned warehouse store parking lot in a town outside Green Bay. They had decided he would ride a freight into town as a hobo. There were more and more of them now, and even though less freight was moving, more was on rail than tires nowadays. He picked up a few items of clothing at a thrift store, old and worn things, and started walking toward the tracks. He was strangely excited, and he thought it was because he had always wanted to hop a train and never did it, but he couldn't pretend on this mission. He had to become a hobo.

By midnight he was rolling through an old business district in Green Bay, and he decided to hop off. It had been fifty years since his last PLF, parachute landing fall, and he did it poorly, but his protesting knees survived and his head only got a little bump. It was the old three point landing, feet, ass, and head.

He tried to blend in, and he thought it wouldn't be that hard. But Green Bay had gone feral. People were wary of anyone or anything they didn't know. He knew he had to find a place, a park bench, an alley, something he could claim. There he could become familiar.

He found a church in an old, downtown neighborhood and decided to hang around. Several Christian-looking people passed in and out of the church without giving him a glance. He was getting hungry, and just a little panicky, so he decided to go hunting.

He noticed pigeons roosting on sills of broken windows in an old abandoned factory, and he decided he could eat one. It wasn't really a hobo thing to do, but he had learned on Grandpa's farm how to climb right up to them at night, grab one and stuff it in his shirt, and climb down. He caught two, tonight. He wondered why no one else was using this shelter, and his gut was in a knot, so he left and headed to the big bridge over the Fox River.

There, under the bridge, he found a small group of ragged people with a fire and kettle. A big fellow put a hand to Kenny's chest to stop him, so Kenny showed him the birds, now dead but still warm. The big fellow took him to a woman sitting on a pail. Kenny laid the birds at her feet. She picked them up and gave them back. "Clean them, please, and add them to our stew pot. We'll draw you a bowl before you put them in." Kenny obliged.

"Down on your luck, mister?" a young girl, maybe fifteen, asked.

"Naw," Kenny answered, "just a little behind on my eating." The teen nodded.

He knew better than to probe, so he waited. When they asked him a few questions, he told them the truth, more or less. "I just left my lovely young lady friend, with her permission, and I've never been homeless before. I thought I might find some people I used to know in Green Bay."

"Are you from here?" the boss lady asked.

"No, ma'am. I'm not. I've never lived here. I just don't know where else to go."

"Not many people are heading into Green Bay right now," the big fellow said.

"I have a couple reasons for coming," Kenny said, truthfully.

"Well, maybe you can tell us about them, then," the big fellow continued.

"Let it be," the boss lady told him. "That's Gus, I'm The Mama. We'll get to know each other piece by piece. What do you like to be called?"

"Some call me Windy," he answered.

"Windy. The curious one over there is Diana, you know, like the princess, and the quiet one up there," she pointed high up under the bridge where Kenny hadn't noticed, "is Mouse. Where'd you get those birds?"

"Some old factory down there," Kenny pointed.

She and Gus exchanged looks, "We don't go there," She said. "Damned butchers do weird stuff in there."

"Butchers?" Kenny asked.

"Those private police in the baggy black uniforms. They get you, they're likely to pull your fingernails out there just for fun."

Kenny was through with the birds, and Diana ladled him a bowl of stew. He slowly lowered the birds into the pot and Diana added some water from a jug. Kenny gazed toward the dirty river and wondered where that water came from, but he ate the stew without thinking about taste.

Sleep wasn't really on Kenny's mind, tonight. He was tired, but not sleepy, so he lay back on the grassy area beside the concrete and watched the river. He did hate cities.

Dawn seemed to wake things up, and Kenny turned around to see Mouse sitting behind him, watching. "You're not like us," Mouse said.

"I'm not?" Kenny asked. Mouse was a slight boy, probably a teenager, too.

Mouse shook his head. "You're shiny," and he motioned to his face around his eyes. "You see things."

"Well, apparently so do you. What do you see, Mouse?"

"I see you looking for something, maybe somebody. Are you a cop?"

Gus walked up and appeared rather interested in Kenny's answer.

"No, I'm not a cop, never have been. I used to be a school teacher."

"He can see things," Mouse told Gus, pointing to Kenny.

"Yeah, Mouse? What kinds of things does he see?"

"He sees stuff, like, what people think, maybe, or where he's going but he's not there yet."

Gus gave Kenny a look, and said, "Okay, Mouse. Let me know if he sees anything I should know about."

"He can't see it now," Mouse said. Gus stopped. "He can't see what he's looking for."

"Are you looking for something, Mister Windy?" Gus asked.

"Gus, we're all looking for something," The Mama said. "When he's ready, he'll tell us."

"He looks like one of those letter guys," Diana said, "You know, lost soldiers or something."

The Mama got interested now, "You mean a Little Guerilla, an LG?"

"Yeah, LG," Diana said.

The Mama looked into his eyes.

"I was an LG," Kenny said. "There are no more LGs. The brass retired us all."

"So, you were an LG," The Mama said. "Does LG really stand for little guerilla?"

"It does," Kenny answered, "to some people. Others called us other things, like little generals—the brass hated that—or, worse. I think the official term is last generation soldier, but I think we're more like the lost generation."

"What are you doing here, LG?" Gus asked. The Mama waited for an answer this time.

"I'm looking for a former student." They all waited, so he continued. "This person is very important in certain places, and I want to talk to him, to try to talk him out of making a big mistake." They still waited, but Kenny didn't know what else to say.

"Does your friend have a name?" Gus asked.

"Yes, he does, Gus, but if I tell you, I could put you in danger."

"With who?" Diana asked.

"I honestly don't know that," Kenny said. He looked around. "Have you folks ever thought of hiring out as lie detectors?"

"No market in that," The Mama said. "Folks around here aren't interested in what's true. They just make up their own stuff."

Kenny nodded, rose slowly, thanked them for a safe night, and started upstream.

Midmorning, 16 September

Kenny found a park by the river not far from the bridge. It wasn't much, but it had grass that hadn't been mowed in awhile and a fairly large spruce tree that had never been trimmed, so he crawled under and slept for hours. He wasn't very good at this homeless person stuff, not in a city, and he woke up real hungry. He decided it must be near dinner time, and he would follow his nose. What he found was a bunch of ragged people standing in line by a door to an old brick building. He decided to get in line.

A little before dark, the door opened and a young woman came out. She touched the people one at a time, counting he guessed, and they stepped inside. When she got to the guy about four ahead of Kenny, she stopped and said, "I'm sorry, that's all tonight," but an older man handed everybody else a white bag with a folded top. Kenny could smell that it was food, and that was good enough for him.

He tucked it in his shirt and headed back to the spruce tree. There, in his little spot, he dined on a tuna sandwich, a dill pickle, a handful of tortilla chips, and orange juice. 'I'm going to remember that place,' he decided.

He woke to the voices of boys playing vigorously in the little park, and he thought back fifty-plus years. 'No good,' he told himself, 'thinking about that today.' He crawled out the other side of the tree and took his bearings, walking past that mission door to looking around for the campaign headquarters. In the alley by the mission he found a dumpster to throw his paper bag.

A campaign poster gave him an address, and a phone booth still had the yellow pages with a map. He found his way to the street where he could see the campaign headquarters sign, but he did not approach. He was feeling pretty grimy by now—city dirt is much uglier than forests and swamps—and he decided to get in line earlier tonight. Maybe they had a cot and a shower. He took one last look at the campaign headquarters before going and noticed across the street, and a little this way, was a dog grooming shop. He decided to stop in when he was cleaned up a bit.

He got back to the mission early and was in a short line. Inside they gave him soap and a towel and pointed him to the showers. Then, they sat everybody down and prayed real hard for their salvation. They gave Kenny a plateful of hot food.

The sleeping arrangements were cots on an old wooden floor and a torn army blanket, but next morning he had juice and a doughnut. 'Maybe if everybody had this experience once or twice, we wouldn't be so selfish,' he told himself. 'Maybe.'

0800 Hrs, 17 September

Kenny walked out of the mission feeling a whole lot cleaner but significantly cheaper. He decided he would send some of his money to this place when he got home. 'Home.' He walked directly to the pet grooming place, entered, and sat down. A woman about Lois's age, only more wrinkled and weathered and with a constant smile, sat behind a chocolate Lab. Kenny sat down within reach, and the young male wiggled right over to him. Kenny showed the dog the back of his hand and let him lick it.

The lady looked at Kenny and said, "He likes you."

"He's a Lab," Kenny said. "He probably likes everybody." Kenny looked at the dog and pointed a finger. The dog sat.

A very busy young woman came to the counter and asked Kenny what he wanted.

He politely stepped to the counter and said, "I'd like to speak to the owner or manager if I could."

"What about?" she asked.

"Well, a job," Kenny said as politely as he could.

"We're not hiring." She looked away.

"I don't mean a real job, I just mean a little something so I can eat every day."

"There's a mission right over there, two blocks down."

"I know, I just came from there, but I don't want a handout. I want to earn my bread."

"I'm sorry, we don't have anything," she said without looking up.

Kenny thought a moment, and said. "Thank you, ma'am. Sorry to have bothered you." He headed toward the door.

The lady with the chocolate said, "Sir, could you hold him for a minute? I need to get something from my car."

"Sure," Kenny answered. "My pleasure." He took the leash and sat by the big boy, rubbing the side of his face with the backs of his fingers. When the lady came back, Kenny sat rubbing the dog's tummy while he stretched on his back.

"See? He loves you," the lady said. Kenny noticed she was dressed in a long, flowing skirt and pilgrim blouse with little flat shoes. He thought of the flower children on campus in his youth.

The busy young gal from the counter came out and took the leash from Kenny, asking the lady, "The usual, Ginger?"

"That would be great," Ginger answered. "Here," she handed Kenny a card as they both walked out.

Kenny looked the card over. Pet Nanny, Ginger Graham.

"Delicious name, ma'am, but I don't have a phone."

"Oh, that's okay. Do you have a minute?"

Kenny chuckled aloud, "Ma'am, time is all I've got."

"Okay, I want to talk to you a minute," and she walked over and opened the side door of her old, blue cargo van, no flowers on it, though. She motioned for him to sit down. She stuck out her hand, "I'm Ginger. Please call me Ginger."

Kenny was surprised at her straight forward manner, and he respected it. "Ginger, would you call me Windy?"

"Windy? You don't look like a Windy."

"What do I look like?" Kenny asked, amused.

"Hmmm. You look like a...Benjamin."

"Call me Ben, then."

"I want to hire you, Ben, to hold some dogs for me when I bring them in, then I don't have to wait for the gals at the counter when they're busy. Where can I find you when I need you?"

Kenny looked around, "At the bus stop," he pointed.

"I'll go tell Karen that Ben is going to pick Hershey up at eleven. Okay? That way I won't be late and I don't have to be early. You just wait for him in there, pick him up, and I'll meet you at the bus stop."

"Okay, Ginger. I'll be here."

"I know you will. Ben, what size clothes do you wear?"

"I'm not particular, ma'am." She nodded and ran into the grooming shop. Kenny got out of the van, walked to the bus stop and sat down. 'I wonder what time it is. A working man should have a watch.'

Chapter Fifteen

Early Morning, 20 September

The dog-holding work was great for Kenny. He ate every day, got some used clothes from Ginger, and spent a lot of time sitting at the bus stop watching the campaign office. He had begun to notice a pattern with Daniel arriving early every morning, then going up the street to church for a half hour or so later. With all the so-called body guards and private security around, he wondered why they let him get routine. Today was Sunday, though, and Kenny had a day off, so he decided he would go to church a little later. His idea was to meet a preacher or elder and maybe get permission to go in the sanctuary and pray in the mornings.

He sat on the bench now, noticing the campaign was shut down today, but there were still Samson Security people around. He could recognize them even in suits because they acted all serious and tough, like the not-so-secret Secret Service. A big black SUV pulled up and four very large men in black BDUs stepped out with serious automatic weapons. Kenny recognized General Richard Williams and looked around without moving his head.

Two men stood outside, Dick and another guy, and the other two went inside while the SUV turned around and parked in front of Kenny. Within minutes, the two came back outside and crossed the street, standing right behind the SUV. At this point, a second black SUV drove by and up the street past the headquarters and stopped, facing the opposite direction from the first SUV. Four BDUs got out and dispersed, two on each side of the street.

Three long, black, shiny limousines pulled in. The center one stopped in front of the headquarters. More big suits jumped out and walked briskly inside. Daniel Sullivan, Kenny's former student, walked out and stepped into the open back door of the limo. The lead SUV reloaded and pulled out, followed very soon by the three limos. Finally, the SUV in front of Kenny spun around again, picked up its crew, and headed out. Kenny sat wide-eyed as they reloaded the SUV, and he felt he made eye contact with Dick, who seemed to pause just a moment. Kenny thought maybe one of the other BDUs noticed the exchange. Kenny would have to make his move soon.

0700 Hours, 23 September

Kenny found the church to be friendly enough, seeing a new sinner to be saved. He played on it a little, stopping in sometimes two or three times in a day to pray while dogs were getting groomed. He knew Daniel would be in between 0730 and 0800, and he knew he would sit next to the aisle in the second pew on the right side. Today, Kenny was in the first pew. He didn't have to fake his praying.

When he heard Daniel come in behind him, he got up and turned around to go, but as planned, their eyes met. Kenny waited for Daniel to make the first move, but he didn't say anything except "Good morning."

"Good morning," Kenny said, and then gave a look like, 'Do I know you?' and calmly walked out. 'I'll be back,' Kenny thought.

Kenny made a point of being seen leaving again the next day just before Daniel walked in. He had figured out that two suits now took positions in back of church about two minutes ahead of Daniel, so he could time his exit. This time Kenny just nodded, but he was certain Daniel thought he recognized him. The next day Kenny went to church after Daniel, just to keep the suits from getting suspicious. It helped, he thought, that they saw him holding dogs for that lady in the van.

0700 Hours, 26 September

Saturday was a less routine day, and Daniel might not show at all, but Kenny was ready. He was kneeling at the altar today and praying hard, loud, and wet. Kenny was genuinely weeping in remorse and praying for forgiveness in mumbled vocalizations when he felt a tap on his shoulder. "Mr. Brewster? Coach?"

Kenny stood up and greeted his former student athlete. "I'm sorry…."

"Daniel, Danny Sullivan," he said. "Can I help you, Coach?"

"Danny Sullivan. You were a teammate of Dick Williams, weren't you?"

"Right, right. What are you doing here?" Daniel asked with concern.

"Praying. Praying for forgiveness." The suits were closing in now, but Daniel backed them off.

"Mr. Brewster, you look…tired. Would you like to come over to my office?"

"Okay, for a few minutes. I've got a dog coming at eight. I'm a dog holder, you know," and just like that he had a bodyguard escort to the inner office of one of the most powerful people in the Fight for Right campaign. Kenny only wished he knew what to do next.

Daniel walked Kenny right back to a big office, telling the staff this was his high school wrestling coach and to hold calls if possible. By the time they got there, Kenny decided to play it as straight as he could.

"So, Mr. Brewster…."

"Ken."

"Ken, how are you? Can I be of any help?"

"Thank you Daniel. There is one thing you might do for me. Is it possible to put a hold on Operation Earth Rescue?"

"What? How do you know about that? It's classified."

"I have clearance," Kenny answered matter of fact.

"How? How do you have clearance?" Daniel looked incredulous.

"I'm sorry, Daniel. You don't have a need to know that."

Daniel appeared to ponder that for quite a while, walking around his desk and sitting in his big brown leather chair.

"In fact," Kenny continued, "I'm wondering how you have clearance."

"Ken, I have government clearance as an advisor to the Vice President. No, Operation Earth Rescue cannot be stopped, and I wouldn't try if I could. It's our only hope."

"Yes, I suppose you're right, Danny, it's way beyond your control, but is it true that it will turn the sky red, just as in Joel and the Revelation?"

"I'm not at liberty to say." Daniel was the political advisor again.

"I believe you. Daniel, do you believe in your heart that this is the right thing to do—what God wants us to do?"

"I am certain of it, Mr. Brewster, Ken. It is all part of God's plan. Man's wickedness in adultery and abortions and liberalism has caused this climate change, and this is the only way out."

Kenny considered one more tack, "Even if it will result in the end of time?"

"Ken, I am not afraid of God's wrath. If this brings The Rapture, praise the Lord. Let me help you be saved, my old friend."

"Does it make any difference to a former student that his former teacher thinks he is terribly wrong?"

"No, Ken, I know I'm not the one who is wrong. Come to the Lord with me, and you will understand."

"God bless you Daniel," Ken said, standing and holding out his hand. Daniel stood up and shook it firmly. "You're a good man, Danny Sullivan. I'll see you in Heaven."

"I'll pray for you, Ken."

"Thank you, and I for you."

Ken turned and let himself out the door, striding through the campaign headquarters like he was the candidate himself. 'Well, that is that,' Ken told himself, and nausea crept upon him until he got outside into fresher air.

He went directly across the street and into the grooming shop where Ginger was looking a bit confused. "Ginger, thanks for everything, but I have to leave now. I still have your card. I'll send you a note someday. I'm really sorry for any inconvenience, but my health is at stake," and down the street he went. He grabbed his satchel from the secret hiding place in the spruce tree, changed clothes, and headed for the bridge. He really didn't know what might happen next.

He found The Mama and Mouse under the bridge, but Gus and Diana were gone. Kenny walked up like he had just been gone for a minute. "Mouse, I may be hot. Do you know a place I can disappear, or maybe get me out of town?" Mouse looked at The Mama, and she at Kenny.

"Sit down, boy, and tell The Mama all about it, and don't leave nothin' out this time." Kenny started talking like his life depended on it, "The butchers may want me...."

High Waxing Gibbous Moon, 27 September

Mouse put Kenny on an outbound freight. Gus even came along for protection. It seemed they liked his story—especially the part about praying for the Fight for Right guy, even though Kenny was serious about that. Maybe they just liked somebody who could walk into and out of a fancy office like that. Maybe they liked the idea of sneaking Kenny away from the butchers. Maybe they liked the few bucks he gave The Mama. Maybe they just liked him.

He had failed, of course. It always was a long shot. He didn't kill anybody, though, or even hurt anyone. He felt satisfied that he had tried his best, as he had always asked his wrestlers to do. He also felt resigned, as completely helpless as that rabbit he saw on video sitting still while a weasel bit it to death. The weasel jumped around it so fast the poor rabbit literally had nowhere to go. He felt ill, as if he had just eaten poison and it was beginning to take effect.

The train slowed considerably as they approached a small town, and Kenny thought that peculiar. He worked his way around the end of the shipping container and thought he saw some activity along the track ahead, so he jumped off. It was a slower PLF, but his legs were stiff from his position, and he laid there a moment before he slipped off the track grade. He worked his way slowly around the little whistle stop town and back onto the tracks. Maybe he was paranoid, but those butchers were to be feared.

Here, in the dark between moonset and sunrise, he stood trying to figure out where he was. He checked the Big Dipper to verify his direction heading away from town and started walking. He was extremely happy to smell the fields and forests, swamps and farmyards. It was all better than city stink.

He was walking to freedom, to Lonesome Pines, all the way if necessary, and away from the shackles of duty and debt. Dick got himself into that mess and he could get himself out. Hadn't he insisted Lois not tell Kenny where he was and what he was doing? Kenny had to find out from an LG he barely knew.

Lois was in Madison minding her own business, now. She didn't want Kenny's help, and she sure didn't want him to feel obligated. He hated feeling obligated. Besides, he didn't know anything about all that brass and intelligence stuff. What good could he do her?

Hadn't he done enough? Hadn't he served in Vietnam when half the country was trying everything they knew to stay out of it? Hadn't he volunteered in old age to keep some kids from getting hurt? Hadn't he lost the best friend he ever had, a daughter, and.... 'Jesus, what more do they want from me?'

He walked slowly now, his mood about as black as the night. He could feel the savage beast of rage right below his sternum, and he felt the black coyote watching, waiting for his chance. He noticed the nice little stream below him, the clean feel of the air, and he recognized the place. He was approaching the crossing ahead a half mile or less, the road that would take him to the Escape. 'Why not keep walking? It's only a hundred miles, one week, ten days tops.'

In the starlight of the clear night, he could see the opening in the trees that meant the crossing was just ahead. He slowed his pace even more.

He stood at the crossing now, the little road to his left went to town and the Escape—and back to Lois in Madison. Behind him, the tracks led back to Green Bay, danger, and Dick. Ahead lay freedom, a slow walk home, and life on Kenny's terms. He stood there, barely breathing.

He looked to the right. The little road seemed to disappear into the big marsh that opens into miles and miles of blackness of Green Bay waters. He saw a light now, ahead of him down the tracks. His mind went back to his narcotic confused vision in surgery or recovery, and his entire being focused on the white light. It appeared to be getting closer. An image of Lois emerged in his mind, cooking in that little cocktail dress and apron. An image of Dick appeared telling the group at Line Camp how he loved them all. A feeling of nothingness seemed to call him from the right, the waters of Green Bay. The light was definitely coming closer.

Choices had been difficult for Kenny for so long he couldn't remember when he had made them in confidence. Bonnie had finally stopped tolerating his days and weeks of inactivity. Vicky had managed him, talking him through the big decisions, like whether he should buy a new lawnmower or try to fix the old one, again. Rick had made a lot of decisions with him, kind of like two cripples sharing three crutches. He felt very alone, and the light came closer.

Oh, how he wanted freedom. He wanted freedom from the beast that burned in his chest and the sneaky black coyote. He wanted freedom from the government and freedom from society. He wanted freedom from comrades, fellow soldiers, and Dick. He wanted freedom from Lois and…he couldn't think what. 'I want freedom from my thoughts.'

The approaching light was clearly not one, but three, and some part of his mind processed the data. He focused on the tightness, the knot that hung below his sternum, at his center. He turned to the blackness of the marsh, but there was no release. He turned to the way back to Dick, but there was no release. He turned to the road back to Lois, and he felt a slight release, but he denied it. He turned toward the way to Lonesome Pines, so hoping for release, but there was none, only three lights approaching rapidly. He stood on the track focused on those lights and thought, 'Maybe I don't have to decide.'

The train was fast approaching the crossing, now, and it blew its whistle-horn. Kenny froze, then jumped and ran, stumbling and falling. The train rumbled by, whistle blowing, and Kenny lay in the dirt beside the road. The train was way down the track when he picked himself up and brushed himself off. He checked for fluid leaks or other malfunctions. His heart rate had not even increased. 'Weird.'

Behind him was the crossing. Ahead lay a town and a way back to Lois. He couldn't help feeling a little relieved by his choice, but he also couldn't help holding a little resentment against Lois for the freedom and life he was giving up. Kenny was like that, he knew it, and he hated that about himself.

Chapter Sixteen

First Light, 28 September

Colors were beginning to appear as Kenny walked vigorously along the straight, flat road, now. Once the decision had been made, he felt an urgency to get to Lois, fast. He did not sense any particular danger, but he imagined it. His mind was churning in undisciplined ways when he posed a riddle for himself, 'When is an Escape not an escape?' He stopped almost in mid stride. 'When it is a trap. Oh, shit.'

He looked about almost in panic and thought of running back to the tracks to find some wild place, a swamp, a little woods. He looked right and left for a cornfield and found none. Ahead on the left, very close to the road, was an old farm house. Maybe he could beg a place to sit and eat a piece of bread so he could think.

The old barn was across the road on the right. He liked old barns. Maybe he could hide out until he thought things through a bit. He walked on, waiting for some lights to come on in the house, or maybe the barn if they still had cows. Nothing.

The closer he got, the more it looked abandoned. The house was small for a farm house, a story and a half with dormer windows, certainly not ideal for a big family. It looked like it used to be white a long time ago. Now he could see windows broken out upstairs. Nobody had mowed or trimmed around the yard for a couple of years or more.

He focused on the barn, almost there now. It was in a little better condition, perhaps, but certainly not being used for dairy. The old milk house door was broken and slightly ajar. The once red barn was small and now old board gray. He headed for it.

He put his hand on the milk house door and changed his mind. Instead, he made his tracking check around the structure. On the west side, the direction he had been walking, he found the drive to the hay barn above the ground floor and a concrete stave silo like his grandpa had. The back was a barnyard where the cows had been fenced when they weren't in pasture. That continued around the east side. He noticed the red sunrise and recalled his grandpa's saying, "Red sky in the morning, sailor, take warning."

He decided to make a quick check of the outbuildings. There was what looked like a hen house, a small tractor shed, and remnants of an old wooden corncrib. Set back a ways to the north was a metal structure newer than the others, but still fifty years old or more, probably a machine shed. He walked around that, too and found vehicle tracks, cars or trucks and tractors, driving through that yard and out to the fields, but they did not look recent, maybe a week or two old. He decided to climb the silo.

The large door on the back of the barn was broken, and he slipped through it. It was dark and dusty smelling inside and full of cobwebs. He paused a moment to get his bearings, then made his way through a stall on his right to the manger and found the door to the silo room. The rotting stuff at the bottom of the topless silo smelled foul. He ignored it and reached for the steel rungs that held the silo together. Kenny pulled himself up into the chute, then climbed twenty some feet to the top.

Memories of childhood adventures resurfaced. He had loved to climb when he was young. Not so much today, but he did it without incident. At the top he could see around the north end of the barn all the way to the bay and even a thin dark line that he figured was Door County land on the other side. The sun was rising red today, and his heart skipped a beat or two, until he convinced himself it was normal water vapor color.

He found no signs of activity anywhere except on the next road to the west, up the hill. He was pretty sure the town was not far over that hill. From his perch here, he could see through a hole torn in the metal machine shed wall. There appeared to be a white vehicle of some kind in there, maybe a truck. He decided to climb down and investigate.

He was right. Kenny found a white pickup truck, maybe twenty years old, with an open stake body useful for hauling a cow or horse. It was in pretty rough shape, but the tires were up. It seemed like it had been used recently, and the key was in the ash tray. He backed away and looked around the shed. There were a few other items in there, a chemical sprayer, an antique tractor with a sickle mower, and a couple of gravity-box grain wagons. Clearly, this shed was storing functional equipment for somebody who worked the fields here. He had to think about this.

Kenny stepped very carefully out of the shed and walked up the drive to the hay barn, pushed the small door aside and stepped in. This smelled a whole lot better with bales of hay stacked up on the north end and some straw on the other. He looked around for an escape route and located an open window, a cutout really, on the east side, but it was a long way down. Near it, though, was a chute to the cow barn below, and he could climb down that, if he had to, and slip out the back door.

He chose the straw, because it might be a little softer, and made himself a hidden fort with the bales, leaving one to sit upon inside. Kenny sat down to ponder. 'What do I know for sure? Lois is in Madison. No, not for sure. Dick is—not for sure. I'm not sure anybody is looking for me. Hmmm.'

Kenny worked on it for awhile and decided he didn't know much for sure. If they were looking for him, he could not go to Lois. Besides, he really didn't know how to find her. He got an idea. He would go to her friends' lake cottage. 'What day is it? Shit, Monday. Well, maybe they're on vacation. Maybe a neighbor will call them for me. No phones. No emails. Not secure. Okay, what are my options here?'

Kenny decided he didn't have that many. He couldn't go to the co-op. He couldn't go to the armory and look for her. He didn't know where she lived, and even if he found out, he couldn't go there. 'I'm going to the cottage. Where is it? How far? Fifty miles? More like seventy five or a hundred. I can find it.'

He paused and took several breaths. How could he get there? If he took the old truck, if it would run, if it had gas—he had no money—he might make it, but would they figure out that he stole the truck?

Young Kenny Brewster had done some of his best thinking in a hay barn. That's where he figured out that he wouldn't die if he asked Bonnie Miller for a date. That's where he decided to join the Army to be a medic, and where he made up his mind to ask Bonnie to marry him before they knew she was pregnant. And after he got out of the Army, that's where he decided to go to college to be a history teacher. He spent a lot of his early life thinking in a hay barn.

'Okay,' he told himself, and he got up, walked out to the machine shed and went to the truck. He popped the hood, checked oil and coolant, battery cables, and belt. He closed the hood and turned the key. It started! He got nervous, now, because he had never stolen anything, not even a pack of gum.

He hopped out, grabbed a gas can sitting by the door and threw it in back, opened the big machine shed door, drove out, and closed the door behind him. When he got back in, he noticed less than a quarter tank of gas. 'Perfect.'

Kenny had an idea. He drove the old truck right into town, turned left at the state highway, and headed south out of town. He took the first county road west and kept heading west and south, wandering through Wisconsin until he knew he was getting close. Then he turned south on another county highway and drove until the truck ran out of gas. He got out, put the hood up, set the gas can by him, and waited.

Several cars passed him by before a young fellow in a tired, old economy pickup stopped. "Need some gas?"

"I believe I do, sir," Kenny said.

"I can give you a ride to town. There's an old truck stop there."

"That would be very kind," Kenny said.

When they got to the truck stop, the young man asked him, "Do you need a ride back? I'll take you."

"You, sir, are a very good Christian," Kenny said. "Thank you, but, no. I'm not ready to go, yet."

The young fellow blinked and said, "You sure?"

"As sure as I am that you've got some place to go besides here. Wish I could give you a couple bucks, but I'm pretty near on empty myself."

"Okay then," he said, and he drove off.

That greasy food smelled awfully good, but Kenny was in a hurry now, and his pockets really were on empty since he gave all his money to The Mama. He set the gas can by the pumps and walked in, stopped in the restrooms and washed up, and walked out the back door on down the road. He could make it from here—not more than ten or twenty miles he estimated.

One thing about September is a guy can find things to eat in Wisconsin. There were alfalfa blossoms and clover flowers. He found a few fox grapes along a fence line by the road. It was a little early, but some were not too sour. There was an apple tree so close to the road he just couldn't resist a couple windfalls. He even snatched an ear of dented corn and nibbled on the kernels as he walked along. He never had considered this stealing. He was just sharing the bounty of the land in a small way.

Late Afternoon, 28 September

It was like the scene in The Graduate where Dustin Hoffman is running and everything seems to be slowing down, like he can't move. Kenny was walking about as fast as he could right now, and the lake cottages seemed to be moving by so slowly. He could finally see theirs, maybe three blocks ahead, but he wasn't sure he would live that long. Of course, Lois wouldn't be there, probably nobody would, but he still remembered her sitting at that little table when he turned and walked out the door.

Finally, he was approaching the door. He knocked, waited, and nodded his head a few quick short nods. He walked around back to the lake, but nobody was there. He walked down to the dock and out to the end because, he didn't know why, he didn't have anyplace else to go, so he turned around and came back.

A woman's small voice from the neighboring cottage asked, "Are you looking for the Petits?" He looked over to see a little lady with garden gloves and a hand cultivator coming around the corner, so he walked to meet her.

"I guess so, ma'am. Actually, I'm looking for a friend of theirs who stays here sometimes, the lady with shiny brown hair."

"Oh, Lois? I think she might be coming tonight."

Kenny's heart didn't skip any beats, it added a few extra. "You think she might be coming tonight? Really?"

"I think so. She stays here most every night lately. Say, are you that fellow who stayed here with her a few days and hardly ever came outside?"

Kenny was speechless, and maybe a bit flushed, but his heart was beating like a teenagers' first kiss. 'Teenager, heck, I was ten.' "Well, yes ma'am, I was here a few days a while back."

"What's your name? Maybe I can let her know you stopped by." Kenny's heart sank a bit at the thought of leaving. He wasn't going anywhere.

"My name is Kenny, ma'am. Sorry for my manners."

"I think she's looking for you. She's up here waiting for something. Would you like me to give the Petits a call?

"Well, not yet. What time does she usually get here?"

"Oh, pretty soon, I think. Do you want to wait?"

"Yes ma'am, I would."

"Well, if you stop calling me ma'am, you can wait over here. My name is Martha. Would you like some cookies? I baked some peanut butter cookies fresh today."

"Yes, Martha, I could eat a cookie or three, for sure."

Later Afternoon, 28 September

Martha sat with Kenny, feeding him cookies and milk. Kenny felt like a child, but he kept his eyes on that front door of the little cottage. After half an hour or so, and maybe half a dozen cookies, Lois's Bronco pulled in and she almost ran to the door. He could see her through the windows moving quickly about the little cottage, but he was at the door before she made it all the way around. He opened the door just as she came back from looking out back and said "Lo." That was all he got out before she knocked the wind out of him.

When she finally let go, and he thought he could, too, they sat down at the table. "Wait a minute," Kenny said, and went back outside. "Thank you, Martha." She waved and smiled broadly, nodding her head. Then she put her hands together, clasping them, and shook them up near her face. Kenny chuckled and waved, then turned around. He almost ran Lois over, she was so close behind him.

"Lo, I need to get cleaned up."

"Sure, Ken." She paused and looked him up and down. "Let me in to get washed up first, and I'll fix something to eat."

Lois was busy at the stove, wearing jeans and a sweat shirt, when he came out. Kenny felt cleaner than he had in two weeks. He put on the jeans and sweat shirt she had laid out for him and sat down at the table. She dished up her warmed up leftover hash kind of stuff, and sat down beside him, patting his thigh. Kenny leaned over and kissed her.

"You look really good," he told her, "Kind of bright and glowing," then added, "except for little shadows under your eyes."

Lois ate slowly, at least compared to Kenny. "Well, Ken, it's been…I don't know what to call it. Our time together was more wonderful than any of my girlish dreams or fantasies. But worrying about you was just horrible. It's like I've been living the best life and the worst life almost at the same time." She paused to watch him eat.

When he slowed up a bit, she began, "Ken, I've heard from General Williams."

"How?" was all Kenny said.

"Well, you know that guy you saw tailing me? It turns out he and another guy work for the general."

"They're Samson Security?"

"No, no, Ken. They're not. They are from a Native American group, Turtle Island Protection, Ted One Bear and Tony Hawes."

Kenny gave her a demanding look, and took both her hands in his. "How do you know this, Lo?"

"They told me."

"Has Dick told you, himself?"

"Yes, he has."

"How?" Kenny insisted. "How does Dick communicate with you?"

"Through Ted and Tony. They courier his notes to me. Nothing insecure like phone or texting. No emails," Lois answered.

Kenny shook his head. "So, all your information about these guys is coming from these guys. Do they know you're here, now?"

"Yes, they know. They block for me so we're sure nobody else is following me. And no, all my information about them is not coming from them. I talked to Mrs. Williams, personally. She's the one who told me about the general hiring them."

Kenny relaxed a bit now, and so did Lois. "Ken, there's something else. Tony gave me this note today," and she pulled it out and gave it to Kenny.

It read, "Got fired again. Need to talk. Can we meet tomorrow? You pick the place." Kenny read it three times, then folded it and gave it back. He wished he had his rock, a cedar swamp, or even a hay barn to sit in.

"You're tired, Kenny. Let me rub your feet. We can talk about it in the morning. Ken, I have to be at work by eight." She nudged him toward the bedroom.

Chapter Seventeen

Predawn, 29 September

Lois was dressed in her uniform at the table drinking coffee and eating biscuits with jam when Kenny came out of the bathroom.

"Okay," Kenny said. "You send the note for Dick to meet you at the office, if you're sure he'll know what that means. I'll be there waiting."

"He'll know what it means." Lois said. "He used to tell me that all the time when he needed to clear his head. He always went to that park on the lake. I knew where to find him if I had to. I figure about 1700 hours, well after work and before the night people might arrive."

"Yeah, your work. How's that going, Lo? Have you got your new boss broke in yet." Kenny waited for her answer.

"Oh, Ken, I'm ready to surrender. Colonel Peiper is driving me crazy. Personally—I shouldn't say this—I think the governor appointed him because he's not smart enough to make any waves the way General Williams did."

"Does the colonel have any suspicions about anything?"

"I don't think so, Ken. That would require abstract thought."

Kenny sat down and ate some breakfast. He looked at Lois watching him before asking, "Lois, where does our governor stand on this? I mean, is he loyal to the party all the way to Operation Earth Rescue?"

"You know, Ken, I think he's half in and half out. He's not running for re-election, and he never had much to do with Fight for Right that I know, but he's caught in the middle of everything. I think he just wants to retire and go fishing." She stopped and looked at him. "Aw, Ken, that's just my take, a feeling. I have no evidence."

Kenny looked away, pondering, then directly at Lois. "Lo, I could use some I.D.—driver's license, bank cards."

"Ken, I don't have your I.D. and wallet here. They're in a safe deposit box in Madison." She gave him most of the money she had in her purse. "Ken, how will...."

"Lois, this is what I do, and I've survived so far. You drop me off at the park on the way in this morning. We can decide what to do next after we talk to Dick."

Lois handed him a grocery bag with something in it. "Lunch," she said as he headed out the door. She locked up, and they were on their way.

They sat strangely quiet on the drive in, Lois patting Kenny's knee a couple of times. Kenny was looking out the window on his side when he asked, "Honey, have you seen Sammi?"

"No, I haven't seen her, but I talk to her almost every day. I think she's doing better. She might come back and stay with me again, at least for awhile. Why, Ken?"

"I was thinking about who might help us, and she popped into my head," Ken said, still looking out the window.

"I think I'll wait until she comes back before I say anything," Lois said.

"Yes, that might be wise. Good thinking, *Kimo Sabe*."

"Yes, Tonto. Thinking is what I do best."

Kenny looked back at Lois with a smile. "You give 'um good foot rub, too."

Afternoon, 29 September

The park was not at all busy today, maybe because school was back in full swing, or maybe because people were not very positive lately. Or, they might be in a lull between summer and fall. It actually felt like September today, like frost might not be far off. The sky was still summery, a hazy blue with puffy white *Cumulo humilis* clouds, the fair weather sign of the Midwest. But, annual plants were turning yellow and brown, and a few of the maple leaves were blushing. This was Kenny's second favorite time, next to spring planting, because it meant the beginning of a long stretch of hunting seasons.

He spent the day the way God intended, he thought, watching the leaves dance in the wind, playing in the lake with the ducks, and reading tracks all around the park. Parks are always full of tracks, and there is no end to scenarios an active mind can generate with them. He also studied the terrain and vegetation, and he designed a plan.

Watching the sun descend now toward University Bay across the lake to his right, he calculated that it was time to start watching. He picked his spot by an old, old, burr oak tree. It was not too far from the refuge of the cattails and marsh along a drainage canal where he had a good view of the parking lot. He did not quite know what to expect, but he was excited. This was so much more pleasant than a bus stop bench in a sad downtown, especially when homeless. The sun warmed his wet toes, and the day generally pleased him.

An older, dusty blue full-size pickup parked, and an ordinary looking man in jeans, western shirt, and leather vest got out, donned a black felt cowboy hat, and walked directly to the lake. He squatted down and touched the water, almost as a caress, like Kenny sometimes did, and then sort of moseyed around. 'Ted or Tony?' Kenny asked himself. 'He looks like a Tony.'

The Green Bronco arrived next, maybe five minutes later, and Lois stepped out, looked around, and pulled out a picnic basket. She looked to the man in the vest, and he pointed at Kenny. 'Ooh, he's pretty good,' Kenny thought. 'Maybe that's Ted.' Lois located Kenny, turned, and walked to the nearest picnic table, set the basket on the seat, opened it, took out a table cloth and put in on a table. Kenny shook his head in disbelief. 'Maybe she's Toni in disguise.'

When a newer model sedan arrived, a tall Native American with long black ponytail and dark suit got out the driver's door, and a large man that had to be Dick crawled out the other side. The two of them walked quickly to the picnic table and Dick sat down. Kenny decided the party was starting without him, so he walked over to join them. Ted or Tony in the cowboy hat disappeared.

"*Gato,*" Dick called when he saw Kenny. That had such a sad, hollow sound without a *lobo* in front of it.

"Nephew," Kenny replied, and Dick had him in a bear hug. He motioned toward the suit and Kenny stopped him. "No, let me try. This is Lois," and he lightly brushed her hair causing her to respond almost like a cat arching when you pet it, "and this is Tony."

"Right you are," Dick said. Tony gave a little nod of approval or something, shook hands, and stepped back.

"Damn, boy," the general continued, "I've got to hear what you said to ol' Danny Sullivan. That place was buzzing like you took a stick to a hornets' nest."

"Sorry about your job, Dick," said Kenny. "The other one too, I guess. I cost you two jobs in two months. Planning to go back to work soon?"

"Not for hire, Uncle Kenny. But there is a whole lot of work to do here. I think I just joined your profession. Got any contacts in Green Bay?"

"Well, sure, general. I gained the confidence of four homeless people and a dog nanny. I know a preacher fellow, too, but I think he might not want to see me anymore, unless I'm coming to be saved."

"Okay, team," General Williams commanded, "let's sit down here and lay out what we've got." Tony backed away, over near Kenny's tree, and the general sat down. Kenny went around the other side and sat next to Lois, picking up her hand. General Williams took notice and smiled approval, then got serious as he said, "Uncle Kenny, give me a brief report of that last mission with Rick."

"They were young Christians, some female. They were singing gospel music and wearing crosses. Some of their tactics were pretty sound moving through the woods, and some might have been cadre for the Fight for Right people, but they sure weren't any foreign nationals working for anybody opposed to Christian fundamentalism. The next day, *Manitowish* showed up...."

"Samson Security," Lois interjected.

"And that son of a bitch ex-governor was there, only he came in a small commercial medevac and landed away from the kill zone, maybe a couple hundred yards from me, and too far from the tags. He had a better than fifty-fifty chance of getting away clean, there. Rick saw that, I figure, and he came out from his position way across the valley dressed in clothes like the dead and pretending to be stunned. He managed to pick up a tag and activate it. Then he walked it right up to the son of a bitch. I only wish I could have heard what Rick said to him before the missile planted."

Lois was squeezing his hand with one of hers and rubbing his thigh with the other. She seemed to be watching him, but she did not cry. The general shook his head. "I knew something wasn't right, but I never expected that. I wouldn't have sent you out there."

"We knew that, Dick," Kenny said.

"Why was the ex-governor there?" Lois asked.

"I haven't figured that out, yet," the general said. "On one hand, he and Samson took out a whole lot of Fight for Right people. On the other hand, Samson is all over their headquarters helping them at every turn. It doesn't compute to me."

"I have a question for you, Dick. Why did you go to work for Samson, and as a boot?" Kenny asked.

"I went to work for them because they asked me, and I thought I might find out something. I started in the ranks because I was being groomed for operational command and needed the experience, but I also thought I could hear stuff that way. They fired me too quick, though."

"Yeah, what was that about?" Lois asked.

"Well, when Kenny put the big move on Danny, it shook him up. He must have been stunned because the storm took awhile brewing, but by late afternoon I was on the carpet. The Big Guy was on a conference call—listening, but I couldn't hear him, or her—and decided it was too much of a coincidence, me being there and Kenny showing up, too. They took my credentials and weapon, escorted me to my quarters to pick up all my other things, and put me on a bus home."

"Did you get anything out of their questions?" Kenny asked.

"Well, it was pretty strange. The Fight for Right muscle—they have some of their own, you know—were all excited about Kenny and me knowing too much. I don't know what about. The Samson people seemed to be most concerned that Kenny and I might be working something together, yet. They knew about him as an LG. So, my gut tells me two different things were going on. I think I was fired because Samson thought I had outside interests, not a complete company man, and it looked good to Fight for Right to get rid of me."

"Sir," Lois started slowly, "you don't know about Operation Earth Rescue, do you?"

"Well, yes, I've heard of it. I mean, I've read of it in some LG report. What do you mean?"

Kenny answered, "Operation Earth Rescue is the reason I was there. I had heard that Fight for Right was trying to convince the White House to push the international community to begin it before the election."

"Holy Mackerel," the general said. "They want to use that to steal an election. Fight for Right is taking over the Presidency," General Williams declared.

"So, you don't know anything about where that process might be?" Lois asked.

"I know the Vice President was in town last week to see Danny. Holy Mackerel." The general sat erect in full alert, eyes flashing.

"That's who was in the middle limo?" Kenny asked.

"Well, yes, the Vice President and somebody big in Samson." The general frowned.

Lois summed it up, "Samson big shot, Fight for Right big shot, and the Vice President of the United States. What does that equal?" There was silence.

"It equals another mission," Kenny said.

"Where?" Lois asked. "How, when, why, and for what?"

"Thinking is what you do best, *Kimo Sabe*." Kenny said. Lois looked at him with no expression at all, but Kenny developed a concerned look. "One more thing, Dick. What is my status with Samson?"

"Good question. Somebody there must know you killed a whole team of their finest, not to mention a favorite son of a bitch. I think there might be a hit out on you, at least, if you come around again."

Lois asked, "What about Fight for Right? Would they be after him too?"

Dick answered, "I believe their muscle would, unless Danny stopped them—if he could, that is."

Lois was really squeezing Kenny now, so he pointed out something obvious. "I am definitely on the wrong list for both. Hello!" Kenny looked sharply at Lois. "Just what other two names do you reckon are right there beside mine?"

General Williams said, "I'm taking my wife to her family far, far, away. I am officially retired."

"I'm putting in for retirement, too," Lois said looking at Kenny. "Let's go to Lonesome Pines and live free as long as we can."

They both watched Kenny, obviously agitated, until he responded, "Well, I don't know the how, what, when, or why, but that's what my commander and handler are for. I'm going back to Green Bay."

"I'm in," the general replied instantly.

"You had me at hello," Lois answered.

Evening Twilight, 30 September

Tony and Ted had company tonight at the little cottage on the lake. Two other cars staked out the road in either direction, Ted sat in the yard on the lake side, near the back door, and Tony watched the front from inside the porch. General Williams, Lois and Kenny sat at the little table inside. These were the arrangements they had made yesterday—that they would meet here for however long it took.

General Williams began, "Lois, you have been the best soldier I ever had the privilege to serve and a loyal friend. Kenny, you have been a great teacher, coach, uncle, and LG. I hope I don't let you down, but this time I have very little juice. I have no troops, no command, and no government support. Please don't call me General anymore." He looked at Lois. "Please, my name is Dick."

"Okay, Dick. I'll try, but forgive an old habit, please," Lois asked.

"Okay, Dick." Kenny looked at Lois, "and, I won't call you Chief anymore. You all know what to call me."

"Windy," Dick and Lois said in harmony.

Kenny smiled and said, "I've been here all day, praying and meditating, and the only thing I know is I have to go to Green Bay alone and see The Mama." Dick raised his eyebrows. "A homeless lady I met. That's it guys, that's all I got."

Dick said, "I've been talking to these security people my wife hired," Lois and Kenny looked at each other. "I think they might be of help. I would need to talk to a commander, maybe even management, but it might be something I could work on."

"I've been thinking," Lois said, and Kenny smiled wryly. "Now that Kenny is back, and Dick is back, and Sammi is coming back soon, and I turned my retirement papers in today, I can think more clearly. So, I've been thinking about those three people in that limo, and I think I may be onto something. Care to hear it?"

Dick said, "Sure!"

Kenny looked at her and said, "Of course."

"Okay, I'm thinking if I'm a fundamentalist born-again Christian advising candidates for the Fight for Right campaign, I want several things. First, I want the President to win re-election because he is closer to our position than his opponent. He's not doing real well in polls right now because of the economy, climate, global instability, and especially the chaos in some of our mid-sized cities. Second, I would like to set up for the future, and enrolling the Vice President could mean a winner next election. Third, I would be interested in doing God's work combating sin and promoting what I believe to be His will. I might believe that I could be a helping hand of God by smiting those guilty of causing all these troubles, including the Global Warming people who have been blaming gases for what I believe sin is causing." Kenny gave her a sideways look.

"Stay with me. I am really looking forward to judgment day, when everybody gets what is coming to them. What is coming to me for serving God? Rapture. Eternal bliss. In my mind, I am helping God bring about what I believe is inevitable, prophecy. I want the skies to turn red, and all the other things in the prophecy, so the rapture will come soon, in my lifetime, now. Operation Earth Rescue accomplishes all of these and makes me a hero to boot."

Dick sat speechless, close to a miracle in itself, grimly alternating between nodding and shaking his head. Kenny sat almost motionless, breathing in careful, controlled rhythm. He took her hands in his. "And, if you were the Vice President?"

"Well, if I were the Vice President, I would want to be the President. The first step on that path is to get re-elected. It looks like something must be done, or my chances end in five weeks. If I get re-elected, I need to develop a constituency for myself in preparation for the next campaign. Fight for Right is giving me both of these. Operation Earth Rescue is a winning ticket for me."

Lois paused, waiting for permission to go on. Getting no objections, she proceeded. "If I were the mystery man, the important person in Samson Security, my interest would be in promoting and maintaining a climate that requires security services, and that means trouble, chaos, faction fighting, all the things we have been watching grow over the past decade. And, I want a political atmosphere, an administration that sees Samson as part of the solution. I don't really care who wins an election as long as Samson is part of their agenda. Parties and candidates opposed to big government tend to hire private contractors. So, in this case, anyway, I see Fight for Right as being good for business because they promote small government and private enterprise, and because they cause trouble. We also have an excellent working relationship already.

"So, I've been thinking, from what you two tell me, in Green Bay anyway, Samson Security is in charge. I like it that way. I like being in control of cities that affect the economy but are not important enough to demand federal intervention, troops, or money. Being in control means Samson can maintain its position. It's job security. It also means other possible income opportunities, legal and illegal.

"Here's where I get confused." Lois paused. "I have trouble being in charge of Samson. Why would I want to kill hundreds of loyal Fight for Right cadre?"

"I can help you there," Dick said. "Balance of power."

"Ah, sure," Kenny said. "Keep the Fight for Right from taking control of Green Bay. If all those people came in, Fight for Right might squelch the opposition politically, cool the unrest, put order to the chaos, and the Guard would be back. Samson Security would be out."

"Wow." Dick said, "This all makes too much sense. Could we be the only people in the country thinking about this?"

"No," Lois said, "I don't think so. How many other cities out there are in similar conditions as Green Bay?"

"Many," Dick answered. "I can get that information for us."

"Man, I wish I had been in that limo," Kenny said.

"Why not?" Lois asked. "You go forward in time to plan an operation. Can you go back in time, too?"

"Yes, but I never did that in such a case—and a moving car."

"It's only moving on the outside," Dick said.

"What?" Lois asked.

"Relativity. It's only moving to an outside viewer, not a fly on the wall inside."

"Interesting," Kenny mumbled. "I need a lock to something or someone inside the car, and a lock on the time."

"Do you actually need to be in Green Bay?" Lois asked.

"Hmm, I think it would help, but…."

"What can we do with that information, Kenny?' Dick asked. "Why risk your life gathering information we can't use?"

"I feel so helpless," Lois added. "This is too big for us. I'd like to talk to Sammi."

"Okay, here's what I suggest," Dick offered. "We spend a couple of days—no more—talking to people, sort of feeling them out for help. I'll talk to Turtle Island Protection, Lois can brainstorm with Sammi, and Kenny…."

"I'll go back to Green Bay and talk to The Mama and, maybe, Ginger."

"Ginger?" Lois asked with more than professional curiosity.

"Ginger Graham—honest to God—the hippie throwback dog nanny. She trusted me and gave me a little job. She must have some important clients. Maybe somebody there can help."

"Okay," Dick was commanding again. "We will meet…."

Lois interjected, "At the office."

"At the office," Dick continued, "in two days."

"Moonrise, full moon on October 2nd," Kenny concluded.

Dick reached out his hands and they formed a circle holding on to each other. One neat thing about three—every body touches everybody else exactly once. There is strength in the shape, especially an isosceles triangle of equality. It is rare and powerful.

Chapter Eighteen

Midmorning, October 1

It was a cool morning but warming nicely as Kenny headed up US 151 toward Green Bay. Tony had not only retrieved Kenny's personal items from the co-op house, he had delivered his motorcycle to him at the office. Kenny would ride right down to the bridge and see The Mama. Then he got an idea.

He pulled into the truck stop at Hwy 41, shook the vibration out of his old bones, fueled, and made a phone call. "Ginger?"

"Yes, this is she."

"Ginger, a friend referred me to you. I'm going to be in town for just a few days on business, and my Lab really needs a bath. The dang fool jumped in the Fox River. I have meetings all day. Can you help me out?"

"Well, I might. Could I have your name please? And who referred you to me?"

Kenny paused. "I'm sorry, this isn't going to work. Look, Ginger, you took a chance on me, now I'm going to take a chance on you. You know me as Ben."

"Ben? Really? How do I know?" Her voice was cautious.

"Well, you helped me and I ran out on you, literally. I came to repay your kindness by asking another favor. Does that sound like Ben, or would you call me Windy?" Kenny waited.

"I'll be walking some dogs in the old park by the river this afternoon, maybe around two. Can you find me?"

"I believe I can. Thanks, Ginger."

Late Morning, October 1

The bridge was vacant, no sign they had ever been there. Kenny had not foreseen this—he had no backup plan. He could ride around town with his helmet on and not be recognized, but taking it off to talk to somebody was risky. 'If they left, there was a reason,' he warned himself, and he put the helmet back over his blue camouflage bandana, walked up to his bike and rode off. 'Where would they be?'

Part of his plan today was to drop an envelope with a little cash at the shelter, so he started heading that direction. It was not as easy to find on the bike as on foot, but he finally pulled up out front by the entrance for donations and helpers. When he parked his bike, he noticed one ragged looking young man, a teenager, slouching against a building. Kenny slipped him a five and asked him to watch the bike. Then he took his helmet off and walked in.

It was a busy place, people moving things, taking some boxes back through one door and some through another. Finally, he just spoke up, waving the envelope, "Who do I see about making a donation?"

A young woman looked up from a box on the floor and stood up. Kenny recognized her and hoped she didn't him, but she was looking into his eyes with interest. She brushed off her right hand and stuck it out, "I'm Sister Maggie. Do I know you?"

"I'm just one of the more fortunate, today, here to share a small tithe," and he handed her the envelope.

"Thank you...," she said, pausing.

"Some call me Windy," he said.

"Thank you, Windy. Come see us again."

"You're welcome, Sister," and he walked to the door, but stopped and turned around. "Sister, I'm looking for some friends of mine, and I seem to have misplaced them. Do you know a solid lady called, The Mama?"

Sister Maggie blinked a couple of times and said, "I'm sorry, Windy, I can't help you. If I see her family, could I tell them where to find you?"

"Oh, I guess not. I'm on the move today. Maybe I'll check back later," and he was out the door. The young man was still standing there, and so was his bike, so Kenny gave him another five. He could actually buy a meal now if he chose.

A small, middle aged lady followed him out the door. "I know you," she said. "I saw you here and once coming out from the bridge. Diana told me about you."

"Can you help me find them?" Kenny asked. The lady looked down, then around, and delayed. Kenny gave her a five, too.

"A dirt bag tried to do Diana under the bridge and The Mama whooped on him. He run off but came back with another dirt bag, and they beat on her, put The Mama in the hospital."

"When?" Kenny asked.

"Night before last."

Kenny looked around, trying to think where the hospital was.

"They right down there at the free clinic," she said.

Kenny grabbed her hands, thanked her, and gave her another five. He was going to have to get some more change.

He looked down the street, at his bike, then at the young man.

"We got it, Windy. Your machine will be here when you get back," the young man said. Kenny waved a salute and hurried down the street.

1223 Hours, 1 October

It was Mouse who recognized Kenny while Diana gave him a sideways look. "Look, Diana, Windy's still alive. You are alive, right?"

"I am alive, Mouse, thanks to you. Can you take me to The Mama?"

"I will," Diana said. "Mouse don't like it in there much." She took him through the clinic to a ward with a few cots. Gus was sitting outside the ward in the hallway, apparently on guard.

The Mama saw Kenny coming and raised her head up, "Ooh, ooh. Don't you look pretty, boy, in that fine jacket and homey bandana? You sit here and tell The Mama your story."

"Hi, The Mama," he greeted her, sitting down and taking her hand in his. "Are you on the mend?"

"Oh, I be up and around, today. They probably chase me away, tomorrow. But I don't want to talk about this beat up ol' woman. I want to hear about you."

"Well, The Mama, I got me a problem bigger than I can handle, even with the help I've got, and I've got some pretty fine help. I got out of town alright, and I made it to my people...."

"To your lady, we think."

"Yes, ma'am, a lady, too. But, I just know too much about some things and not enough, too, if that makes any sense."

"Boy, that's my life story. How can I help you?"

"The Mama, is there someplace a little more private we can talk?"

"Windy, you just grab me up and we can walk out to the alley. There be a couple ol' chairs out there." Kenny helped her up—she wasn't nearly as heavy as he had thought—and walked her out back. There were some people sitting out there, but she shooed them away with kindness.

"The Mama, I know stuff about important people, people in Samson—the butchers—and people in Fight for Right, maybe even people in the White House. There's some bad stuff coming down, and we, some friends I used to work with and I, are trying to put a stop to it." He paused for her reaction.

"I knew you weren't really down and out. But you're still one of us, I think," she said.

"I think so, too," Kenny said. "I'm sure not one of Samson or Fight for Right."

"If listening will help, I will help," The Mama offered.

Kenny opened right up and told The Mama about Operation Earth Rescue, that last mission, and his dream of living free in his woods.

When he finished, she asked simply, "What can we do to help you?"

"The truth is, I don't know. I really don't. I'm just looking for ideas from somebody I trust. Now, what can I do to help you? You can see I have a few resources."

"The Mama don't need nothin'. I been livin' free for two, three year now." Then she looked real serious at him. "But if the moon comes up red, I will be with you and your lady in the woods," she said with impeccable diction.

Kenny smiled at her, "I'd really like that," and he helped her back inside. When she lay back on her cot, he stepped over and gave Diana a kiss on her forehead just because he figured she needed one. He gave Gus a sturdy tap on the shoulder, and Mouse he thanked politely. Now he needed a place to put his bike down by the park to wait for Ginger.

Early Afternoon, 1 October

The bike was parked out in the open in front of Kenny's favorite spruce tree with his helmet sitting on the seat so anybody would think the rider was close by. He lay hidden under the prickly tree waiting for Ginger. She said she would be walking dogs, so he imagined her with one or two on a leash, but when he saw her come around the bend, she was being followed by six well behaved animals. She had dogs of various sizes, colors, and breeds, and there was no dissension at all. Kenny thought she would make a fine school teacher, middle school maybe.

He was a little concerned about how the dogs might react to seeing him, thinking they might lose their discipline and get into trouble, so he crawled out behind the tree and walked down toward the river across their path, allowing them to come to him. He needn't have worried.

Ginger waved to him, "Hi, Ben," and walked directly to him, all the dogs staying behind her. When she got to him, she turned around and they all sat before she said a word. She stuck her hand out and shook his. "It's good to see you. I was worried about you."

"Thank you, Ginger. I was worried about me, too, but here I am."

"Yes, you are, looking a little different. Are you in disguise now—or then?"

"Both, I guess," he said, looking around. "There are some people not too happy with me right now."

She sat down right there, and the dogs all lay down. Kenny sat facing her.

"Then, why are you here?" She asked in her direct honest way.

"I'm looking for help. You trusted me when you had no reason, and I don't know many people I can trust, here. Do you have time for a listen?"

"Are you kidding me? I love a good story. What's yours?" Ginger smiled.

Kenny told her everything he could in a few minutes, just as he had with The Mama, and waited for her reaction. She sat still for a few moments and then said, "That's sad. It's like the Hopi prophecy of world changes. I believed it would happen someday, but not to me." She paused, and a terrible look came over her, "What about all the dogs?"

"I don't know, Ginger. I have only been thinking about the people. I don't know what to do." He hung his head and shook it.

"You know, Ben..."

"My name isn't really Ben."

"Yes, I know. Mine's not really Ginger, either, but I've been called that all my life, by my parents and everybody, so I guess it is my name now."

Kenny looked at her with some amusement, "I'm Kenny, or Ken. You were really close."

"Okay, Ken?" She paused. "Wow. This is too much for me to absorb all at once."

"Ginger? I have a question for you...well, two." She nodded. "One, do you believe me? And two, if so, why?"

"Sure, I believe you. Absolutely. Why? I just have feelings about people, that's all. There isn't any more to it that I can explain. Why do you trust me?"

"I have to trust somebody, and I really don't have time to check anybody out. I wouldn't mind hearing some of your story, though."

"Oh, I'm sorry, but I am on a schedule. Call me in the morning, maybe about five, okay?"

"I will call you at five," Kenny said.

As Ginger walked away with her charges, Kenny wondered where he might spend the night. He thought immediately of Mouse and Diana. Gus, he figured, would stay with The Mama. He looked at his motorcycle and became weary of it, but he would need it tomorrow. He had to find safe public parking. He would take a ride.

This bike liked to go fast and far, but he started in a slow circle around the clinic and kept widening it until he found a Walmart. It wasn't perfect, but at least they had some all night security. He parked it as close to the grocery door as possible, walked in, and went out the garden center door. He had a mile or more to walk back to the clinic.

When he arrived, he asked Mouse and Diana, "If you had the money for a room and bath, tonight, where would you go?"

"We go over to the Bradmore," Diana said without hesitation. "Sometimes we hit a score and we all go. Sometimes we take turns, just one or two at a time."

"I need a place to sleep where I won't be found, and I want to smell good tomorrow. Anybody want to share a room?"

Mouse and Diana looked at each other. "I'll go talk to The Mama," Diana said. Kenny followed her in. Just as he figured, Gus wanted to stay, but The Mama sent the others to clean up and sleep soft tonight.

"We'll be back in the morning," Diana told her. Kenny nodded.

0500 Hours, 2 October

Diana and Mouse were sleeping soundly when Kenny slipped out to make a phone call. "Ginger?"

"Oh, Ben, I mean Ken, I had this dream and I have to tell you about it. You were in it."

Kenny paused to think for a moment, and Ginger continued, "We can talk about it when we meet. I'm free from eight to nine. How about the coffee shop by the groomer?"

"Oh, no," Ken said. "Too visible. How about the Bradmore?"

"The Bradmore? Are you sure?" Ginger asked with skepticism.

"I'm sure. I'll be waiting in that cubby they call a lobby," Kenny assured.

"Okay. Eight o'clock. See ya."

Kenny went back to the room and prepared for the day. By six, Mouse was up and ready to go, but Diana awoke slowly, like she had slept hard. She spent a long time splashing in warm water in the tiny bathroom but finally came out awake and looking happy. Kenny asked them to make a run to the coffee shop for him while he contemplated this day. 'Where do we go from here?'

Mouse and Diana were gone a long time and didn't have any change for Kenny, but they did bring him coffee and a muffin. "We stopped by the clinic," Diana said.

"Did you take care of people there?" Kenny asked. Mouse had a broad smile and Diana backed away, looking worried. "Thank you for doing that," Kenny reassured them. "How are Gus and The Mama?"

"They're getting out later this morning." Diana bubbled.

'Such a frail little baby,' Kenny thought, looking at her. 'What was so bad to put her out here on the street?'

"Great," Kenny said. "Where are you going now?"

"The Mama says a way will be shown to us," Mouse said. He didn't talk much, but when he did, it was worth hearing.

"How can we stay in touch?" Kenny asked himself out loud.

"Cell phones?" Diana asked.

"Maybe," Kenny replied, "but they're not very secure."

"Tracfones," Mouse said. "Keep changing numbers." Kenny thought about that and considered it. He would take that idea back to his mastermind group, Dick and Lois. It was past seven fifty, so Ken needed to get downstairs, soon.

"Mouse, Diana?" he asked, "Can you wait here for a little while? I'm meeting someone downstairs around eight, and I would like you all to meet. Okay?" They looked at each other and around the room. It was a big decision to make without The Mama, or even Gus, but they looked at Kenny and nodded.

0756 Hours, 2 October

The light air Ginger usually carried seemed to have evaporated as she opened the Bradmore door and looked around the little lobby, but it came back when she spotted Kenny.

"Hi, Ginger. Now, that's punctuality," Kenny said.

"Interesting place," she replied. The quiet man behind the counter watched with apparent amusement.

"Come on upstairs and meet some friends of mine," Kenny said.

"O…kay," she hesitated, but followed Kenny up the dark stairway.

Kenny gave his knock and Mouse opened up. Ginger followed Kenny and stood while he sat on the bed.

"Ginger, these are my friends, Diana and Mouse. This is Ginger Graham."

"I know her," Diana said. "She's the dog lady." Ginger brightened noticeably. The room became quiet.

Kenny explained, "I talked to The Mama and Ginger both yesterday about something bad that might be happening. I'll let The Mama tell you about it, but we're all in this together." Kenny noticed Ginger's curious concern, and explained, "The Mama is a brave lady who helps Diana and Mouse, and Gus helps them all."

Ginger's face seemed to make a connection now, as though she knew the little group. She spoke up, "Okay, so I want to tell you about this dream I had. We were living wild and free in the woods, lots of people I don't know, but you were there with a wife, maybe my age with dark hair, and another woman who was tall and blonde. I think she had a baby. Do you have two wives, Ken?"

"No, and I don't plan to," Ken said, more than a little surprised at her description of Lois and Sammi.

"And we had dogs, lots of dogs. I think they helped us hunt and carry stuff and guard our camp, too. That was my job, taking care of the dogs." Then she got a strange, almost rapt look, "And, talking, I mean communicating, with the other animals in the forest. It was wonderful."

It was quiet again until Diana said, "Cool."

Yes, it is," Kenny said. Mouse was smiling broadly.

Ginger waited before telling them, "Ken, I had a thought. One of my clients is a retired TV news director. Do you think he might be of any help?"

"Interesting possibility, Ginger. Do you trust him?" Kenny asked.

"I don't know. I sort of do, and I sort of don't. Would you like to meet him and decide for yourself?"

"Okay, can it be today though? I'm due back this evening."

"Possibly. I'll call him and see if he needs me to work his Rottie today." She popped out her phone and called, stepping over by the window to talk. When she finished, she said, "Okay, I pick up his dog at three-thirty. Would you like to be my assistant, today?"

"Sure. Where should I meet you? Hey, can you pick me up at the Walmart? My bike is over there. That reminds me, I should move it before security calls the police."

"I'll give you a ride."

When Ginger and Kenny went out the door, so did Diana and Mouse.

1033 Hours, 2 October

The clinic released The Mama, and Gus walked her out to the street. Diana and Mouse greeted her while Kenny waited. The Mama gathered them all in and said, "Family, let's take a little walk," and the group flowed down the street with Kenny following. They walked about two blocks when Gus helped The Mama to a bus stop bench to sit down.

"I've been thinking," she told her little group, "That old bridge was our home. We hadn't oughta let weak-minded people scare us out. Diana, how's that for you?"

"It's okay, The Mama. I'm not afraid. Besides, I'm pretty sure those guys aren't going to come around again." The Mama looked at Gus.

"They went away," Gus said.

"They weren't from here," Mouse added. "Maybe they went back."

"I'm not leaving you two there alone, again," Gus said, and he helped The Mama up and on their way back to the bridge.

Kenny pulled Mouse aside to ask him a question. "Is Gus a veteran?"

"Abu Ghraib," Mouse answered.

When they got back by the clinic, The Mama stopped and motioned for Kenny. "You know where to find us," she said, "and we'll be looking forward to seeing you. Bring that lady friend," she said, and they turned to slowly walk away. Diana looked back, threw Kenny a kiss, and waved.

Chapter Nineteen

1530 Hours, 2 October

Ginger rang the doorbell at the large, white house while Kenny stood back. Mrs. Pendergrast greeted them and invited them in. As soon as they were in the house, a very large Rottweiler male walked out to greet them. He looked at Ginger and walked right over beside her, but never took his eyes off Kenny.

Mr. Pendergrast came out behind the dog, and Ginger greeted him and introduced Kenny. "This is my friend, Ken, and he will be helping me out today. Nixon, say hello to Ken."

The big dog stood up and walked over to Kenny and looked him in the eye. Kenny held the back of his right hand out so Nixon could smell it.

"Hello, Nixon," Kenny said in even, calm tones. "How are you, today?" Nixon did not respond. Kenny had dealt with a Rottie before and understood Nixon's way. The dog would accept him in time, his time. Kenny went down on both knees, standing as tall as possible that way. Nixon stepped closer and smelled him some more. Kenny made both hands available and Nixon licked them.

"Wow," Mr. Pendergrast said. "He's warmed right up to you. Have you worked with dogs long?"

"Oh, not really," Kenny said, "I have always loved animals, and I've had several dogs, myself. How about you? Have you always had Rottweilers?"

"No, this is my wife's baby. He was her protection when I was working those late nights."

"Oh," Kenny said, "have you not been retired long?"

"It seems long," he said, "but only about a year and a half."

"It seems long? You'd rather be working?" Kenny asked.

"I miss the excitement of the story," he said, "and watching those young reporters break their first big one."

"Oh, sure. What was your favorite big one?"

"Oh, I don't know, there have been so many. I had a new reporter, middle aged lady, but new to journalism, and she uncovered some graft in city hall. Gutsy gal. She took down several greedy politicians. Put her right in the big time, working for CNN, now."

"That's impressive," Kenny said. "It must have felt good to have been a part of that."

"It was great. I hired her over some objections upstairs. They like young people, you know, to mold them."

"Sure. Mr. Pendergrast…," Kenny continued.

"Ed. Call me Ed, Ken."

"Thank you. Ed, if you were still working today, where would you point your best reporter?"

"Oh, good question, Ken. Have you ever worked in news?" Kenny shook his head. "Well, I'd like to know more about the connection between Fight for Right and Samson Security. That is a strange marriage."

Kenny glanced at Ginger who was staring back at him. Before she could say anything, Kenny spoke up. "Well, I suppose we had better get going or we'll have to short Nixon here." So, they took the big dog in her van and headed to an open field where Ginger could run some drills to reinforce his command responses.

"Ginger?" Kenny asked, "Would you take me back to my bike now? I need to report home."

"Well, sure, Ken, but what are you going to report about Ed?"

"I'm going to report that I see some possibilities there. I think he might be helpful." Kenny looked far away, in thought.

She stopped the van at the Walmart garden entrance, and as Kenny was getting out, she asked, "So, how close was I? In the dream, I mean?"

"Ginger, you saw my Lois, my lady, and her friend, Sammi, but I think the baby was pure imagination."

Ginger smiled. "Call me."

Moonrise, 2 October

The full moon was rising over Kenny's left shoulder, and he still had fifteen or twenty miles to go with no simple way to get there. He knew they would be worried about him, but he really didn't want a speeding ticket running through the system with his name on it, so he rode within the law. When he pulled into the park, Lois was sitting with her back to the table, watching the parking lot.

She took him by the hand to the waiting group. Dick was there, and Sammi, and, tonight, Tony was at the table, talking with Dick, who waved to Kenny. Sammi came up and hugged him. When she pulled back and looked at him, she said, "I know, Kenny. Thank you for being there and for coming back," and she hugged him again.

Tony stood up, shook Kenny's hand and moved around the table next to Dick so Kenny could sit with Lois and Sammi. "Tony is joining us," Dick said, "and his team's services are free from now on. And, get this, he used to work for Samson Security—at the regional office in Chicago. I talked with the chairman of Turtle Island Protection by secure phone, and we will get whatever information they get. He's had suspicions about Samson for years, and the concept of OER, Operation Earth Rescue, alarmed him. He also knows some other people around the country with suspicions. How about you, Kenny?"

"I made some contacts, shared OER with The Mama and with Ginger." Lois gave him a look. "They are both willing to help, but I don't know how. The Mama's little family will pick up what they can on the street. I don't know about Ginger, but she has a client who is a retired TV news director. I met him, and I think he will be helpful. He did mention he thought there was a story in the strange relationship between Fight for Right and Samson. What have you got, Lois?"

"I brought Sammi, and she brought the ideas. Tell them, hon."

"Well, what Lo and I thought was how we might use technology to share information. We went to a library out of town and I searched for stuff on Fight for Right, and Lo searched for stuff on Samson. We found out several blogs are already posting things like you guys have been saying—strange connections with the White House, militant involvement in cities, rumors of violence. Lois found several scary stories about Samson Security, all posted anonymously."

"But, nothing on the connection between the two," Lois added. "Then we both searched Operation Earth Rescue and got absolutely nothing."

"So," Sammi continued, "we thought we could start some blogs about that—and connecting Samson to Fight for Right."

"But we were concerned about security," Lois went on, "and Sammi got this great idea. You tell them."

"Well, we can use pre-paid cell phones, and we can connect those to some hand computers. Our phone numbers can change frequently and our ISP's also. Combined with libraries and Internet cafes, we can be fairly invisible for some time. We may need some bank cards with false names, though."

"I can do that," Tony said.

"Let me get this straight," Dick said. "We're going to reach out through the Internet to tell others of our concerns and to ask for ideas. Is that right?"

Lois and Sammi looked at each other and nodded.

"What is our objective?" Dick asked.

"Stop Operation Earth Rescue," Kenny said.

"Why?" Dick asked. "Will that prevent the end of our age?"

Nobody answered.

"Stop Fight for Right from taking control of America." Kenny said.

"Why?" Dick asked.

"And stop Samson," Tony said, "and no, I don't know why—except it seems like the right thing to do."

"Yes," Dick mused, "the right thing to do."

Lois said, "At least we can let other people know what we know, and we can give them somebody to talk to about their concerns."

"Okay," Dick said, "our objective is to blow the whistle on Samson and Fight for Right because it is the right thing to do. How do we know when we have accomplished that?"

"When the media picks it up," Sammi said.

"Our mission is to blow the whistle?" Kenny asked.

"If we blow the whistle," Lois said, "the people may put a stop to this Operation Earth Rescue, and that will undercut Fight for Right's manipulation of the election, and Samson might even get investigated by Congress or Justice."

"That works for me," Kenny said.

"It's the best we can do," Tony added. Others nodded agreement. The full moon was now ascending, bathing the isthmus and Capitol, and reflecting off the waters of Lake Mendota. They paused to watch it.

"I just had a terrible thought," Sammi said. "Watching this beautiful full moon rise so pure and white, what if the next full moon is red?"

"Then, we do what we can do, Sammi," Lois answered, "together."

"I hate to mention this," Dick said, "but we should consider the possibility that blowing the whistle will prod the powers to pull the trigger on OER sooner."

"Maybe a week or two," Tony said. "It's still the right thing to do."

"Okay," Dick concluded, "we are agreed on a strategy. Now, let's get down to tactics. Where will we meet next?"

"Prairie du Chien Library," Tony answered. They looked at him. "Why not? Random choice is the hardest behavior to predict."

"Oh, he's good," Kenny said. "Ten hundred hours tomorrow?"

All agreed.

"Ken?" Lois asked, "where are we going?"

He thought a moment, "On a random road trip in Sammi's car—the three of us."

1000 Hours, 3 October

It was a fall day with a cool damp wind blowing in low blue clouds from the northwest, a serious cold front. It would freeze hard tonight in the coulees between the limestone bluffs of the driftless region. Kenny was glad his bike was in a parking garage in Madison. Tony and Dick drove up right on time. Kenny got in the back seat and asked them to drive off.

"What's up, Kenny?" Dick asked.

"Those gals have been busy for an hour already in there. You won't believe it. Sammi has a blog up and running on her computer through the library's wireless. Lois is posting with all kinds of pseudonyms on other blogs around the net through the library's computers. These gals are pretty good. I think we're onto something. What's new with you two?"

"Tony got a call from a friend in Duluth," Dick said, "and they are seeing similarities to Green Bay with Samson and Fight for Right plus ethnic clashes disrupting the docks. I called a friend in Yuma, Arizona, and they are practically shut down except for Samson Security protecting the vegetable harvesting and processing. This thing is bigger than we imagined."

"Where is Homeland Security in this, Dick?"

"Yes, indeed," Dick said. "Well, officially, our resources are in the bigger, more important cities and regions…wow. This looks like a well-planned strategic campaign to focus all the state and national attention on big targets while the real operations are elsewhere. I need a list of those cities like Duluth, Green Bay, and Yuma and a big US map."

"I'll get the map and a list from our information," Tony offered.

"The girls and I will work on a list from the blogs," Kenny said.

"Uncle Kenny?" Dick asked seriously. "Do you really think you can handle those two girls yourself?"

Kenny laughed, "Fortunately I don't have to. They're the handlers, I'm just a pet they don't share."

Tony asked, "Do you want to go back and pick up the girls now?"

"Yes," Dick answered, "let's take them for a little ride and plan the next step. Then we'll drop you off a little ways from Sammi's car. Okay Kenny?"

"Yes, sir," Kenny answered. "Say, what do you think about me calling Ginger and trying to get that news guy on this?"

"What do you think, Tony?" Dick asked.

"I say if there's a chance he'll help, and you think it's not dangerous, ask, but see what the ladies think," Tony answered.

"That sounds good," Kenny said, "and I'll see if I can get Ginger to have him call me or give me his number, so I can keep her out of danger if possible. I wonder...."

"Wonder what?" Dick asked.

"I'm not sure yet, Dick. I might have an idea, but I'll get back to you."

1504 Hours, 4 October

Fall colors were showing on the East Bluff at Devil's Lake as Kenny, Lois and Sammi climbed Potholes Trail to the top. As they stopped to catch their breath, they saw Dick and Tony waiting on a bench up the trail. It was a real October day after the cold front had passed through, crisp this morning, but pleasant and dry this afternoon. Kenny noticed a couple of other men studying vegetation and rocks, 'Tony's men,' he thought.

"Good afternoon, ladies, Kenny," Dick said. "So glad you could make it."

"Me, too," Lois said. "I'm not as young...."

"Ha," Kenny commented.

"We started a list with some demographics," Lois told them, taking a paper from her pack and handing it to Dick.

Tony looked over at the list, "Uh huh."

"Interesting list," Dick said. "We came up with some of the same and a few others. I'll put these on the map and research your demographics. What's your take, team?"

"Relatively unimportant cities, politically," Lois began, "small, poor, almost insignificant places in small, poor, or unimportant states with some exceptions like the Packers."

"It's almost like these are places where they could get away with stuff they couldn't get away with on the coasts, near D.C. or in major cities," Sammi added.

"Generally, away from the really big military bases, but often near important transportation routes or unique economic areas." Kenny offered.

"Places important for special reasons, but not on some priority list," said Tony.

"Let's see what we have," Dick said, then he turned to Kenny. "Anything new from Green Bay?"

"Ed, the news guy, is hooked, I think," Kenny answered. "I spoke with him in some general way about Samson and Fight for Right, but I didn't open up. He is poking around. I'm thinking about heading up there tomorrow."

"What about Ginger?" Dick asked.

"Ginger wants to meet with Ed and me. I think she had another dream, but she wouldn't say on the phone. I have some phones to take with me," Kenny said.

"What is the online buzz?" Dick looked at Sammi and Lois.

"Oh, wow," Sammi said. "It's like all these people are coming out of nowhere to talk about a big secret they thought was only happening to them."

"There's a whole network building," Lois said. "It's amazing."

"Dick, Tony," Kenny started, "if the team agrees, I'll turn Ed onto these sites after I tell him about our own observations."

Dick looked around and got consensus. "Team says go, Kenny. Now, one more thing. It won't be long, probably, before something hits the airwaves or print and Fight for Right and Samson are going to be all over this. We need to have a plan. Next time we meet may have to be our last as a whole group. I take it you three are an inseparable unit." It was a question directed at Kenny, Lois, and Sammi.

Lois answered, "We are, Dick, except Kenny is making the Green Bay trip alone."

"Good," Dick said, "on both counts. My family is gone out of town now, and I'm as mobile as Tony and just as protected.

You three are the ones hanging out there, so I'm glad you're hanging together."

He took out a card and gave it to Lois. "I want you to call this number and ask for me when you have a time and place for our next meeting. I want an inside room big enough for eight, some kind of marker board or poster paper, and an exterior that can be guarded."

"Yes, sir," Lois replied.

Chapter Twenty

0935 Hours, 5 October

It was drizzling all the way to Green Bay. Kenny had to wear a rain suit, and now he sat under the bridge alone and chilled. If he were in the woods, he would know where to find dry wood, but here he was lost. His black coyote usually couldn't get control when he was this focused on a mission. Feeling lost is feeling vulnerable, and that is a big trigger for his PTSD—which tends to turn to anger, then dread, and finally depression. What kept the coyote away today was Mouse.

He was dragging a broken pallet in from somewhere, and they got busy making a fire. 'Nothing like a little motion to manage emotion.' Within minutes Kenny had his rain suit off and his jacket open to the radiant heat of the fire. He liked Mouse.

By the time Kenny was warming his back side, the other three returned, Diana with a big smile holding a butchered chicken. The Mama was walking much better now, and Gus was, well, Gus.

"Where did you get such a fine chicken?" Kenny asked her.

"From a fine chicken shop," Diana answered. "Me and Mouse saw this chicken hanging from a window over in the Hmong part of town, and I walked in and asked the guy if he had any work for me to earn that chicken. Well, now I know how to butcher chickens. His help didn't show up today, so I worked for a couple of hours and helped him out. He gave me a whole chicken and asked me to stop by again. How cool is that?"

Kenny had to chuckle, "The coolest thing is I just heard more words from you than the whole time I've known you. Diana's got a job."

"What's this world coming to?" The Mama asked. "We've got fire in the stove and a chicken in the pot. But you didn't stop by for dinner, did you boy?"

"No ma'am, but I brought you a couple of presents," and he gave her two packaged phones. There just happened to be a few small bills in the boxes. "How are you, The Mama?"

"I'm being well cared for, and a body can't ask for more than that. Gus has some news for you, though."

Gus looked up, "I heard a couple butchers talking in that bar they like to brag in, where I sweep up sometimes for the change I find. They were talking about you, Windy. They know your name and what you look like."

Kenny felt a little weak. "Thanks, Gus. Did they say anything about what I'm doing now or who I hang around with?"

"No. They were talking tough, liquor, you know, but they were talking like if they saw you, and someday, and stuff like that."

"Thanks, Gus. I'll call you as often as I can on that phone and you can tell me if you hear anything else, okay?"

"Sure, Windy."

"Guys, I have to go now, see if I can cause some more trouble. Bless you."

Kenny's mind was racing, but not a swamp or hay barn within miles. Besides, there was no time. He had to meet Ginger at Walmart in fifteen minutes.

Ginger was there in her van, waiting. Kenny parked his bike and hopped in.

"Hi, Ken," Ginger bubbled. "I had another dream, but this time not about you. I dreamed that I fell in love with a friend of yours when we were living in the woods all wild and stuff, and he fell in love with me." She looked at Kenny, "No babies, though."

"Hold that thought, Ginger," and he set two phones down for her. "It might be a bumpy ride today." She looked at him again, but didn't say anything.

They met Ed at his house, just walked in and sat down, with Nixon's permission, right there in the living room. "Ed," Kenny started after greetings, "it's been bugging me since we met. How does a beautiful big dog get a name like Nixon?"

Ed chuckled, "My dear wife named him that because he was too big for the media guys like me to kick around, anymore."

Kenny really liked that one. He felt a whole lot better about Ed, now. "Ed, have you ever heard of the LG program?"

"Yes, it's a kind of special ops program for old Vet volunteers—like you, I suppose."

"Like me. I don't know how to say this, so I'm going to go right at it." Ed watched him intently as did Nixon. "My partner, Rick, died on our last operation. He died making sure the second part of that mission was accomplished." He paused before continuing. "I'll just say that mission left a whole lot of Fight for Right people, some young ladies, dead—along with many Samson people including one ex-governor." There, it was out.

Ed must have been a very good poker player because he showed no obvious reaction, unlike Ginger who was covering her mouth and beginning to tremble. Kenny thought they might have to bolt, but Ed slowly looked up at them both and nodded. "Why did the Fight for Right people die?"

"Sir, they died because that son of a bitch ex-governor lied to us in his intelligence reports, saying they were going to be somebody entirely different—foreign nationals, in fact." Ed nodded some more and shook his head. "It didn't make sense to me for awhile, either," Kenny added.

Before Ed could get all tangled up in details, Kenny asked him right out, "Sir, have you ever heard of Operation Earth Rescue?" Ed's face went white. Now Kenny was sure he had made a big mistake, that somehow Pendergrast was connected to the administration or Samson.

"Ken," Ed spoke softly, "That is a term I had dearly hoped I would never hear again. I had a young reporter who came in all wound up with that story he said he picked up from a babysitter of the Sullivan family. One day that young reporter and the babysitter were found in his car in the river. I retired very soon after that."

"Ed," Ginger said, "you didn't know, then. Would you like to help us, now?"

He was watching his feet and looked up very slowly, as a very tired man. "I'm no LG," he said. "I have to talk to my life partner."

"We understand, sir," Kenny said, "but if you're curious, here are some web addresses you might find interesting." Kenny handed him an envelope. Kenny studied Ed a moment and looked him in the eye. "Ed, is Ginger safe in this town with you knowing this?"

Ed returned Kenny's look and responded, "I will protect her with my life, and I will be in contact with her." Kenny and Ginger said goodbyes and left.

Ginger was still a bit shaky when she got behind the wheel, but they drove off toward Walmart. Kenny had her stop at a supermarket. He pulled out one of the phones and asked Ginger, "Please call my Lois and tell her...say this exactly, 'Tonto will be at the second rest stop.' That's all. Do not give her your name or mine. Can you do that?"

"Of course I can. Give me a minute." She took out her notebook and pen, wrote down a script to read and wrote the number on top. "Does that look good?"

"Great. Thank you, Ginger. I have another favor—sorry, it seems to be a one-way street here—would you check on The Mama and family for me?"

"Every day, Ken, and it's not a one-way street. I'm going to have your friend for my love. Besides, this is my country, too."

1638 Hours 5 October

The weather had brightened considerably so Kenny could ride without his rain suit. By the time he approached the park-and-ride lot near I 90/94, he had formulated a primitive plan, but he really wasn't looking forward to telling Lois about it. Anyway, it was something for the team to discuss. But, Kenny knew he was poison and had to go into some kind of isolation, or the mission would be a failure and somebody would get hurt.

Some days, time seems to go so slowly, and other days, it is so fast. Today it seemed jerky, sometimes slow and sometimes fast, but never quite right. His mind went round and round, but at the center was one thought, 'I hope Lois is right, that love really does last forever.'

It seemed like forever before the women got there. When Sammi drove in the lot, Kenny could see the concern on Lois's face as she sat in the passenger seat. She got out and opened the rear door before giving him a hug and crawling in back with him. He noticed their bags in the back on the floor and seat. "Sammi, find us someplace secret with two rooms tonight," Kenny said.

"Yes, sir."

"Actually," Lois said, "we already have an idea for a place. It will take a couple of hours though. Have you been waiting long?"

"It feels like long," Kenny said.

"Care to talk now?" Lois asked. Sammi turned her stereo off.

"Gus told me he heard Samson boys talking about what they're going to do to me, by name."

"Oh, God. We were afraid of that," Lois gasped.

"There's more." Lois sat without breathing, holding and patting his hand at the same time. "My news guy knew about OER because a young reporter got a lead from Danny's babysitter and they both ended up in the river."

"Oh, Ken, what are we going to do?" Lois asked. Sammi looked at them in her mirror.

"We're going to discuss it with the team and decide, but I'd like us, you and me *Kimo Sabe,* to have a plan worked out. Have you scheduled a meeting yet?"

"Well, tentatively, yes. We found a place," Lois answered.

"Lo, Lonesome Pines won't be safe anymore. The deed is in a trust, but the neighbors know me by name."

"I'm sorry, honey."

"I have money, but it's all visible, and they're probably watching it."

"We can use mine, Ken." He didn't answer that. "Ken, honey, what are you thinking of doing?"

"I'm thinking of leading them away from you, all of you, so the mission doesn't get swamped."

"You're going to be bait?" Lois asked, eyes wide.

"I'm going to be an LG again. Other than that, how was your day?"

"Damn, Kenny, I was really getting used to having you around. My day? I don't know. We have a lot of posts on our blog. I'm surprised the media hasn't picked up on it, yet."

"Have you posted on media blogs?"

"No, we haven't, but we did suggest that today on our blog."

"Smooth, Lo. Tomorrow should be interesting in many ways."

"Ken, where will you go?"

"I'm thinking Yuma. We visited Vicky's family there, and she always dreamed of retiring in Arizona. I know the area pretty well, and I think I'm going house hunting."

"Kenneth Brewster, there are Samson people all over that place."

"Yeah, I figure I can take them by surprise. They won't be expecting it."

"God help me, that almost makes sense. Ken, I want to go with you."

"Lo, I want you to go with me, too, but we both know we're not going to do that."

"I know, I know," Lois resigned. Sammi wiped her eyes.

2100 Hours, 5 October

When Lois and Kenny had finished explaining things and Sammi was getting ready to go back to her room, Kenny said, "Sammi, I want to take your computer with me. In the morning will you show me a few things when we're ready to go?"

"Sure, Kenny. Are you planning to be the blog master, too?"

"Yeah. If nobody is wise to you two, yet, let's not tempt them. I think you can do enough damage now just posting on other blogs—and mine, of course."

"Okay, sure," Sammi said. "I'll go get breakfast. What time?"

Kenny looked at Lois. "Six? No, seven. Okay?" he asked.

"Seven, sweetie. Goodnight," Lois said.

Sammi waved and opened the door. Kenny was on his way to the shower before Sammi had closed it. Lois was right behind him.

They lay in bed for awhile after, watching some old comedies for distraction from motel sounds. Kenny felt surprisingly relaxed lying there with Lois cuddled up on his left side as though this was just another day. But, he knew it wasn't.

Softly, Lois said, "Thanks, Ken."

"For what, dear?"

"For being you, and for sharing you with me. I'm really happy right now all wrapped up in you like this. I just know everything is going to be okay. Well, not okay like nothing is wrong, just okay, you're going to come home to me, again."

"I'm never going to let go," Kenny said. Lois tilted her head up to look at him. "I mean it. No matter where I go or what happens to me, you're always going to be lying right here on my heart."

She put her head back down over his heart where she could feel it beating. "Should we go to sleep, soon?" Lois asked. "I scheduled that team meeting for noon tomorrow, and we have miles to go."

"Nah. Sammi can drive, and we can do this all the way there."

1200 Hours, 6 October

August weather returned warm and humid with a haze in the sky. Kenny couldn't remember weather events like this, but he wasn't yet convinced the climate change concept hadn't been blown out of proportion for political ploy for decades, already. Still, he had an uneasy feeling about the weather.

They were late, about fifteen minutes away, and Lois held his left hand tight in her right hand, patting his left thigh with her left hand. Kenny knew they would part in little more than an hour, and he was pretty sure she knew that, too.

They passed an SUV changing a tire as they turned down a town road by a real estate for sale sign, passing another car parked there with a man talking on a cell phone.

"The realtor is a friend of mine, okay?" Lois said. "You are an eccentric friend, and if you buy the place, I split the commission."

"You lied to a friend?" Kenny asked.

"No, I am hoping to buy it, with Sammi, of course." That gave Kenny an idea.

It was a long lane over a knoll, and when Sammi pulled up to the house, Kenny wondered what she saw in it, except a lot of work. It looked like that abandoned house where he found the old truck. Dick and Tony were waiting outside with plenty of other help around the yard. Lois unlocked the house and led them to an interior room decorated as an office/library. They sat around an old, oak library table.

Dick held a rolled up map but put it down when he got a good look at Lois, Kenny, and Sammi. "Do you want to go first today, Lois?"

"Dick, Samson is after Kenny by name, and we're thinking he should leave for Arizona for awhile, maybe lay down a scent." She explained what she and Kenny had talked about with Sammi. When she was finished, Dick didn't say anything, at first.

After studying them, Dick said, "Let's hold on that for now. Tony's got something."

"Some of our people around the country are picking up signals that there is a lot of dissention among the Samson people," Tony said. "Many of them are coming to us looking for work. We think Samson's tactics are scaring them, or maybe their extra-curriculars."

"Any particular places?" Kenny asked.

"Yes," Dick said as he rolled out the map. "Here are the cities from our combined lists. Except for Erie, Gary, and Green Bay, they are all under a hundred thousand and mostly ignored nationally. For the most part, they are out of big electoral states, away from capitals and major universities, and one more thing. They all have some racial or ethnic tension and gang activity, but no dominant power—except for three." He pointed to Grand Island, Nebraska, Grand Junction, Colorado, and Yuma, Arizona. "These are not city powers; they are large rural areas with urban hubs. Each has a strong ethnic base, and Samson is having trouble. Their people are looking for jobs in all three."

Kenny said, "I'll be visiting each of those places in the next three days. Can I do any good there?"

"Yeah," Tony said, "maybe. Let's think about that."

"Another thing," Dick said. "I called an Academy classmate who works for Army Intelligence as a civilian, now. I asked him if he had seen any of the blogs about Samson and Fight for Right or Operation Earth Rescue. Of course he didn't answer, but he did ask if I was looking for a job. He knows about all of it, I'm sure."

"Team," Lois started timidly, "is it time for me to make another call to the Senator?" There was a pause.

"Make it generic, Lo," Kenny said, "Maybe emails to senators in general." Sammi was already writing in her notebook. "You can follow with a call tomorrow if he doesn't call you first."

Sammi said, "We can suggest that on the blogs today, write your senators and congressperson, and remind them about posting on media blogs."

"This thing is accelerating," Dick said. "Keep your wits about you. Anything else?"

Tony said, "Maybe...could we use Kenny to drop some leaflets or posters on his way out of town?" Sammi was writing again.

"Got it," Lois said. "We'll have generic email scripts posted on blogs this afternoon and leaflets for Kenny by morning," she said.

"I need them by 1800 today," Kenny said.

Lois starting tearing and nodded her head. "You'll have them by then. I'll leave them at the co-op."

"Do you really want this farm?" Kenny asked Lois, then looked at Sammi, "It would make a nice secure operation center."

"Sure, but…," Lois said.

"Give me your account numbers and I'll have the money transferred to both of your accounts by anonymous intermediate routing from Rick's business account, today." Lois and Sammi just stared blankly at him, mouths open.

"Gentlemen," Kenny said, looking at Tony and Dick, "I'd like a moment with Lois, and then I'll need a ride to Madison."

"Sure," Dick said and walked to the door.

"You want that bike picked up and delivered somewhere in Madison?" Tony asked.

"Great," Kenny said, giving him his extra key. "Leave it at the co-op. I'm leaving tracks today." Tony nodded and walked out with Dick and Sammi.

"If the sky turns red before I get back, I will come straight to you, here," Ken told Lois.

"I will be here, Ken, waiting for you. I know you're coming back." One more hug and a simple kiss, just like that first one, and Lois walked out.

'This is getting really old,' Kenny told himself, 'but, it's got to be done.'

Chapter Twenty-One

1348 Hours, 6 October

Tony and Dick dropped Kenny at the Internet café on the capitol square. The first thing he wanted to take care of was the money transfer. Rick and he had set up their business accounts so each could access the other's in case of just such a circumstance. Death certificates without bodies are difficult anyway, and when the only witness is the only beneficiary, well, there are complications. Kenny wouldn't touch Rick's Social Security. That went to his personal account and could rot there for all he cared. This was residual income from Rick's business that he had shared with Kenny through Vicky. Somewhere, Rick was smiling now, Kenny could feel it.

Now he needed a car, no a van, and he needed cash. He wondered if his bike was back, and the co-op was only a few blocks, so he walked over. There it was, already, and the jacket and helmet, too. He headed his bike out East Washington Avenue to find a van. At the third used car dealer, he found a suitable older conversion van with the remote start option. Kenny took it for a test drive out on the highway.

Satisfied, he talked to the salesman. "Here's the deal," Kenny told him, "I have a long, unexpected trip to take, and my old bones don't like that bike for trips, but I need it in two hours."

"We can do that, sir," the salesman said. "Will you be trading the Honda then?"

"Oh, okay," Kenny said, like it was the salesman's idea. "What's your deal?" The salesman named a price and Kenny said, "Okay, but, I need four new tires, new belts and battery under the hood, all top quality, and two full tanks of gas. Oh, and plates on it. What time can you have it ready, today?"

"I'll be right back," the salesman went inside and returned in a few minutes. "Six o'clock today, but we'll have to add the tires and stuff to the bill." He showed Kenny the total.

"Write it up," Kenny said, "I'll be back in one hour with the money and a pen."

In an hour he was back with a bank check and plenty of cash for his return trip. They already had the tires, belts, and battery changed, and it was full of fuel. He signed all the papers, legal and proper in his own name, using his co-op address. "I'll be back at six sharp," he told the salesman and his boss.

Kenny hopped on the bike and rode around the block, stopped, and walked into a coffee shop to wait where he could keep an eye on the dealer. As soon as they took those papers to the DMV, the clock started. Samson could have that information in hours, if not minutes.

Within an hour, Kenny saw them mounting the plates on the van parked in front of the office. He was there in minutes, gave them the keys and title to the bike, and was out the drive. He had to pick up those pamphlets and personal items at the co-op, but his gut was screaming caution. He approached through the back alley from one street west. His roommates were eager to help him load. One of them told him about a car parked down the street in front for half an hour or so. Kenny took a look. He was sure the two guys in the car were on stakeout.

"Say, Willy," he said to a tall, middle-aged guy living there, "do you think you can pretend to be stoned and talk to those guys for me?"

"Oh, I'm pretty sure, Ken," he answered.

"Well, ask them if you can help them. If they ask anything about a guy like me, tell them you think they missed me, that I was going north, hunting, this week. Okay?"

"Sounds like fun," he said, heading for the door.

"Wait!" Kenny said. "Give me about fifteen minutes first to clear some traffic. Thanks guys," and he was on his way. Ten minutes later he was heading southwest out of town with an uneasy heart. 'I hope you're riding with me tonight, Rick.' He felt strangely better.

First Light, 7 October

Trucks were pulling in and out around him at the Des Moines truck stop. Kenny stretched himself awake and decided it was time to leave some more tracks. First, he updated his blog and checked others. Lois and Sammi had posted on several, yesterday. He used his bank debit card for breakfast and again for gas, and he was on his way. He smiled a little bit at the thought of what detectives would do with this data. One nice thing about Des Moines is that it is a hub, a crossing of two major interstates with this truck stop right there. It might look like he was turning south on I-35 for Kansas City, but he headed west on I-80 instead.

He reached Grand Island by early afternoon and found some hungry souls on the streets. He gave them each a bundle of pamphlets and a few dollars to distribute them. He found some teenagers at a mall and did the same. Then, he fueled again and headed up the road to Cabela's to shop. He had a good time there, using his bank card again. 'One more stop,' he thought, 'and they should see a pattern.' He headed for Cheyenne.

He decided to set the pattern by sleeping in a truck stop again, having breakfast in the morning, and buying gas, all on plastic. He listened to the TV news in the truck stop, but heard nothing of interest to him. 'That channel probably won't run anything until the government tells them it's okay,' he told himself. Then he turned left for Denver and west on I-70 over the mountains. Well, that was his plan. Mother Nature had another plan, and Kenny saw the weather coming down the mountains to greet him. He decided on a detour. He pulled into Greeley and found a small, old motel where he could park around back and pay cash for his room.

0514 Hours 9 October

The cable news on TV was talking about Internet blogs and the Fight for Right Campaign. They mentioned Samson Security, but nothing specific. Operation Earth Rescue was not mentioned at all. The Weather Channel showed improving weather to the west, and Kenny was really uneasy, so he was out the door without coffee. Even though he paid cash for the room, his license number and vehicle description were on record.

The weather may have been improving, but the roads were a sloppy mess, and that old van was not safe. 'Why didn't I get AWD?' he asked himself. 'Oh, yeah, the remote start,' he remembered. He had to take it very slow and easy, following trucks down the mountains and hardly staying ahead of some of them up the shorter pulls. He was a happy man when the Grand Junction exit sign come into view.

He left leaflets in Grand Junction much the same way he had in Nebraska and headed west into Utah. He left tracks again near Green River for gas and food, but he doubled back to Moab and south on US 191. It might be a long cold ride, but he had fuel for more than six hundred miles, and he figured about that much energy. He made it all the way to Flagstaff where it was snowing again.

Kenny did not dare stay here or leave any tracks. He paid for gas and food with cash and headed toward Phoenix where he knew it would be warm and dry. Kenny used to like solo road trips, but not when he was the fox and the hounds had big guns. He needed to sleep, but there was no time or place, and caffeine was making him anxious.

1426 Hours, 10 October

Montezuma's Castle was a favorite place for Kenny. He had visited it twice before, amazed at the concept, craftsmanship, and the simple beauty of the dwelling overlooking the garden valley below. He walked around almost in a daze between the caffeine buzz and the sleep deficit. This place relaxed him and he decided on a little nap in the van. Even with windows open, he woke up sweating and seeking air to breathe. Although the air temperature was pleasant, the sun had heated his van quickly.

Looking at his road atlas, he found a rest area south on I-17 and decided to stop again there for a couple of hours to nap. The sun would be getting low and it should be comfortable. Phoenix traffic should clear by the time he would wake up, and he could head toward Yuma. He was beyond tired though, but he did not want to register anyplace. Rest areas made him nervous, too. 'I don't even know for sure if anybody is after me, at least before I spread those pamphlets.'

He decided on a rural route instead. It is legal to camp in most National Forests for free outside regular campgrounds if you are a quarter mile off the main road. He could find a spot near here, park his van, and actually sleep in his sleeping bag and poncho a couple hundred yards away for security. 'Good. I have a plan.'

Dawn, 11 October

There is something peaceful, comforting, and so right about waking up with trees standing guard around you. Kenny was at home here. The species were different, the rocks were different, even the air was different, but it was a forest, and he was in love with forests.

He stirred and stretched quietly in case his van had been found. He was feeling jumpy, almost paranoid, and he did not like that about himself. Oh, how he missed Rick. Just thinking of him seemed to ease his mind, again.

The very best thing to do in the woods is walk. Kenny packed his bedroll and made his clearing circle around the van back to his bivouac. Now, he could pick up, pack the van, and head around Phoenix to Yuma.

There was no easy way around Phoenix. An alternate route might be less predictable, so he decided to head for Prescott, through the mountains, and south later. He knew he could find a place for breakfast and a wash-up on this route. Near Prescott, he found a National Public Radio station with a news hour, but there was no mention of the topics of interest—except for one thing. The President had scheduled a rare news conference for nine Eastern Time tonight.

Kenny had a sick feeling about this. He wished there would be more news. Then, toward the end of the hour, he heard the announcement that their guests this afternoon would be Ed Pendergrast and Senator Brad Dickenson. Oh, how he wanted to hear that. He started trying to figure where he could be at that time, 'What time was that, again? Three this afternoon? What time is it now? Seven ten. I should be in Yuma before then.' He picked up the pace and decided no more stops except to pee, and no more caffeine.

Well before noon he was approaching Yuma, and he was getting more nervous all the time. He would not be able to avoid a Border Patrol checkpoint. They might find his large amount of ammunition reloading supplies interesting, but he had his receipts and all was legal—well, except for the detonators, but they were really well hidden. He was getting downright twitchy about Yuma. 'This might have been a bad idea,' he told himself.

Where was he going to hide out? If they were after him, probably every Samson gun had his license number, van description, and a photo of him by now. He thought hard about turning around and running away. He kept driving, breezing through the checkpoint with a few sniffs from the dog and a peek into the van. 'Good old Wisconsin plates.'

Now he was approaching the city and he had no idea where to go. His elaborate plan, the one that made him smile, had to be scrapped now that the snowstorm had slowed him down so much. He came into Yuma too tired and too late. He could not remember the last time this had happened to him—

then he remembered he couldn't remember a lot of his missions at all. He saw a mall up ahead and decided to pull in. Driving around a bit, he found a relatively quiet lot in back. He stopped to think. Nothing came to him.

A big, black SUV drove by with four men wearing black inside. Kenny could not see if they were looking his way or not. He almost panicked, but stayed still. They passed. He started up and drove out. 'Where to go? Where to go?'

He turned onto US 95 toward I-8. He went up the ramp west bound on I-8. 'Where am I going?' He waited for an answer, across the Colorado River now, into California. That felt good. He headed toward San Diego, and there it was. The casino. Tribal land. They would have their own security, not Samson. He was sure of it, so he exited.

Driving into the casino lot, he made another decision, valet parking. He gave the attendant his van, took his belt pack, and headed inside. Maybe a plan would come to him there. Suddenly, he remembered the radio program. How could he do that here? He checked his cell phone—one thirty-five. 'Okay, maybe there is time.'

There was an old-fashioned quarter slot machine with the fruit and diamonds like he used to play. He dropped a fifty in the slot and worked it so as not to attract any attention. He played it mechanically so he could think.

He needed to buy a different car, a little SUV this time, but from a private party so it still had plates. That was part of his original plan as was the distribution of pamphlets. But the part about leading them to the van and hoping they would wire it for a bomb might have to be scrapped. 'Wait. Maybe I have an idea.'

He kept playing while he observed people around him. He noticed a lone man, perhaps late thirties, clean clothes and well-groomed, who looked desperate. Kenny saw him first sitting at a slot machine, not playing at all. Later, the man was walking around, apparently checking machines that still used tokens for loose change. Kenny decided to approach him, so he cashed out with a voucher.

"Excuse me, sir," Kenny said, "but I found this voucher. I think maybe you dropped it."

"What do you want for it?" the young man asked.

"A ride into town listening to your radio. There's some cash in it, too, if your car has FM."

The guy looked him over, and Kenny could almost see his mind churning. Finally, his eyebrows bounced up and down into a little frown, his lips pursed, and he sighed with a slight shrug as if too say, "What the hell?" and he took the voucher. "Shall we go now?"

"Now is good," Kenny answered. "I'm Ben."

"Tom." They shook hands. The young man had a nice sporty car with an Arizona plate, and Kenny found NPR on the radio. As they crossed back into Arizona, Kenny asked him to stop someplace where he could pick up an advertiser. Tom obliged, turning in at the mall and stopping by a department store with papers in boxes outside. Kenny grabbed one and hopped back in the car.

"Tom, I noticed a lot of black BDUs around. Is that what your police wear?"

"Private security," Tom answered.

"Not Samson Security," Kenny said as he paged through the used car ads.

"Yes," Tom said, "do you know them?"

"I've heard about them. Are they big around here?"

Tom turned to look at Kenny as he wheeled his car around and stopped. "Did you want to go someplace else?"

Kenny was riveted to the discussion on the radio now. Ed and Senator Dickenson were addressing concerns over links between Samson Security and Fight for Right. Ed also introduced the Operation Earth Rescue term, but the senator did not comment. Kenny was sure the President's address tonight was going to relate to that.

"I'm sorry," Kenny said, putting his focus back on the advertising paper.

"Did you want to go someplace else?" Tom repeated.

"Yeah, well, maybe." He put his finger on an ad. "How far is it to the foothills?" Kenny could see Tom was getting nervous or impatient.

"Ten to twenty miles," Tom answered.

Kenny placed a fifty on the dash. Tom picked it up. "I have a nephew who went to work for Samson last year, and we haven't heard from him since. Do you know where they are located here in town?"

Tom changed lanes, "Sure, about half a mile up here on 16th Street in the old bank building," and he drove Kenny right by it.

"Thanks, Tom, maybe I can locate my nephew. So, can you drop me somewhere near 13000 East 44th Drive?" Kenny asked. Tom obliged, turning back to the highway and east to Foothills Boulevard.

Kenny gave Tom another fifty and wished him luck. Now, he had to find this address on foot and hope the old Jeep Liberty was still available. It turns out he found the car on the street before he located the address.

Kenny had just begun looking the car over when a lanky fellow about his age came out. "She's a beauty," the guy said, "been in the family since I was your age."

Kenny gave him a second look. "You are my age. Call me Benny."

"Dewey," he answered, shaking hands firmly, "as in, 'do we have a deal?' What would you give me?"

"Well, what are you asking?" Kenny said.

"I'm asking for an opening bid," Dewey answered. "I used to be an auctioneer."

"Really," Kenny probed, "I thought from that handshake, you used to milk cows."

"I did that too, and bought houses."

"And cars," Kenny finished for him.

"Oh, no, this really was my wife's car, but she bought a new one. Will you give me a thousand for openers?"

"One thousand," Kenny answered.

"Do I hear two, two, two, I've got two. Do I hear three?"

"I didn't hear anybody bid two," Kenny said.

"Takes good ears to be an auctioneer," Dewey answered.

"Uh, huh. Are the tags good?" Kenny asked. He began to wonder about a natural law that whenever it is really important for a guy to get something done quickly or simply, the universe puts a comedian or other hazard in his path. 'Maybe I'm being told to slow down,' Kenny considered.

"Tags are good until next year. Can I get three thousand?"

"Three thousand," Kenny said.

"Three I've got, and thank you for your help. Do I hear four thousand, four thousand dollars one time? I've got four, how about five?"

Dewey gave Kenny that 'I've got you now,' grin. "Want to take her for a drive? First guy who bids five thousand can have a test drive."

"I'll bid a conditional five thousand—based on the driving condition." Dewey gave him the keys and eased into the passenger seat. When they got back, Kenny made a point of checking the radio, battery, belts, fluid levels, tires, and owner's manual. He was beginning to enjoy this game and thought about dropping his bid, but then decided that Dewey needed a win of some kind to close the deal. "Okay," Kenny offered, "Five thousand dollars."

"Five thousand here, I've got five, five, five, do I hear six," and he watched Kenny who tried to remain deadpan. "Well, give me fifty five," he told Kenny.

"I'm in at five," Kenny said. "You want me to raise my own bid?"

"Hey, every bit of help is appreciated," Dewey told him.

Kenny pulled a wrapped bank bundle of fifty dollar bills out of his belt pack. "If your other bidder can top that, sell it to him."

"All done? All done?" Dewey asked the air. "Sold to the gentleman up front. I'll get the papers". Dewey was back in two minutes, and he had a marker pen to check every one of those bills. "It's a good car, Benny. I hope you enjoy it as much as I enjoyed selling it to you."

The remarkable thing is Kenny felt significantly better. Whether it was being out of a marked car, or whether Dewey had relaxed him, he was beginning to believe he might make it out of Yuma alive. Still, he had a couple of dangerous things to do, and he hadn't worked out the details. He decided to take his new ride to the Bureau of Land Management area and into the mountains for a think. He parked where he could watch the sun dropping toward the sand dunes far across the river with all of Yuma laid out in front of him. He prayed and meditated, and another plan began to develop.

Chapter Twenty-Two

1747 Hours, 11 October

Kenny called a cab to pick him up at Burger King. He parked the Jeep on a residential street nearby, around the corner, walked over and waited inside. The cab dropped Kenny off outside the casino hotel, and he walked through the lobby into the casino, wandered around the games and to the front door with his valet ticket. He got in his van and drove back into Yuma. This would have to be a quick and dirty operation. He had a box of pamphlets to deliver and a new plan.

He stopped at a few churches and dropped bundles of pamphlets at their office doors all the way from downtown out to Foothills Boulevard and back. He set a bundle on top of each newspaper stand he saw. Then, he headed for his final stop.

At the abandoned discount store across from Samson headquarters, Kenny parked in the middle of the empty lot, set his bomb under the driver's seat, his box of ammunition reloading supplies on top of the seat for a booster, and his detonator on the ignition. He tossed the remaining pamphlets around the van, grabbed a couple bags of belongings, and walked around the corner and through the alley. He got into his Liberty and drove around the block so he could see the entire lot clearly and would be able to pull away easily. He hit the remote start and blew the van to pieces.

Kenny headed out of town to California with the radio tuned to NPR, rather unhappy about the untidy exit, but happy to be going home. He would take a different route through Las Vegas, Salt Lake City, and The Black Hills. He had no deadlines now, and nobody chasing him, so he could wait for weather as necessary. The news conference was beginning.

As suspected, the President denied any program called Operation Earth Rescue, claiming that terrorists were trying to disrupt our electoral process. He then went on to say that a major coalition of nations around the world—he did not say who or how many—were in the process of finalizing a plan to reduce warming trends and, therefore, improve the global economic climate. This plan would be announced in a major event at the United Nations later this week, and it had full support of the scientific community.

Kenny found it interesting that the President completely avoided any mention of Fight for Right or Samson Security. Of course, he promised that this United Nations plan would solve all of our serious problems, that help was on the way, and hope could once again replace fear. It was a great speech, but a very contrived news conference. He only answered a few questions and deferred those he found off-topic to pertinent secretaries and agencies.

Sunset, 14 October

The Black Hills beckoned Kenny to stay, but he knew people in Wisconsin were worried about him. News of his exploded van may have reached them, and even though they knew about his plan, they could not be sure he had escaped. He loved these hills deeply and spent two days walking and resting. Tonight, he would go home.

NPR news finally gave a date for the United Nations event, tomorrow afternoon. 'Interesting,' he thought. It was not during prime time. 'I'll bet our President schedules another evening speech.' Sure enough, the announcement came that a special joint session of Congress would include a Presidential speech tomorrow night. Now, Kenny was in a hurry to get home, wherever that was.

He knew he could not go to Lonesome Pines, not yet, anyway. He wondered if Lois and Sammi had closed the purchase on the little run-down farm outside Madison. He set that as his destination. Twelve hours, Kenny figured, in time for breakfast, maybe. Oh, how he wanted to call ahead.

I-90 is an open road without much traffic, dark and lonely on a cloudy night. Kenny drove a steady legal speed, listening to talk radio as much as he could. Then, he found an oldies station, and that took him all the way across southern Minnesota. He couldn't resist stopping when he made Wisconsin, for a little break, gas, and some snacks. His mind began to entertain intrusive thoughts about all sorts of unpleasant scenarios, so he put the caffeine soda aside and drank water.

'Lois would be much better off without me,' he told himself, and he agreed. 'Maybe it would be better if I really were dead.' Maybe Lois and Sammi had plans for that farm that might not include him. Maybe they didn't believe the prophecy about red skies. Maybe they believed it would not happen, or it wouldn't be that bad. He had never intended to be involved with a woman again after Vicky, and now he was feeling tied in knots. Maybe he was now free to go to the wilderness by himself. That, however, was not his Vision.

Traffic picked up as it grew light and he reached the junction with I-94. He considered that a blessing because he could keep his mind occupied with driving. Having some scenery, again, helped, too. But sunrise was always a time when he had to fight sleep while driving. He stopped at a wayside, washed his face, and took a little walk. 'One more hour.'

Breakfast Time, 15 October

The old Jeep Liberty started down the long driveway to that farm, Kenny feeling like a high school kid about to ask for a prom date. The real estate sign was gone, and he could see lights on in the house. 'That's a good sign.' Sammi's little car was there, but not Lois's Bronco. There was also a red pickup truck he didn't recognize. He stopped and looked around before getting out. He felt he was being watched, but he didn't know from where.

The porch door opened and Sammi came running out and gave him a big hug. Kenny had a lump in his throat and a knot in his gut. Something was wrong. He pushed Sammi back, and she looked fine. "Oh, Kenny," Sammi said, "Lois is going to be so happy to see you. She's been so worried."

"Where is she?" Kenny asked.

"She stayed with friends in Madison last night. She had a doctor's appointment late yesterday and decided to stay over and do some shopping. She should be back pretty soon. We're planning to work on the barn today."

"Doctor's appointment? Anything wrong?"

"No, nothing's wrong, Kenny. She should be back pretty soon."

"Whose pickup?" Kenny asked.

"That's our farm truck," Sammi said. "We're going to work this place." Kenny had nothing to say about that.

"Sammi," Kenny said, "I have the feeling I'm being watched."

"Oh, you are," she said. "One in the house and one in the barn, Tony's guys." Kenny nodded approval.

Just then, he heard a car and Lois's Bronco appeared, driving up like a NASCAR pit stop. She grabbed Kenny, giving all indications she was more than happy to see him. When he was able to separate enough to get a look at her, he noticed she looked positively radiant, although those dark circles under her eyes bothered him.

"So, Lois, what did the doctor say about those circles?" He brushed her face with the backs of his fingers. Lois looked at Sammi and smiled. Sammi was smiling back.

"The doctor said I need iron and some vitamins." She kissed him and took his hand. "Help me bring some things in and we'll make breakfast. What would you like?"

Kenny said, "Oh, I don't care, uhm…a sausage and cheese omelet with onions and peppers. How's that?"

"That's a challenge," Lois answered, "but I'll come as close as I can. Come, tell us about your trip. We read about the van on the Net."

"Got your TV set up so we can watch the President tonight?" Kenny asked.

"No," she answered, "but we can see it live on the computer."

Evening, 15 October

News all afternoon had been about the big announcement at the United Nations of an agreement to initiate a scientific project altering the atmosphere and dampening the changes in climate trends. Most nations had agreed to support it, and the UN would fund the project with support from large industrialized countries. Tonight, our President would give us specifics at the exact same time as leaders around the world would be announcing them to their people. Kenny was afraid that he knew the specifics.

Dick and Tony joined Lois, Sammi, and Kenny for the Internet broadcast. In uncharacteristic fashion, the President began right on time, "Good evening fellow Americans. This afternoon, the United Nations announced an agreement among nations of unprecedented scope and importance." He went on and on about what a big deal it was and why it was necessary, blah, blah, blah. Finally he got around to the details.

"Tomorrow afternoon at 5:15 p.m. Eastern Daylight time, there will be simultaneous launches of space missiles from several locations around the world carrying chemical payloads that will change the carbon dioxide and other greenhouse gas chemistry in our atmosphere. Initially, we will notice little or no effect; however, in the days or weeks following, there will be a temporary, I repeat, temporary, darkening of the atmosphere that will give the sky a reddish hue and may make many stars seem to disappear.

"This condition is temporary and the sky will return to normal in a few days. The red color is our proof that the chemistry is working as we planned. The result will be a stabilization of our atmosphere, a cooling of surface temperatures, and a return to more normal conditions. This will drastically reduce severe weather, allow our agriculture and commerce to stabilize, and stimulate our economies to become robust again as hope returns, replacing fear.

"Governments around the world and here in America already possess sealed documents brought by trained scientific experts who will elaborate on details and answer specific questions. My fellow Americans, this will be the greatest scientific achievement in the history of mankind, and we are here to celebrate it in our time. Thank you, good night, and God bless America and our whole world."

"Hallelujah, God save the king," Kenny said. "This is the end of our world."

Lois squeezed his hand, "Maybe not, Ken. Maybe it will work out." Kenny felt serious nausea and went outside to barf. The others stayed inside to discuss it, including Lois, which left Kenny feeling empty. His mind went back to his Vision of prophecy and what his role must be in this event. He knew he had to go home to Lonesome Pines, whatever the risk. The moon was gone with the sun, so Kenny celebrated the stars for a long time before he heard the porch door open.

Lois found him sitting on the lawn, leaning against a silver maple tree. She sat silently beside him and reached for his hand. Finally, she snuggled against him and waited for him to talk.

Kenny started, "I have to go home, Lo, to Lonesome Pines."

"Can we talk about it in the morning, hon? They're all going home tonight, and we'll be alone. Come in and say goodbye?"

Kenny stood up carefully. "You told them about the prophecy and my Vision of helping people survive in the wilderness?"

She squeezed his hand and led him inside.

First Light, 16 October

Lois remained curled up beside Kenny, head on his chest and shoulder. Kenny remembered Sammi this way with Rick at Line Camp before that last awful mission. He thought he should say something but couldn't think of anything. His mind wanted to cry, but his eyes wouldn't cooperate. No word was spoken, but he knew she wasn't going to go with him. She, like the others, did not really believe the prophecy or his Vision. Kenny wondered if he had been this sad even when Amy died, or Vicky.

"Thank you for the farm, Ken. Sammi thanks you, too."

"It wasn't me, Lo. Rick gave you this farm."

"We think it was both of you." She looked up at his face, then lay her head back down. "Did you know Sammi and I had shared this dream of a little farm since we were in high school?"

"No," Kenny said, "but I'm not surprised."

"We always wanted to raise goats and rabbits along with earthworms and organic vegetables, feeding them the scraps. We are living our dream, Ken." He couldn't think what to say.

"I'm going to shower and fix breakfast," Lois said, and got up without asking him what he wanted to eat. He figured he'd shower too, but waited until she finished. He saw she was distancing herself from him, and though confused, he knew enough to give her space.

At the table, Kenny decided to come right out and say it. "Lois, I love you, but you don't owe me anything." She grabbed his hands and started to cry. "I'm very happy you and Sammi are living your dream. You know my thirst for the freedom from duty and expectations, but…."

"It's okay, Ken."

"Lo, if there is anything you want or expect from me, please tell me. Please."

"Ken, I love you, too, more than I ever dreamed possible. That's why I have no expectations. You owe me nothing at all. Everything we have had, I feel we have shared equally, something unbelievably amazing to me. Of course I want to sleep with you, make love with you, and wake up with you. You are always welcome here, but I don't expect you to stay—especially when I know you believe so deeply that you must go." She started sobbing now, and Kenny held her.

"And, I cannot expect you to give up your dream, your Vision, to go with me. You are always invited but never expected," Kenny told her.

"Oh, shit." Lois said, "Is mature love supposed to be so sad?"

"I don't know, Lo. I don't know nuthin' anymore. Hon, I don't know what to do."

"Well, I'll tell you, Kenneth Brewster, you just come right back upstairs and get naked with me, and we'll see if we can figure something out."

"Well, at least you fed me first, this morning."

Kenny left for Lonesome Pines before the others came back. He had been wrong about his eyes, they could cry some more. 'It's only two hundred miles,' he told himself, but he knew there would be no casual visits, no more of these awful goodbyes. 'Damn it!'

Chapter Twenty-Three

Sunset, 16 October

The new moon would set with the sun, and Kenny would see it from his own fire pit at Lonesome Pines. The stars on a clear cool fall night in Northern Wisconsin are breathtaking, so brilliant that the Milky Way looks like a thin cloud overhead. Operation Earth Rescue had already tarnished the beauty, however, not because it had begun, but because every time Kenny looked into the sky, he feared seeing red. It was almost like watching a loved one die, knowing it is coming soon, and there is nothing that anyone can do.

But the stars were beautiful tonight, so even though he was chilly, he kept the fire as embers—his favorite fire anyway—to keep from polluting the beauty above. The dread he felt for the coming horror the world would know could not diminish his reverent awe, and he had to sing "How Great Thou Art." He didn't even care if somebody heard him off-key, shaky, and squeaky. His soul was singing, and his voice just needed to join in.

Behind his couch he had found a comb Lois left, and he had taken the few hairs, tied them together, and put them in the little, leather medicine bag he now wore around his neck. He laid the comb beside his bed, and he held it every night when he went to bed and every morning when he awoke. In his mind, he could see her when he held that comb and know she was well.

Evening Twilight, 31 October

A natural consequence of the rhythms of sun, moon, and Earth intersecting with the constructs of human time is what some call a blue moon, the second full moon of a calendar month. Tonight, on the Hallowed Eve of All Saints Day, which this year came two days before the Presidential election, that moon would rise. Since his return to Lonesome Pines, Kenny had watched the sky with dread.

Tonight, he celebrated the appearance of the stars as dark preceded the tardy moon rising later each night by some fifty minutes. Behind the trees across his valley, above the wisps of fog in the cold air over the warm stream, it began to rise gloriously white, and he clung to hope.

Kenny thought he was to be treated to the veils of thin clouds covering a shy moon—until he noticed the stars disappearing in patches across the sky. When he finally braved a look, behind the black silhouettes of grace, the moon ascended blood red. Kenny vomited in wretched horror. "My God, they did it."

He was grateful there was no bottle in camp.

He walked in somber misery to his special rock to visit the spirit of Summer Moon, and they wept together.

Dawn brought an indescribable view of the most unnatural color to the sky that Kenny questioned his sanity, again. But his tears were gone. There was nothing he could do, but the helplessness brought a kind of relief, a release from his need to fix things. Perhaps he had found his peace, his freedom from the blood chit, after all.

Tuesday, 3 November

Kenny stepped into the voting booth, treating this act as he had the sex in old age, savoring what was very likely to be his last time. He believed it was futile, that Operation Earth Rescue had sealed a victory, if one dared call it that, for the Fight for Right campaign and the President they endorsed. He voted anyway, just in case his candidate might lose by one vote and he would feel responsible.

At home, he went back to the woods for what had become his way. He went to the woods to pray and meditate, only something had changed. He now combined them in one communion. There had been that evening by the fire, as he savored the memory of a moment of eternity with Lois, when something occurred to him. Oh, he admitted that that had not been his only eternal moment, he was not that romantic. There had been a few such times with Vicky, and perhaps even with Bonnie, but he had been too self-involved to be aware of them, then. What occurred to him was that such a moment of intimacy with another human soul was so wonderful that he wondered what such a moment of intimacy with God might be. And, so, that is what he sought.

Now, he touched eternity daily, usually once early in the morning, once late in the evening, and one or two other times during a day, depending upon Nature. The result was that, in this most tragic time, his black coyote stayed away. He accepted his smallness and relevance at the same time. He began to believe, deep down, that the mortgage had been paid. Still, there was a feeling, not really like a nagging, not an obligation so much as an opportunity, maybe like a genuine tithe of joy. There was something left for him to do. He did not know exactly what, but that no longer mattered. He had faith, now, that when the time came, he would know what to do and how to do it.

0812 Hours, 4 November

The newspaper was full of expected election coverage and lots of excitement about the great positive effects of Operation Earth Rescue around the world, quelling fears and reducing crime. There were predictions of a new age of discovery and industry, and the evolution of mankind to a higher order spiritual being. Kenny ate his omelet at the diner and said goodbye to town. He was going hunting.

Most years he was content to take a few grouse and one deer, but this time he wanted more, although he wasn't sure why. He filled his propane freezer and made venison jerky. He even canned meat the way his grandmother had taught him on the farm. He made sauerkraut and pickles of many kinds. He tried things he had never tried before, studying ways to preserve food.

One day around Thanksgiving, when the woods were orange with deer hunters, he stayed home and made a plan, and that showed him his obsession. He was preparing to teach again, to live that Vision to help people prepare for the wilderness. So, he laid out a curriculum for himself through the winter and into spring. It focused on basic survival at a spiritual level.

The sky had cleared within a week after Blood Moon, but Kenny couldn't seem to predict the weather, anymore. Well, maybe he could because it changed so little. The autumn pattern of storms of the upper Mississippi River Valley was absent, and week after week it seemed to stay moderate. Oh, it gradually got colder, as November does, but there was no bitter cold and no Indian summer.

Day after day he stocked up for winter and studied basic survival. He tanned hides and made snowshoes. He made bows and arrows, hatchets and knives. He kept no calendar except by sun and moon.

He built and stocked caches around his place and beyond with food, blankets, weapons, and ammunition. He stored garden seeds in paper-lined glass jars. He cut wood and filled his shed. Some days he just wandered the land for miles, studying places for people to camp.

Chapter Twenty-Four

Afternoon, Early Second Winter Moon

Kenny thought of Lois, again, today while he was cooking his own dinner. He remembered her feelings about Sammi missing her opportunity with Rick. He remembered their concerns about turning forty. He remembered Lois's passion and thought about their first time when he had been so worried—no, scared. He remembered her hips on the pillow and his arousal at the thought of her pleasure. Finally and suddenly, it occurred to him, deep in the icy grips of the north woods winter so many moons later, that what she had wanted then, more than anything else, although maybe subconsciously, was a child. 'But, why would she want my child?'

He decided to see if he still had the ingredients to make some mocha.

Kenny sat by his fireplace, gazing down his little valley and holding Lois's comb. He imagined her with a child, but he couldn't see her anymore and that saddened him profoundly.

Recalling their brief conversation about Rick's tattoo and daggaboys, his love for Lonesome Pines, and the urge to live free of the blood chit, he got a strange feeling. Lately, The Dream was recurring, only now the big faceless shadow was more important, and it was starting to develop. Suddenly it occurred to him that his dream shadow, his nightmare, looked a lot like an old Cape buffalo bull.

He thought of another line from Jeremiah Johnson when Robert Redford asked what month it was, March or April.

Kenny knew it was neither, and spring was a long, lonely way off. He sipped his mocha and wondered if he were crazy, so he got dressed and went to the woods to commune, again.

Midmorning, Late Second Spring Moon

Nothing, absolutely nothing, not mocha, not forest leaves falling, not even Lois's subtle scent, was as comforting as the smell of freshly tilled earth. Anything that can make a person feel this whole is a blessing, and finding an activity that is productive and useful while evoking such a feeling is cause for celebration. Kenny planted his seeds as though his life depended upon it, but with reverent faith and joy. He was so engrossed in his project, he was not aware of the approaching vehicle until it came into sight some thirty yards from him.

A tall, middle-aged man stepped out, "Kenny Brewster?" Kenny stood up slowly to face whatever he must. "Mr. Brewster, I'm Randy Jenkins, one of your students a long time ago. Would you like to meet my family?"

"Sure, you bet. Please, come into my camp and pull up a log," Kenny told them.

"This is my wife, Susie. She was in your class, too, but a couple years later. Our son, Jacob, about my age when I was in your class, and our daughter, Molly, almost seven."

"What a wonderful family, Randy, Susie, and yes, I remember you both—not well, maybe, but I do remember. Would you like some coffee, tea, cocoa?"

"Thank you," Susie said, "but we just ate at the diner. That's how we found you."

They moved to the fire pit where Kenny had arranged some logs for seating for several people, even though he lived here alone. "It's really nice to see you both," Kenny told them, "and your children."

"Mr. Brewster...," Randy began.

"Ken, or Kenny."

"Okay, Ken. We, Susie and I, remember your class well and your discussion about this red sky prophecy. We have thought about it often, and now, since last fall, we can't get it out of our minds. All winter things seemed to be going pretty well, but now there's more trouble than last year."

Kenny thought awhile. He knew they wanted an answer, but he didn't have any. "I'm sorry, but I don't keep up with the news, anymore. What's the problem?"

Susie answered, "Ken, there are bombings and assassinations of local officials in places around the country. Samson Security sometimes has open firefights with police—well, that's what we've heard. That's not on the news."

"Where have you been living?" Kenny asked them.

"Madison," Randy said. "We've always been pretty much spared, but it's even starting there, now. Ken, we are here to prepare for the wilderness."

Kenny's mind did some kind of involuntary gymnastics. He had anticipated this, it was his Vision, but now it scared the hell out of him. Suddenly, and for the first time, really, the enormity of responsibility hit him, and he asked so weakly it surprised him, "How can I help you."

"Do what you do best," Randy told him. "Teach us how to live in harmony with Nature, how to survive for ten years in the wilderness."

That's how it began one glorious spring day in Northern Wisconsin, with one small family and one old man. They pitched a tent and pitched in living and learning. Within two weeks they were building their own wigwam using cordage made with their own hands and young aspen cut and trimmed with stone axes they also fashioned. Randy and Susie worked hard and learned well. Molly was gifted at reverse wrapping and braiding cordage, and Jacob took to primitive skills like Kenny took to planting garden.

Little plants were coming up in rows in the garden, and Kenny was busy cultivating when another car arrived with another family of a former student. Randy and Susie showed them around, and a clan was born.

Kenny wandered off in the woods to commune, but his heart ached for family. He prayed his gratitude for the gift of useful service that had come to him and for the health and safety of Lois and Sammi on that little farm.

When the third vehicle arrived, Kenny was alerted by one of the young scouts-in-training with the call of a crow. He recognized the old blue van and prayed his gratitude for family before the vehicle stopped. Ginger was still smiling and The Mama was walking just fine. Mouse and Diana seemed much more mature now, but Gus was still stoic, although he shook Kenny's hand with meaning. The second family showed them around.

And so it went through spring. More families of former students arrived, some in phone contact with those already here, and the clan had soon outgrown Kenny's few acres. They had also outgrown family politics, and it became evident that some kind of government was necessary. Kenny waited until they came to him and then suggested a council meeting at his fire pit.

He began with some drumming which he kept very quiet because of the neighbors. He then taught them the pipe ceremony and discussed the importance of ritual and ceremony. He told them some stories connecting spirituality to such daily chores as starting a bow drill fire or making cordage. Then he asked his students, "Do you remember the assignment I gave you in class to design your own group spaceship?" Yes, they remembered.

"Do you remember that I also asked you to design a set of rules, and some of you chose to have no rules?" Yes, they remembered that also. "Do any of you remember me saying that this was not a pretend exercise, but that it was real?" Susie remembered. "Well, I didn't always say that, so don't feel bad if you don't remember. You may not have heard it. Well, now is time for you to develop your own method of governance, of making and teaching rules, and perhaps enforcing them. This may take some time. Go, talk with each other, and come back for another council four days from now. That is my counsel to you."

"Ken," Susie asked, "can we have a prayer circle here, now, for those who wish?"

"Well, of course," Kenny answered, "although you may want a break to put little ones to bed, but that is all up to you. I'm going for my vespers, now."

Chapter Twenty-Five

Rise of First Summer Full Moon

The first clan had sold their cars and other worldly goods and moved out a few miles into the national forest. They lived their practice of avoiding people and living off the land, and they kept in daily contact with Kenny's camp where a second clan was building. Members of the first, who called themselves the Ravens because they read the signs of the times and tried to tell others, sent members to teach the new clan.

The full moon rose over his little valley, reflecting off the fog drifting along the stream. Kenny sat alone in silence, feeling awe and gratitude mixed with concern for Lois and sadness for himself. She had been good for him and he missed her, tonight, as much as ever.

'Thank You, Grandfather, for the love of three good women. I don't know any man who deserves that, certainly not me, but if it is in Your plan, I sure would like to have a little more time with Lois. I can't see her anymore, and I fear for her safety and her health.'

He held her comb to his heart again, and for a fleeting moment, tonight, he could see her cooking in their little kitchen at the farm, and he saw Sammi too, holding a newborn baby. And then it was gone. He puzzled over the meaning, but rejoiced that they both seemed healthy.

Kenny thought back to that time last summer, so long ago, when he found Lois waiting here for him. He recalled his coldness and her warmth, his black coyote days, her birthday he didn't know about. 'Her birthday,' he thought. 'Wasn't there something about her visiting me for her next birthday? I think I'm supposed to make her a present with my own hands.' He thought it strange that he would even consider that she might come, but it was hope, and he needed that, tonight. 'What should I make?'

Rising Waning Crescent First Summer Moon

Ten days had passed since the full moon and Kenny's last vision of Lois, but he had worked daily on her birthday present. It looked a little like an empty nativity set, a manger, only it was round. He had decided to make her a place to keep a few goats while she visited. He knew it was silly, but it gave him and three young boys a chance to practice some skills.

The design was that of a wigwam, but only a little more than the back half was covered. The front was a woven fence high enough to discourage climbing. Kenny felt good, like this project had satisfied some need he hadn't recognized. The little birthday present amused him. He worked until dark finishing a gate, and then he sat alone by the embers in his fire pit and remembered.

There were many warm memories of Lois, but his favorite was the first time they felt forever in a moment. 'She was right, love does last forever.' He could almost feel her touch his knee, and he looked to see if she were there. Of course she wasn't, but he really could feel her presence. Kenny went into his cabin, grabbed a couple of blankets, and slept by the fire, again.

By dawn, he was preparing for a visit to the Raven clan. He told the people in his camp where he was going and that he would be back in the afternoon. It was a good visit. Scouts picked him up and guards escorted him to the quiet greetings of Ginger's dogs. After lunch, he was on his way home. About a mile from his cabin, one of the young boys who had helped him build the goat yard came running to meet him.

"Uncle Ken, Uncle Ken, more people came to camp."

"That's wonderful, nephew," Kenny said, "and what can you report?"

"There are two ladies with some goats and a tiny baby."

"What can you tell me about them, nephew?"

"Well, two mama goats are milking, and they have three babies, and there's one papa goat."

"Excellent report, young scout, and how about the ladies?"

"Well, Lois has shiny, dark hair…."

"Lois? Are you sure?"

"Yes, Uncle, Lois and Sammi, she's the tall blonde lady holding a baby. They put the goats in our pen."

Kenny found a burst of energy so that the young lad could not keep up without running. Within minutes they were approaching camp and Kenny could feel his heart racing. He saw Sammi first and she was holding a baby, but before he could reach her, Lois found him. When she was through hugging him, Kenny noticed she looked a little different, a little rounder and softer maybe, but seriously happy.

"I made it here for my birthday," Lois said, "and thank you for my present. Would you like to meet baby LG?"

"You call a baby LG? Why?"

"His name is Lucas Gerald, in honor of his grandfathers." Lois watched to see if Kenny made a connection, but he was already approaching Sammi. He stopped and spun around, looking at Lois to see if he had heard right.

Lois stepped forward and took the baby from Sammi. "Ken, would you like to hold your son?"

There is an old saying that motherhood begins at conception, but fatherhood begins when he first holds his baby. Kenny was in love again, immediate and complete love. There would be a celebration in camp tonight, and Kenny would dance around the fire like a young warrior.

Shortly after full dark, in deference to neighbors, they quieted the camp and sat around the fire talking. Kenny listened as Lois and Sammi described the terrible things that were happening around the country, the race riots, food shortages, energy blackouts. Lois said there were rumors that the President was indisposed much of the time, a nervous breakdown kind of thing, and the Vice President held the power. And, often standing next to him was his close adviser, Daniel Sullivan.

Samson Security had become a Gestapo. Militant vigilante groups were popping up like mushrooms. Our southern border saw open combat on a daily basis, and many Americans were going north to Canada as refugees—unwelcome guests. Stores were being looted and entire cities burned to ashes. There would be more people coming to this camp, they all agreed.

When they dispersed, the people left with confused hearts. They celebrated new life, and they mourned their friends and families who chose to stay behind. Kenny sat at his little table in front of the fireplace and watched Lois feed LG. He could not reconcile his flood of mixed emotions. He could not, so he chose to stop trying. Still, he must ask, "Lo, how long will you be staying?"

"As long as you will have us, Ken—at least that long."

Kenny muttered something like, "Oh, good. I was afraid...," and he trailed off.

When LG was asleep in a chair next to the bed, Kenny held Lois again, and they cried tears of joy and fear together. They both knew that a baby in the wilderness is at risk, but anybody staying back was at much greater risk. They learned tonight that it is possible to touch eternity together, to make love without sex. Kenny thought that was a very good thing to learn.

Lessons and preparations for departure became more earnest, bordering on desperation. Summers are short in the north woods, and they had much to learn, and others kept coming. The Raven Clan departed for wild places but kept contact through their scouts. The second clan now called themselves the Bear Clan, because they enjoyed the berry seasons and worked so hard preparing for the first winter. They moved to the national forest.

The Mama's family, including Ginger, elected to stay in the national forest to help the Bear Clan adjust. There is a profound credibility to a group that has survived the concrete wilderness and adapted to the forest and clan life. They moved freely between clans, visiting Kenny's camp frequently to meet newcomers.

A third clan was growing to maturity, and a fourth was born. Lois, Sammi, and LG chose to stay with the last clan until the very end. Kenny began to feel restless as colors kept changing on the ferns, grasses and the tops of a few trees. He knew what autumn felt like, and his life was approaching winter while Lois was in full season.

First Hard Frost

The Bear Clan had departed for the wild places with the last new moon. Now, the third group, calling themselves the Wolf Clan because their hunters worked well in groups at night, was already preparing to depart. The fourth group called themselves the Puma Clan. They said it was because they were so sneaky, but Kenny knew it was in honor of him. He had not yet had the heart to tell them he would not be going with them.

There had been no new arrivals for many days, half a moon now, and The Puma Clan was anxious to get to wilder places. Many of them had been here a long time, and the insanity of the outside world was even reaching the small northern towns. Kenny stayed in his cabin with Lois and LG as long as possible, giving his son as much chance to grow as possible.

Lois made Kenny mocha one evening and sat at the table with that body language that told him she had something to say and he had better listen. "Ken, the Pumas are ready to stage in the national forest. Hunting season is coming. They need your counsel." She paused and Kenny nodded. "Talk to me, Windy."

He could put it off no longer. "Lois, you know my Vision has always been to help people learn to survive in the wilderness. With the help of so many wonderful people, I have been blessed to live that Vision." He stopped, but Lois waited patiently, rocking LG in his little rocker crib with her left hand. "I have been blessed in so many ways, dear, I can ask for no more."

"What the hell are you not saying, Brewster? I know when something is on your mind."

"Lois, my Vision has always been that I help other people go to the wilderness. My job is to stay behind, protect your trail, and wait for others who may come and need help."

"Oh, no, Ken. You cannot leave me again. You have a son to take care of, now."

"I know, Lo. That's what I'm trying to do."

"Oh, God, Ken, come with us. Enjoy what time we may have, whatever it is. Let's live it together." Tears streamed down Kenny's face, and Lois reached out to him. It seemed like they touched eternity again, but not in a pleasant way, because the silence felt like forever.

"Kenny, do you remember our talk about you wanting a life free of duty and obligation, no more expectations, no more—what did you call it?"

"Blood chit."

"Yes, no more blood chit, no more mortgage on your life, no more feeling like you owe somebody your service."

"I know, Lo, but...."

"But, your ass, man. Sorry. Look, Kenny, honey, you've done enough. God knows you have done enough. You have lived your Vision." She stopped there, studying Kenny, slumped in the chair, head hanging down. She was weeping in silence, now.

"Alright, Ken, we're staying with you."

"No."

"Yes."

"Does LG get a vote?" Kenny asked.

"Oh, damn it, Ken."

"His only hope is with you in the wilderness. Sammi needs you. The clan needs you, Lois. You're the strongest person in the clan, except for The Mama, and she's going to need all the help she can get. They're barely ready to live in the national forest in contact with camp here. You have to go. I'm sorry, but that's your blood chit." Kenny watched her eyes flash dark and her lips purse.

"Okay," Ken said, "I get that you're mad at me. That's okay. Hell, I'm getting sort of used to it." Lois had to laugh just a little at that. "But, Lo, you really have no choice."

"Well, you do, you...," she stopped herself. She stood up, took his cup, even though he thought he wasn't finished, and cleaned up the kitchen. Kenny loved watching her work in the kitchen.

"Hell, Lois, I won't live another ten years in the wilderness...."

"Oh, you grumpy old fart, you'll probably outlive me. You're too damned stubborn to die." That articulated fact made them both laugh so hard they thought they might wake LG. "I think you could use a foot rub, Kenny, dear."

"It'll put me right to sleep," Kenny counseled.

"That's alright, hon. You'll wake up in the morning, and I'll be there."

Morning Light

Lois was there this morning, and Kenny did wake up. LG woke up, too, but Lois fed him and he went right back to sleep. She snuggled onto Kenny's chest and shoulder and caressed him, and he responded.

When they held each other, again, Kenny enjoyed his soft warm bed and his soft warm wife. He considered her his wife now, and decided it was too early to go outside. He knew October mornings, and this one was foggy and wet. A slight drizzle was falling, sort of hanging out with the fog. Kenny thought he would stay in bed for awhile. Lois thought he would go to the forest today.

She wasn't very talkative this morning, and Kenny figured she had a plan. They packed up their belongings and prepared to move out, Lois, LG, Sammi, and six goats, to the national forest camp with The Mama. When the other clan members saw it, they decided to begin their departure also. Kenny chose to go along with Lois that far.

Once they arrived at the new camp, there was no time for talking. They had to build shelters and a pen and a cache and.... It wasn't that Lois wouldn't talk to him, or cook for him, or cuddle with him, she just had a mouthful of something she refused to spit out. Kenny noticed The Mama watching them.

Once the Wolf Clan was gone and the Puma Clan settled in, a council was called, by whom Kenny didn't know. He suspected some collusion between Lois and The Mama. He approved of that relationship. So here they sat on a pleasant autumn afternoon, red sugar maple leaves beginning to fall, around a tall fire.

The Mama opened the council, "Puma Clan, it is late. The woods will be filling with hunters, and we must prepare to go to wild places very soon. Our scouts tell us the other clans before us are doing well and living free. We will do the same, and in spring we will all meet for a happy time. But now, we have some sadness to hear." She looked directly at Kenny, leaving him no choice.

Kenny spoke, "You have done well, learning and growing, and you will continue to do well. You go soon, and my friends and family go with you. My wife goes with you." Lois looked up in pleasant surprise. "My son goes with you. My city family goes with you. My dear friend, Sammi, goes with you. But I will not go with you." He tried to continue, but the group was murmuring and more, protesting.

Kenny stood and turned to face each in turn. "All that was my Vision has come to be. You have come following the Blood Moon, and you have become a clan and a tribe. The part of the Vision I have not shared with all of you is that my job here is not yet finished. I must protect your trail when you leave and wait for others who may come. My heart goes with you, but this thing I must do. I have spoken." He sat down.

Lois stood up. "My husband, my dear friend, speaks his heart. Each of us must live our own Vision, and he must live his. Even though our humanness may sometimes confuse our interpretation of that Vision, it is for no one to interpret another person's life. I will miss him. LG will miss him. We will miss him.

"Our clan will have a hole in it. My heart will have an empty place. My hut and my bed will have a lonely place for him. But, my heart knows that he will return, and many moons before our son is weaned. I have spoken."

Many people spoke that day, and much was said that needed saying. Something happened inside Kenny's heart, and he began to wonder about the difference between duty and Vision, between obligation and choice, responsibility and freedom, walking life and walking death. Lois sat beside him holding his hand and slapping his thigh. He had ways of telling when she was angry now, but he knew she was not so much angry with him as angry at the world that made this all necessary. Kenny understood that anger.

In a subtle little flash of insight, Kenny realized how angry he had been at Fight for Right, Samson Security, politicians—

many, many politicians—for forty years. A tiny question began to form in his mind, but he could not put it into words, or even pictures, just a feeling. So, he slapped Lois' knee, not too hard, but she understood. He knew that because she now patted his thigh gently. 'Oh, shit,' Kenny thought as The Mama stood.

"Windy, you watch our backside. Lois tells me you enjoy that. You wait for stragglers. You live your Vision. Then you get your skinny butt back to us. Ya' hear?"

She sat down, and Kenny felt relieved.

He looked at Lois and asked, "What now?"

"Kiss me, Ken. Then, go play with our son."

Chapter Twenty-Six

Rising Full Hunting Moon

While Sammi rocked LG, Lois and Kenny took a little walk to watch the full moon rise behind the trees across the small lake. They sat on a blanket and wrapped another around them, holding each other. Both knew this would be the last full moon here because the Puma Clan would move out during the dark before the new moon. It didn't last long, however, because the low clouds moved in slowly. First, the stars disappeared, then the moon. They waited like children for it to reappear, but they both knew better. They had seen the warm front coming before dark.

Morning brought a magical day of foggy mist and a slow rain of colored leaves. The whole forest was hushed and one could walk almost silently on the wet leaves. Kenny carried LG, showing him the falling leaves, and Lois delighted in their delight. As far as you looked, there was magnificent color of yellows and reds punctuated by dark wet trunks and the greens of pine, spruce, and fir. But one could not see far, for the fog dimmed the view in a few hundred feet. They were living in a jigsaw puzzle.

Such a day is for making memories, and they were making some. "Lois," Kenny started, "today makes me think of so many days lost to the drugs…." She stopped him with one robust squeeze of his hand.

"Ken, we are here, now. Let's not waste time in the past or the future. They do not exist."

Kenny smiled at her and nodded. "Thanks, Lo."

"Ken, I want to ask you something, and I don't expect an answer. In fact, I don't want you to answer, now. Answer when you are alone, after we are gone. Okay?"

He looked at her. "Okay, Lo."

"Well, I remember you telling me about your experience when you were recovering from surgery, those things that kept you from the light." She paused to look at him. "It's kind of complicated in my mind, so bear with me. Those things you hold onto are keeping you from the light. Are they not keeping you also from your freedom from that debt? Don't answer! When you chose, that day, to come back, what were you coming back to, or to do? Don't answer.

"Okay, I don't want to hurt you or get you upset. I really don't want you to be angry with me, but what is holding you back from your freedom, your family, your life today? Don't answer that, now! Is your treasure, your anchor, your sail, or whatever you call it that catches the wind of light that blows you back, the obsession of your daggaboy dream, is that thing your land, Lonesome Pines? Please, Kenny, don't answer, now. Don't even think about it now. File it away in that memory that is so important to you. Answer when we are gone and you are all alone. Today, just love me, love us, all day, as much as you can."

Kenny asked, "Is it okay for me to talk, now?"

"Please do."

"Thank you, Lois. Let's go collect some acorns. What do you think, LG?"

High Waning Crescent Moon of Morning

There were feelings in the air today, and the entire clan knew it. There was a feeling of change in the weather, of a storm coming, maybe a big one with some snow. There was a feeling of excitement as everyone prepared and packed for the exit to wilder places north and west. There was a feeling of finality, the feeling that Kenny had known so many times with death, a feeling he never really understood. 'Does anybody ever really understand a feeling?' he asked himself. 'Good question,' he answered.

There was a feeling in his gut that Kenny knew too well, a feeling that something bad was coming. There was a feeling in his throat like he couldn't swallow. There was a feeling in his heart that hurt, and a feeling in his eyes that they were about to run over.

He sat holding LG, rocking him back and forth, watching Lois pack. Oh, how he loved watching her work, especially from behind. LG relaxed his grip on Kenny's neck and fell asleep. Kenny breathed in his smell and held him as what he was, the most precious thing in the entire world.

The Mama came over and sat down on a stump nearby. "Windy, you are a good man, maybe even a great man. You have helped more people to hope in these dark times than I could have dreamed. I want to give you something before we go."

Kenny looked to see what she was going to give him.

"I'm going to give you a story. There was this cat who lived in a laboratory and worked in a box. He did not like the box, and he dreamed of his freedom and a way out of the box. But the scientist always fed the cat in the box, so every day the cat went back in the box to eat and spent hours trying to get out again.

"That cat knew there was a way out, and one day it did a back flip and a spin and accidentally brushed the lever that opened the box. In glorious freedom, that cat explored the laboratory all day and all night, but the next morning it went back into the box to eat, and the door closed. Windy, do you know what that cat did?'

"Well, The Mama," Kenny answered, "I'm guessing it did a back flip and a spin move."

The Mama looked at him with a little surprise. "You are exactly right. But the cat missed the lever and the box did not open. So that cat did another back flip and spin move, and another, and another until he accidentally hit the lever and the box opened." She studied Kenny. "You know what I'm talking about, don't you Windy?"

"Yes, The Mama. It's called superstitious behavior. I used to teach psychology. Tell me about your education."

"I practiced clinical psychology a long time ago. Ken, I watched Gus come back from Iraq as angry and confused as any human being I ever counseled. He was in a rage at the treatment of the prisoners in Abu Ghraib, and he was even angrier at the treatment of the low-ranking soldiers who were punished. He lost his job, his family, and for awhile, his mind." She paused to observe Kenny.

"I've been watching you, Ken. You are a very good man, and you are on your way to recovery from your trauma. Come back to The Mama and let her help you, but don't wait too long." She gave him a hard look. "You wait too long, boy, and you might never find your way back." She stood up and invited him to do the same, and then she hugged them both, LG and Kenny, and walked away.

Kenny tried to swallow that lump, but it seemed even bigger now. He decided to watch Lois, but she was gone. Sammi caught his eye and motioned a direction. There Lois was talking with Ginger and one of Kenny's former students, Robert. He hadn't noticed before, but they seemed to be paying a lot of attention to each other. Kenny smiled at his recall of Ginger's dream—actually, at her dreams. He decided to join them.

As he held LG in his arms and his knees protested, it made sense that children are usually born to young people. He walked right up and joined their conversation. Old people can do that. "So, Ginger," Kenny asked, smiling at her and looking at her friend then back to her, "have you had any more dreams?" Her face dropped.

"Yes, Kenny, I dreamed you were giving meat to some people I don't know, and then you were very, very sad. I wish I had dreamed of you coming back to us, but I woke up with your sadness and couldn't get back to sleep. I'm sorry, Kenny."

"Thank you, Ginger," Kenny told her. "Live your dream and be happy."

Lois reached out to take LG as he stirred. "You are coming back to me, Brewster. I can feel it just like I could when you went out west. You don't have to be so sad."

They walked away from the little group and wandered. "Kenny," Lois started, and then she changed her mind. "It's going to be okay, Ken. We've been through all this before, and it has always been okay."

Oh, God, how Kenny tried to believe that, but he was looking at ten lonely years he did not expect to survive. But, he kept trying to believe his wife.

Next Morning

The Puma Clan broke camp in a cold rain with gusts of wind. It was not pleasant weather for moving, but safe. There would be few hunters about. Their move would be quiet, and the rain, or even better, the snow, would cover their tracks. Kenny stood off in the woods and watched them pass by, saying a prayer in his heart for each one, until they were gone from his sight, all except Mouse.

He came and stood silently beside Kenny, and they watched the rain begin to turn to snow. "Good," Mouse said, "snow will hide the tracks." He reached for Kenny and one last hug. Mouse's job was tail scout, and he had to know where the clan was at all times as well as who might be coming up behind them. He had to start his sweeps now, back and forth, up to their left flank, back around behind them, and up to their right flank. It was a job only for people who could see some things the way Mouse could.

He stopped a distance off and turned to face Kenny. He pointed to his chest, then his eye, then at Kenny. 'He will be watching for me,' Kenny concluded, and he took a long deep breath and let it go completely. Oh, how he wanted to go sit in a cedar swamp and watch the snow accumulate, but he could not take his eyes off the trail. He stayed until there was no light, and then he listened with what hearing he had left.

Chapter Twenty-Seven

Dawn, Day One

Day came so slowly that Kenny feared it was a dream. When he awoke, he feared even more that it was not. He was tired, cold, stiff, and lonely. He was also hungry, so he decided to make a sweep across their trail like Mouse did and head to the cedar swamp to hunt. It was a slow process because of his stiff body and the weight he carried. Besides his pack and bow, he still carried a rifle and two handguns, a .357 magnum on the front of his left hip, and a .22 magnum on his belt in the middle of his back. It was much too much, but nobody was going to follow his clan.

Relieved at finding no sign, he made his way into the swamp and settled down. Not long after he arrived, he began to notice movements of animals from the south. 'Somebody is out there, probably hunting,' he told himself. He closed his eyes to commune. In his mind he saw four young hunters crashing and thrashing in desperation for meat and finding none. Kenny decided to get some for them.

Animals kept moving through the swamp away from the young hunters, and a young doe with no fawn soon came by. Kenny's arrow hit her hard, and he watched as she ran off. He knew it was a good hit, right in the vitals, and she would die soon. He sat still and waited. There was no snow falling, easy tracking, so he let her die in peace.

By the time he thought it had been long enough, the animals were settling down, and Kenny figured the hunters had left. Now he had two jobs. He had to dress this deer and get her to a place where he could camp, and he had to find those hunters. He tracked the deer, quickly field dressed her, and began dragging her out in the direction she had come in, exactly where the hunters had been.

Kenny laid the deer at the edge of the swamp near a large boulder he could see from some distance and started scouting. He found a nice place to camp up the ridge less than half a mile from the swamp, and he found tracks all over the place between. He followed the tracks far enough to see that there were four men, and that they were heading southeast. He figured they would be camping nearby and making loops out from the camp in hopes of jumping a deer. It's a hard way to hunt, but young people are like that.

He purposely dragged the deer across the hunters' tracks up the ridge and into his camp. He set his load down and built a fire. He would cut and hang the deer tonight and cook in the morning. He worked deliberately, and as dark settled in, he finished the task. He reclined on spruce boughs and stoked the fire.

Kenny spent most of this night wrapped in blankets in prayer and meditation. Many times he had faced crucial moments in his life, and often he had sensed them coming. It was like he was being given opportunity after opportunity to make a choice, and one of these times he would make the right one, even if only by accident, like the cat in a box. Tomorrow would be another opportunity, of that he was certain.

Midmorning, Day Two

All four quarters of the deer hung safely in the tree with the hide still attached. The tenderloins and back straps sizzled slowly on the spit that Kenny turned periodically. Scent of venison permeated the forest over the soft, first snow of the season, and Kenny knew the four young hunters would find him. If they could not track him with the fresh snow covering his drag marks, they could surely follow their noses. He knew they were coming, and he knew it would be soon. He chewed slowly on the small piece of tenderloin, savoring every moment, every taste, every breath. Kenny had faced such times before, but today was different.

The young man crested the ridge and stopped still, surveying the scene, holding his rifle across his thighs in front of him at arms length midway between his waist and knees. 'Interesting,' was the only word formed in Kenny's mind. The young man raised his rifle carefully into a port arms position across his chest, still not pointing it at anything, and began walking slowly toward Kenny—eyes fixed on Kenny's eyes.

"Come on in, son," Kenny called with calm resolve. "I've been waiting for you."

The young man stopped again, looked quickly over to the spit and back, then to the hanging quarters and back to Kenny's eyes. "There's a quarter for each of you, and some tenderloin to take the edge off," Kenny offered.

The young man stared at him. Within his peripheral vision, Kenny could see two other young men slowly approaching among the trees, one on his right and another on his left. The fourth, he knew, was behind him. He could feel it. The first young man approached now, close enough so Kenny could see his blue eyes. "We'll take them," He said hoarsely, and he cleared his throat.

"Good," Kenny said. "That deer can feed your families for weeks. You can certainly take them, with or without my permission. Or, I could teach you how to hunt, and you could feed your families for a lifetime." The young man gave a look of utter disbelief, appearing to start talking but no words came out.

Kenny's heart rate slowed noticeably. Everything around him seemed to slow down—or maybe his mind was speeding up. He looked at Blue Eyes but saw bodies bleeding on the forest floor. He saw flag-draped coffins and weeping families. He saw insanity and futility and tragedy about to happen. He saw—no, he felt—a different way. A feeling welled up inside him, like a bubbling spring in his belly, a spring that flowed warm light instead of water. Well, it felt like light, and when it filled his head he knew exactly what to do. He did not form words in his mind, and he did not know what would happen—the consequences—but, he knew that whatever happened would be right.

Kenny felt a little smile creep up his face. It was not a grin, just a simple smile. He could not remember the last time he felt so clean.

The .357 magnum in his holster would do him no good—not because it could not fire, but because he would not. The taking of a human life, especially a young, hungry life, was no longer a choice. So, he looked away at his rifle leaning against a tree several feet away, and unbuckled the holster belt with both revolvers. He gently tossed it away to his left, out of reach but in plain sight. As he sat quietly leaning back against the basswood tree, savoring the tenderloin, no words were spoken in his mind.

"The tenderloins are done," Kenny said, "and the back straps soon will be." He was surrounded now, and all four held rifles, but none yet pointed at him. Kenny looked directly into the blue eyes of the first young man. "The choice is yours, son. I know. They will follow your lead. But, I have to get up now and turn that spit, or it'll burn."

Kenny rose slowly, stretching the kinks out of his back and legs, and turning his back on Blue Eyes. As he stepped toward the spit, he took one more deep breath and exhaled. From behind him came a soft but audible click.

Chapter Twenty-Eight

Evening, Day Two

The night chill was setting in, but the fire pit remained cold. Kenny sat against the tree breathing in, breathing out. The four hungry, young hunters had taken his meat but spared his life, declining his offer to teach them what they thought they already knew. They attributed his hunting success to luck rather than skill—the skill of being in the right place at the right time. He had given them his rifle and revolvers also. He was free, at last.

His family, his clan, his only tribe were two days out into their ten year wilderness journey. He sat here alone, a genuine daggaboy retired from his duty to protect his herd. There were no demands on his time, no responsibilities to anyone but himself, or perhaps some unlucky young hunters. Nobody owned a blood chit for him anymore. He felt the night chill and started the fire.

Here he sat, the wilderness survival teacher, with no shelter. He went to work staking a log fence reflector near the fire across from his place. He built a quick debris wall on his northwest and southwest sides around the tree he would lean against. He cut a few more spruce boughs to sit and lie upon, and some more to cover him later, if needed. He was ready for one chilly night, but much more work was necessary before winter arrived.

Kenny would not sleep tonight. For so many years, he had sought this moment, this goal, this dream of what he considered freedom, and now, here it was. His mind went to Jeremiah Johnson when he was asked if it were worth the trouble. "Huh? What trouble?" Jeremiah lived this freedom after his accidental squaw and family were killed, but Kenny's family was out there, somewhere, tonight. He added another piece of dry wood to the fire.

No, Kenny would not sleep tonight, but he would dream. The Dream came without angry faces, only the big shadow which was clearly a very old cape buffalo. Thoughts and images shaped themselves somehow around the fire and glowing coals. He dreamed of arriving at the City of Light, the destination of the white light that enthralled him. He dreamed of the wind that would not let him approach and the baggage still tethered to his gripping hands. He dreamed of letting go, of releasing all his worldly attachments and finding the solace he sought.

His conscious mind recalled that exposure to cold brings a subtle death, that one gradually loses sensibility so that the pain of frostbite and hypoxia may not penetrate the mind. He imagined being paralyzed so that his arms would not add wood to the fire. Then a coyote howled, and his mind came back to the physical now. He wondered if coyotes ever got depressed.

He tried to remember those questions Lois had asked him to answer, later. It was later, now, but he could not remember them. Perhaps he had made a mistake. Perhaps there was no freedom, as he defined it, short of death itself. That would mean the choice is simply to die or to not die in this moment. That is all.

He looked at his log reflecting wall across the fire and remembered The Wall.

He did not hear a voice say it. He consciously drew all the pieces of his fractured self together and made one silent statement to the universe. 'The difference is I still have a choice. Those soldiers did not.' Somebody chose to end their lives. Nobody was choosing to end his life, except, possibly, Kenny.

'The choice is mine, and that is all the freedom there is. The wind that sends me away from the light is keeping me alive. My attachment to Earthly things is keeping me, sustaining me. Freedom from attachment to anything on Earth is death. Why didn't anyone ever teach me that?

'Kenneth Brewster, you fool. You have let every wonderful thing in your life slip away, sometimes because you were holding it too tight. You thought you were savoring sex, but did you ever think of savoring all the other things? A little laugh? A silly fight? You had wonderful times with Bonnie, but you didn't really live them because you were afraid. The same is true with Vicky, only her strength of soul brought you along, sometimes. Now, Lois and little LG are out there and you are here. Here is your freedom. How do you like it now?'

'I would rather be with them.'

'Then why do you stay here?'

'Lonesome Pines?' Kenny wondered if his little piece of land had come to represent his freedom from duty and guilt, his daggaboy territory. Was that attachment now keeping him from people he loved? From people who loved him? Staying here or going back to Lonesome Pines alone, either one, was another form of suicide, the freedom of nothing left to lose.

'I would rather be with my family, my clan, my tribe. That's all there is to say. I don't owe anybody else a path to freedom. I don't owe anybody else a rear guard. I don't owe anybody else anything. I am free, and I always have been. It has always been a matter of choice.'

Nights get long in the north woods after September, but dawn did come. Kenny began his walk following no tracks at all except in his heart. He knew if he went northwest far enough, he would be spotted by one of their rear guard scouts. He would be reunited with his family and their clan.

Afternoon, Another Day

Today, he did not hurry. He chose to savor the cool, brisk wind, the crunch of frost, the brown trees, and the green ones. Not since he was a child wandering his grandpa's farm had he felt so, yes, free. When he found game, he killed it and ate. When he got tired, he rested. When he wondered which way to go, he closed his eyes and let his gut point the way. When he felt doubt, he prayed, and when he felt gratitude, he prayed some more.

He did not note time, not even days. It had taken him all these years to learn to live. God, he was happy. "This," he told himself aloud, "is life beyond the blood chit."

Thank You

Dear Reader,

This is my first novel, and I enjoyed writing it so much, I decided to write another. If you have enjoyed Beyond the Blood Chit, you might love my second novel. It is a sequel, following many of the same characters into the wilderness, only this time I tell the story from the viewpoints of Lois and Sammi. Two other related novels are planned as well as some nonfiction.

Your book club or reading friends are invited to challenge me with questions. For information, please contact me through ErvBarnes.com. Teaching is my passion, and I love talking with people about writing and other concepts.

If you would like to read more about some of my ideas, I invite you to http://ervbarnes.wordpress.com. It is a blog not about any one thing, and certainly not about everything, but focusing on the whole thing—the connections that make life meaningful. Thank you for sharing my journey.

Erv Barnes

CPSIA information can be obtained at www.ICGtesting.com
Printed in the USA
LVOW050926270612
287781LV00002B/3/P

9 781614 344834